When the Past Kills

M J Lee has worked as a university researcher in history, a social worker with Vietnamese refugees, and as the creative director of an advertising agency. He has spent 25 years of his life working outside the north of England, in London, Hong Kong, Taipei, Singapore, Bangkok and Shanghai.

Also by M J Lee

DI Ridpath Crime Thriller

MJ LEE

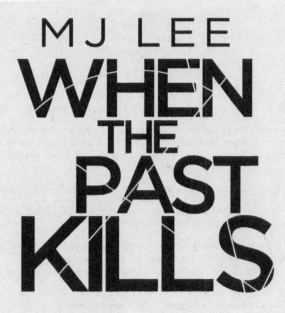

WHEN THE PAST KILLS

CANELO CRIME

First published in the United Kingdom in 2020 by Canelo

This edition published in the United Kingdom in 2021 by

Canelo
31 Helen Road
Oxford OX2 0DF
United Kingdom

A CIP catalogue record for this book is available from the British Library.

Print ISBN 978 1 80032 015 4
Ebook ISBN 978 1 78863 745 9

Look for more great books at www.canelo.co

Printed and bound in Great Britain by Clays Ltd, Elcograf S.p.A.

Chapter 1

The scream came from the Coroner's Office.

Ridpath glanced quickly across to Sophia, before leaping from his chair and running down the short corridor. 'Mrs Challinor, are you ok?'

'He's going to kill him...'

Ridpath shoved the door open.

The coroner was sat at her desk frozen with fear, her hand covering her mouth, staring in horror at her computer monitor.

Ridpath ran to the other side of the desk. On the top left-hand corner of the screen, a timer ticked over remorselessly.

9:01:53.

9:01:54.

An old man was standing on a chair with a noose round his neck. In front of him, another man with his back to the camera was reading from a sheet of paper.

'You have been charged and found guilty of the crime of negligence in public office. How do you plead?'

The old man on the chair slowly lifted his head. His eyes were glazed as if he didn't know where he was.

'It's Brian...' said Mrs Challinor.

'Brian?'

'The former coroner.'

Sophia had joined them in the room along with the office manager, Jenny Oldfield. 'What's going on?'

They both rushed round the desk to look at the screen.

Jenny leant in to take a closer look. 'What's Brian doing?' she whispered.

As if answering her, Brian's lips moved.

'Speak up please, for the court.' The man with his back to the camera ordered.

Brian spoke slightly louder. 'What do you want?' The voice was slurred and slow.

'That is not the correct answer. Guilty or not guilty?'

'What do you want?' Brian repeated.

'What the hell's going on?' Jenny asked looking across to the coroner.

'I don't know,' she answered without taking her eyes off the screen. 'I received an email and clicked on the link and this came up on my computer.'

9:02:12.

9:02:13.

9:02:14.

Ridpath glanced at the clock on Mrs Challinor's wall. Just after nine a.m. This was being screened live.

'Brian Conway, you have been accused of negligence in the execution of your duties as coroner. Are you sure you don't want to plead?'

The former coroner mumbled something and shook his head. The noose around his head writhed like a snake.

'In the absence of a plea, the sentence will be carried out.'

Without waiting any longer, the man stepped forward and kicked the chair on which Brian Conway was standing. For a second, the old coroner was frozen in mid-air, before gravity took hold and his body plummeted down, bouncing twice as it reached the end of the rope, then stopped, the toes of his shoes almost touching the carpet.

Brian Conway's eyes were bulging from his head as he kicked his feet and struggled to free his hands.

Instantly, Mrs Challinor and Sophia looked away. Jenny continued to stare at the screen as if transfixed.

'Do something, Ridpath!' Mrs Challinor shouted.

The man was still kicking his feet. The rope had pulled tight and twisted his neck to one side without breaking it. The tip of his tongue appeared between his teeth and his face grew larger, taking on a blue tone.

9:02:34.

9:02:35.

The coroner slowly looked back at the screen. 'It's his home. I recognise the painting on the wall.'

'Where is it?'

'Saddleworth somewhere, up on the moors... Do something, Ridpath!' the coroner screamed.

'Jenny, do you have his number and address?'

'I think so...'

'Get it!'

The office manager ran out of the room.

Ridpath picked up his mobile and dialled 999. The phone rang and rang.

On the screen, Brian Conway was struggling less. His movements becoming slower and smaller, his face turning a bright blue. After a minute, all movement stopped and he hung there, the rope swaying slightly under the weight of his body.

9:03:35.

9:03:36.

9:03:37.

The operator finally answered. 'Emergency, which service do you require?'

'Police and ambulance. This is Detective Inspector Thomas Ridpath. I'm looking at a crime being committed at—'

Jenny ran back into the room, a filing card in her hand.

Ridpath snatched it from her. '—At 10 Penfold Lane, Saddleworth.'

'What is the nature of the crime?'

'Murder. It's murder, code red.'

The call sign produced an instant reaction.

'Officers have been dispatched to the address and a call out has been sent to the ambulance.'

On the screen, Brian Conway was still, his body hanging loosely from the end of the rope, a dark patch staining the crotch of his trousers, the upended chair lying a few feet away.

The man who had kicked the chair was standing, watching, doing nothing.

The operator interrupted. 'ETA, seventeen minutes, Inspector Ridpath. Are you in any danger?'

9:03:55.

9:03:56.

Ridpath dragged his eyes away from the screen. 'I'm not there. I'm watching the murder on a computer screen. You need to get there quicker, a man is dying.'

'The message has been passed to the response vehicle. ETA is still seventeen minutes.'

'What the...?' shouted Ridpath.

On screen, the man, still with his back to the camera, picked up the chair, placing it against the far wall. He folded up the charge sheet and placed it in his pocket, then walked towards the door. Before he left the room, he turned back to camera, staring directly at it.

His face looked like a wolf.

9:04:19.

9:04:20.

4

Four Days Earlier...

Chapter 2

He parked the car near the Stone Mason's studio on Barlow Moor Road, at the mid-point between the street lights.

There was no point in taking unnecessary risks. Keeping to the shadows was better. Hadn't he always lived his life that way?

Taking the holdall with the tools out of the boot, he checked the road and the nearby shops, before hurrying across.

Just past a deserted bus stop, he climbed onto a low sandstone wall and swung his leg over the short iron railings guarding the exterior.

He'd chosen this place to enter because it was close to a path leading to his destination. Security was always lax around here. There was no likelihood of anybody escaping or trying to break in. It was, after all, Southern Cemetery.

He jumped down, stepping between the gravestones close to the road, deliberately avoiding his uncle's on the left, and reached the path. People joked this was the dead centre of Manchester but it would be a sacrilege to walk all over a dead person's grave, wouldn't it? You had to respect the dead, they were once like us; living, breathing, laughing and loving.

He had once taken the tour of the cemetery, one of Europe's biggest. Ten quid to be shown the graves of celebrities; Matt Busby, John Alcock, Tony Wilson and L S Lowry. Of course, he had been back a few times since to make sure he understood the layout, reconnoitring the place so he could navigate his way to the grave easily even in the dark.

Planning was everything.

There was security here and it occasionally patrolled the grounds, but the cemetery was large and the likelihood of meeting one of the guards was minimal. He had austerity to thank for that.

For a second, he stopped, raising his head and breathing deeply to inhale the atmosphere.

He loved visiting here at night: the shadows cast from the Victorian monuments, the scent of freshly turned earth, the way the light from the street lamps filtered through the bare branches of the trees, throwing twisted shapes across the gravestones.

On his left, an owl hooted from the old Lodge, obviously on the lookout for prey.

He had a target of a different sort.

He glanced at his watch. Twelve minutes left to finish, time to move.

Scurrying down the path in the dark, he took the left-hand arm of the crossroads. The grave, his destination, was three rows in on the right-hand side.

He glanced over his shoulder, checking the area was clear, before striding across to stand in front of the black marble headstone. He read the words.

Charles Whitworth
Born 30 July 1966
Died 30 April 2019

He found it amusing that this man was born on the day England had last won the World Cup. Had his father cursed him because he missed the game?

He reached down and pulled up the weeds that had begun to grow in profusion at the base of the gravestone, revealing a carved message.

Greater love hath no man

He didn't remember this man with love. His only image was of a moustachioed face, a body like it had been put through a mangle and breath smelling of rotten food with an edge of whisky.

Not a fond memory.

He wished the man were still alive, it would have been better to have punished him properly. But he wasn't and he was no longer part of the plan.

Shame.

He took out the hammer and swung it hard against the marble of the gravestone. The shock, as it struck home, reverberated through his arms and echoed round the surrounding trees.

But there was nobody to hear him.

Not here. Not now.

He swung again. This time there was a sharp crack as the marble shattered into four pieces, collapsing over the dark, Manchester earth.

He lifted the hammer once more and brought it down on the largest lump of marble, shattering it into tiny pieces. Again the hammer rose and crunched down.

And again. And again.

He was breathing heavily now, with shards of marble lying at his feet.

He arranged the broken stone into a small cairn, carefully placing a handmade wooden cross upside down, nestled between two of the shards. From his bag, he took out the flyer and placed it under the wooden cross, knowing at least one person would understand his message.

Then he took out the red can of paint, opened the lid and painted one word on the shards of shattered gravestone.

SCUM

The paint dribbled down the cairn looking like blood from a fresh cut. Exactly the impression he wanted to give.

Finally, he reached into his holdall for the four-litre bottle of bleach, twisting the cap and pouring the contents all over the small patch of earth that would remain forever Charlie Whitworth.

The stench of ammonia rose from the sodden earth. Now the bastard would have to be dug up and reburied somewhere else.

'You're going to become one of the walking dead, Charlie,' he said out loud. He laughed, hearing the sound of his voice being swallowed up by the night.

None of the corpses joined in his laughter.

He packed the tools he'd used into the holdall and carefully retraced his steps back to the main road.

On the pathway between the graves, he took a glance backwards. The cairn of black stone was reflecting the light of the moon towards him, the red words still shining wetly, like tears of blood.

Would they make the connection?

Probably not.

But after the next one, he would make sure they did.

After all, they had to know who it was, didn't they?

And so it would begin.

Chapter 3

Detective Inspector Thomas Ridpath had burnt the toast for the second time.

'Shit... shit,' he said pulling out the charred edges from the toaster and tossing them towards the sink. A heavy aroma of burnt bread lingered in the kitchen. He opened one of the windows to let some fresh air in.

It was one of those lovely Manchester mornings in February – blue skies, a hoar frost stinging the lawn, the naked branches of the trees reaching up to soak-in the unexpected sun and a fresh, cold zip to sting the nostrils. By midday, it would be raining no doubt, with a wind howling directly from Iceland. But he'd enjoy this for now.

He took the last two pieces of Warburtons and put them in the toaster. The scrambled eggs were done, sitting forlornly in the pan waiting for a slice of non-burnt toast to sit on.

It wasn't like him. Normally, he was a half-way decent cook, able to follow a Jamie Oliver recipe and produce food looking vaguely like the picture in the cook book.

He liked making breakfast for his wife and daughter. Firstly, because neither of them were particularly active in the morning. Zombie was the word that most accurately described his wife, with comatose probably being a more useful description for Eve.

A few cups of strong coffee would bring his wife back to life while food seemed to do the trick for his daughter. And anyway, breakfast was the most important meal of the day, wasn't it?

While the toast browned, he took the blister pack down from its place in the cupboard and pressed out a single tablet of Revlimid.

One a day keeps the cancer away, his doctor had joked. Now he would be taking these pills for the rest of his life but at least it was better than the fear and the chemo.

The myeloma had been in remission for two years, three months and six days. He'd fallen ill at work, collapsing during a major investigation. His GP had sent him to the cancer hospital, Christie's, almost straight away and, within two weeks, he had commenced his treatment.

For six months it had been touch and go, but finally, after what seemed like years of daytime TV, he was pronounced as being in remission. Now just one tablet a day kept him that way.

He placed the pill on his tongue and washed it down with the last dregs of his coffee. For a second, he flashed back to his first holy communion, the priest placing the wafer on his tongue and his seven-year-old self closing his mouth reverently, desperately trying not to bite into the unleavened bread. Hadn't his mother said if you bit into it you went straight to hell with all the other heathens?

'Is something burning?' his wife, Polly, shouted down from upstairs.

He glanced across at the toaster. A thin trail of smoke was rising from the open grills. He lunged across and pressed the levers. The toast shot up and was the perfect shade of brown.

'It's nothing, dear, making scrambled eggs,' he shouted back as he placed the toast on plates and covered it with the cooked and now crusted eggs.

Upstairs, there were some mumbled shouts followed by the loud slamming of a bathroom door.

It meant Eve was awake and even better, she was up.

He put the plates on the table on hearing his wife's footsteps clatter down the stairs. As the door opened he handed her the coffee.

She sat down at the table and stared at the food. 'Do I have to?'

'You're supposed to set a good example for Eve.'

'What about you?'

'I've already had mine,' he lied.

The kitchen door opened and Eve stumbled in, sitting down next to her mum.

'I can't eat this. I'm vegan.'

'Since when?' he asked.

'Since last night. I saw a documentary on how they treat the chickens who lay these eggs in the factory farms.'

'These are free range,' Ridpath lied again.

'Go on, you need to eat something Eve, look at me.'

Polly was tucking in to the scrambled eggs and managing to smile and grimace at the same time.

'Why's there burnt toast in the sink?' asked Eve.

'Is there? How did that get there? Perhaps, I should call the police... hang on, I am the police, maybe I should investigate.'

Eve rolled her eyes in the way only eleven-year-olds can do. 'Dad, it's too early...'

'But it's not too early to eat.' He pointed to the food.

She stared at her breakfast for a while before gingerly picking up the toast and its burden of scrambled egg with the tips of her fingers and biting down. 'Mmmm, it's good, what's in it?'

'Herbs and a smidge of paprika.'

'Jamie Oliver?'

'The man himself. Listen, I have to go now. We've got the weekly status meeting at the Major Investigation Team and I want to have a chat with Mrs Challinor in her office before I go.' He picked up the cafetière of coffee and poured another cup for his wife. 'Anything else before I'm off?'

'Has she found your replacement yet?' His wife asked between mouthfuls of coffee and scrambled eggs.

'I don't think so, it's one of the things I want to talk with her about this morning. She's rejected all the coppers and is now advertising for someone to become the new coroner's officer.'

After his illness, he had been seconded by Greater Manchester Police to work with the East Manchester Coroner, supposedly a cushy desk job that would allow him to work regular hours. But Ridpath had no desire to sit back and just pick up a salary. Luckily, the coroner, Mrs Challinor, was determined to 'represent the dead in the court of the living' as she described her job.

Ridpath had enjoyed the challenge of working with her and even managed to solve a few important cases. His successes plus the continued remission of his illness had encouraged his boss at MIT to ask for his return.

He had managed to avoid making a decision on his future for the last three months but the arrival of a new DCI, Paul Turnbull, meant he could no longer put it off. He was due to return to Police HQ in two weeks' time.

'Will you miss working there?'

Ridpath didn't answer, rinsing out his cup under the tap. 'How many weeks does Eve have left before half-term?' he asked changing the subject.

'A couple of weeks. You don't know how much I'm looking forward to the holiday.'

'And me,' Eve mumbled.

Both his wife and child went to the same primary school. One as a teacher and the other as a pupil. Luckily, it had never been a problem for either of them. But that would all change after the summer. Eve had passed the exams and was set to join Altrincham Grammar School for Girls in September.

Everybody in the house seemed set to change. Even his wife was talking about applying to move to a new school, the petty rules of her headmistress destroying any joy she had at work.

'Anyway, I'm off.' Ridpath kissed both of them on the top of their heads.

'Can you pick up some milk on your way back? I have end of year reports to write plus a mountain of admin to clear. There's a rumour we're going to be Ofsteded before Easter.'

'Again? They visited you a couple of years ago!'

'To keep us on our toes, apparently. Sometimes, I think the old witch enjoys the visit of the Inspectors. Makes her feel powerful.'

'Mum, you're not supposed to call Mrs Hardacre an old witch.'

Polly zipped up her mouth and slapped the back of her hand.

'I'll get the milk. I'll be back early this evening.'

He put on his coat and did another round of kisses. Since the diagnosis of cancer, he always made sure he said goodbye properly. Cancer had a way of concentrating the mind. What if he never saw them again?

Chapter 4

'Morning, Sophia, is the coroner in?'

His assistant was sat at her desk already. 'Of course, Ridpath. When is she ever not here? I think you'll find her in the ante-room to court no. 1. She's preparing for today's inquest. It's due to start soon.'

He nodded and walked back out of the office. Both the coroner's courts were in a separate building to the administrative offices where he was based. It was a short walk across the courtyard. Ridpath debated whether to go up the front steps into the main entrance of the court or take the rear steps directly to the coroner's ante-room.

He chose the latter, quickly climbing up the stairway and stopping to rap once on the door before hearing the magic word.

'Enter.'

He strode in to find the coroner sat behind her desk, typing on her laptop from notes in a file next to it. She was dressed in a crisp white shirt with her black jacket draped across a chair.

The ante-room to court no. 1 always reminded Ridpath of something Dickensian, out of *Dombey and Son*, perhaps. A wall of legal books and texts was stacked behind Mrs Challinor's desk with filing cabinets, an escritoire with bottles of dry sherry slowly gathering dust and two side tables the only furniture, all made from a dark wood. Georgian sash windows gave a view over the assorted warehouses, Victorian terraces, executive offices and shopping malls of Stockfield. At one side, a door gave a private entrance to the court itself.

Only one thing smacked of modernity; the coroner's laptop. It was the latest model owned by Mrs Challinor herself rather than the council.

'Good morning, Ridpath,' she said looking up from her reading. Caught in the early morning light, Mrs Challinor reminded Ridpath of one of the pre-Raphaelite paintings he'd seen on a school trip to Manchester Art Gallery all those years ago; long, curled grey hair surrounding an alabaster skin and the lightest of light blue eyes.

'Good morning, Coroner, if you're busy, I can come back.' He gestured towards the myriad files lurking on her desk.

She stared down at the them. 'The Wentworth Case. An alcoholic who, despite being seen by doctors, social workers, an outreach worker and a church group, still managed to drink herself to death. Everybody was on holiday and nobody followed up.'

'Family?'

'A disaffected daughter and a long-gone husband.'

'Do you want me to look into it?'

She shook her head. 'There's no criminality here, just laziness, stupidity and workloads fit to breaking. What do we charge them with? Having so much work they can't look after all their cases properly? Sophia has liaised with the family, but even they don't seem to miss her.'

'Sad way to go. Why hold an inquest?'

'Somebody has to hold them to account. It won't save this woman but it might scare the council into resourcing their outreach services properly.' She paused and stared into mid-air for a moment. 'Then again, it might not.' She switched her gaze back to him. 'Sometimes, I feel I'm pushing a rock up a tall mountain and, as I get to the top, it rolls all the way down to the bottom again.'

'It's a feeling we all share, Coroner.'

She shrugged her shoulders. 'Anyway, thinking in that manner doesn't help anybody. We do what we can. How can I help you, Ridpath? But before you tell me, help me carry these files into court.'

Ridpath picked up the three heaviest and followed Mrs Challinor through the door into the empty courtroom. The same soft February light suffused the place through large Victorian sash window on the left.

In an hour or so, this would be full of people, all gathering to either give evidence, watch the proceedings or help the coroner reach a conclusion by sitting on the jury. The court itself wasn't large. Mrs Challinor's desk sat on a raised dais overlooking a few tables for counsel in the centre, a witness box on the right and a jury box on the left.

In two of the corners, CCTV stared down at the participants in the inquest. These were a recent addition, requested by Mrs Challinor to provide a visual record of the proceedings. Today they were going to be used for the first time.

'I do hope Jenny manages to work them out,' the coroner pointed to them, 'we're having problems with the sound. The recorders are back in the main building. Apparently, there's a problem with the technology.'

'Isn't there always,' he said, plonking the files on her desk.

She immediately set to work, sorting them into the correct order for her inquest.

'I have the MIT meeting this morning, anything you want me to bring up with them?'

Once again, she paused for a moment. 'I don't think so. Nothing has crossed my desk which I need to flag with them.'

'Right.' He stood there, staring down at the worn carpet.

'Was there something else, Ridpath?'

'Well, I'm seeing Claire Trent and the new DCI, Paul Turnbull, and I wondered if you had any news on the new coroner's officer.'

'How is Detective Superintendent Trent?' said Mrs Challinor avoiding the question.

'She's fine, I think. But she doesn't often confide in me the state of her health.'

The coroner appeared to consider his answer. 'No, I can guess she would probably prefer a more transactional relationship.'

'Actually, she prefers a master–slave interaction or at least a commander–subordinate. It is the police after all.'

'Hierarchies, how we love them. And hate them.' Mrs Challinor stopped speaking and stared out of the window. 'To answer your question, not very well, I'm afraid. GMP gave me a list of chancers, no-hopers, incipient alcoholics and those with their slippers already on their feet, doing the pension tango. The names are with Jenny if you want to check them before you go to MIT. We've put the job out on the website and I thought we may have had an existing coroner's officer from Derbyshire but he's pulled out. Too far to travel apparently. There's a couple of others I'm going to interview over the next few days. You're a difficult man to replace, Ridpath.'

'I'm sorry, Coroner, it's just the job back at MIT is open and if I don't take it now...'

He didn't finish the sentence.

'Can you buy more time from Claire Trent?'

'She's not the problem. It's the new DCI, Paul Turnbull.'

'Ok, I'll go through the police applications one more time, there may be a gem amongst the dross.' She looked across at him. 'We're going to miss you, Ridpath,' she paused for a moment, 'I'm going to miss you.' She looked away as if slightly embarrassed at her admission.

'Not as much as I'll miss you, Coroner.'

She looked at her watch. 'You'd better hurry otherwise you are going to be late.'

Ridpath pursed his lips and nodded once. 'I'll let her know, Coroner.'

He left the office, closing the door behind him, feeling as if he had let Mrs Challinor down somehow.

It wasn't a feeling he enjoyed.

Chapter 5

John Gorman's back was killing him.

Spending the whole day on the allotment yesterday was a mistake. He was too old to be bending down, digging and carrying. But the winter cabbages needed to be cut and the trenches for the potatoes had to be re-dug after their winter break.

Perhaps he shouldn't be such a workaholic in his retirement, but that was easier said than done. He had always been busy throughout his life, he couldn't stop now. These days though, the problem was not doing too much but finding enough things to do.

Somehow, as he aged, the days had grown longer. He found it difficult to sleep at night, lying awake in his bed staring at the ceiling, hearing the wind whistle through the trees.

When he did find something to do, like digging the allotment, it was all so hard and painful. His mind was willing, but the body was weak. Nobody helped any more – he couldn't tell people to do things like he used to.

He missed the sense of control he used to enjoy. The good thing about being a Detective Chief Superintendent in the Greater Manchester Police was you looked after your team and they looked after you.

The only job was to put away criminals. Nothing else mattered.

As long as you did your job, nobody got in your way. And he had been good, very good, at his job.

He swung his legs off the bed, glancing at the picture of his wife, Annie, on the bedside table. This morning, he had woken up, feeling the curve of her back as she lay on the other side of the bed.

But he knew it couldn't be.

She had been dead for two years.

They always planned to go travelling together once he retired from the Force. The Gormans on a tour of the world, they always joked. Annie had even gone as far as to research those round-the-world cruises to find out which one was best.

But then she had her first heart attack and, before he knew it, she was bed bound, unable to travel. Being forced to retire from the police was the best thing he could do for her so he didn't fight it. He was grateful for spending the last three months together before she died.

He heard the scratching at the door. The dogs were up and waiting for him. 'I'm coming, I'm coming, hold your bloody horses.'

The scratching at the door increased in tempo, followed by a short yap of impatience. That was Big Charlie, the Jack Russell, all piss and vinegar in his tiny frame.

He reached out and touched Annie's photo with the tips of his fingers as he did every morning after he woke up and last thing at night before he slept.

She was always there with him, every day.

He levered himself up on to his legs, feeling a twinge in his back as he did. Should he go to the doctor? No point, there wasn't a lot they could do and they were busy. It was only age, the incurable disease, catching up with him.

As a young copper, he'd been able to run and fight with the best of them. One day, a scallywag had snatched a bag and he'd ran after him, eventually catching up with the bastard near Old Trafford. Must have been all of two miles he ran, in his big copper's boots. The poor bastard never knew what hit him.

Outside, the sun was peeping over the roof of next door's shed, cracking through the haze of a Manchester morning.

It looked like another beautiful February day. If the weather held, he should push on today in the allotment. Perhaps later in the afternoon he'd take the dogs to visit his wife's grave in the cemetery. He could tidy it up and add some fresh flowers. It had been a while since he'd had a chat with her.

More fevered scratching at the door.

'I'm coming, I'm coming.'

He took off his pyjama bottoms and reached for the trousers hanging over the side of the chair. One foot in and then the other. 'Careful lad, we don't want you falling like last week.' He often talked to himself these days, when he wasn't talking to the dogs.

He knew why of course, loneliness, the need to hear the sound of a human voice even if it were only his own. A twinge of sadness welled up in the middle of his chest. He'd always loved solitude when Annie was alive. Now he was just alone.

He slipped into his slippers and shuffled over to the door, opening it to be greeted by a yapping Big Charlie and Cora, the Golden Retriever, turning circles in the hall. Despite being three times Big Charlie's size, she was dominated by him with a few well-placed nips to the back legs.

'Come on you two, time to go out in the garden.'

He didn't know what he would have done without the dogs since Annie had passed. They had been his support, his pals, his mates. These days, he didn't even see anybody from the police. They didn't come to visit any more.

Why should they? He was retired and life and the Force carried on doing what they had always done; putting away the bad guys, holding back the curtain of darkness that often threatened to overwhelm the city. He was proud of the thirty-five years he had spent on the Force. It had been a good life.

He shuffled into the kitchen to put the kettle on. He couldn't do anything before his first cuppa in the morning. It was almost as if his body was like a car in winter – slow to start.

He leant over to turn on the radio. Another habit; listening to *Today*, Radio Four's news programme. When he was working, he used to switch it on in the car on his way to work. Now, he found the voices comforting in the morning as they talked about the latest happenings in the world. Not that he cared any more, they could all bugger off as far as he was concerned.

The dogs circled him, getting under his feet, before racing to the front door. It was like this every morning, their routine. As soon as he woke up, he let them out while he sat down for his cuppa.

He opened the front door and they raced out into the garden, Big Charlie nipping at Cora's heels, desperately trying to be first to pee.

It wasn't great for the lawn or the shrubs, but they needed to go first thing as much as he needed his cuppa. He would take them for a long walk in the afternoon to see Annie.

He stumbled back to the kitchen and poured the boiling water into the tea pot throwing in two bags of PG Tips. As the tea brewed, he opened the back door and listened to the birds singing against the sound of the voices coming from the radio.

A blackbird had already started staking out his territory from the aerial of the house opposite, lulled into a false sense of spring by the glorious sunshine.

In the kitchen, the voices were discussing some illness in China. 'Tell me minister, are we prepared to fight this disease if it ever comes to Britain?'

A soothing, emollient voice answered the question. 'Listen, Tom, we have our scenarios if this disease, ever, and I emphasise, ever, should come to these shores. We are world-renowned for our work in these sort of infections and I am sure we will combat this disease in the same manner in which we fought two world wars; with resilience, resolve and the British bulldog spirit.'

'Is the bulldog spirit much of a defence against a pandemic, Minister?' asked the interviewer.

John Gorman zoned out of the words on the radio and poured out his mug of tea, adding a splash of milk. He walked over to the back door, breathing in the morning air. This was a time he loved even when he was going off to Police HQ every day to fight crime and his bosses. A time when the air was fresh and the morning light gave everything in Didsbury a soft glow.

At the front of his house, he heard a car engine starting. The neighbour was leaving for work early this morning, not like him. Either that or his wife had kicked him out again like she did last week.

John Gorman chuckled to himself. Young couples these days didn't know how to work at a marriage.

What was he going to do today? Read *The Times* when it was delivered and do the crossword. That should take until ten, and afterwards? He didn't know. Perhaps he wouldn't go to the allotment but travel to see Annie this morning instead of this afternoon. Make a day of it, take the dogs for a long walk and tire them out.

Where were they?

He listened for their usual sounds – digging, yaps from Big Charlie and plant pots being knocked over by Cora.

Nothing.

The car had gone too.

Strange. Had he left the gate open when he came back yesterday?

He put his mug of tea on the table and rushed to the front door. The dogs weren't in the garden.

'Big Charlie… Cora,' he shouted.

Nothing, not even the smallest yap in answer.

And the bloody gate was open. He was sure he had shut it last night but now it was open and the dogs were nowhere to be seen.

'Shit.' Now he would have to go up to the allotment and bring them back. That's where they always went when they got out. Big Charlie in the lead, head held high, with Cora wandering dumbly behind.

He grabbed a coat and closed the door behind him. He felt the pathway through the thin soles of his slippers. Should he change into shoes? No point, the allotment wasn't far away.

'Big Charlie… Cora,' he called as he closed the front gate and walked towards the allotment, hoping they would hear him and come rushing back.

Nothing.

He noticed the neighbour's car was still in the driveway. Strange, he could have sworn he heard him drive off this morning. Perhaps, his ears were playing tricks.

'Cora… Big Charlie…' he called again.

Still no dogs.

He walked to the end of the road and turned left, Bradford Fold Allotments were around the corner. He listened for the dogs and called out once more. A young kid on his paper round looked at him strangely.

Bloody dogs. Big Charlie would get a proper telling off when he got home. John Gorman hadn't been known as the hairdryer for nothing. He used to enjoy taking down young coppers a peg or two. A few well-chosen snarls usually had the desired effect. They didn't screw up again, not when they were working for MIT anyway.

He turned the corner and walked down the path to the allotments. His was on the right at the far end.

He called once again. Usually there was an excited yap from Big Charlie, followed by the clumsy, tail-wagging Cora rushing up to greet him.

This time, nothing.

He hurried along the path, stumbling over a sod of earth somebody had dumped. Stupid buggers, he'd report them to the management committee.

Where were the dogs? Were they here?

'Cora… Big Charlie…'

He thought he heard a whine from the other side of the hut. They were there, digging up his earth as usual. He called again but still they didn't come.

He narrowed his eyes. All his copper's instincts told him something wasn't right. He rushed forward along the path feeling the damp earth beneath his slippers. 'I'm coming,' he shouted.

He rounded the corner just in front of his allotment and shed.

No dogs and no noise.

'Big Charlie... Cora,' he shouted once more, striding towards the shed.

The door was slightly ajar. He pushed it open, hearing the hinges squeal in pain as the early February light crept across the floor, slowly illuminating a stack of plastic plant pots, three seedling trays, an earth-covered spade and a twitching leg.

He followed the leg upwards. The dogs were hanging from the eaves of the shed. Big Charlie's neck was broken and Cora had a look in her eyes that said, 'help me.'

John Gorman, a man who had put hundreds of Manchester's most vicious criminals behind bars, screamed.

Chapter 6

Ridpath walked into the weekly status meeting at MIT carrying a latte and a Danish from the canteen.

The latte was really a milky coffee and the Danish a bit of puff pastry with jam in it. There was a new caterer at Police HQ in Newton Heath and the descriptions of the food had improved even if the food itself hadn't.

DCI Paul Turnbull rose from his seat next to Claire Trent and clapped his hands. 'If we can get started, people, we've got a busy day and I would like this meeting to take no more than...' he checked his watch, '...thirty minutes. Let's finish by ten-thirty, shall we?'

He ran his hand over his perfectly shaven head, as if combing back hair that was still there, staring across at the assembled detectives sitting in front of him.

He'd been poached from a senior position at Cheshire Constabulary, or nicked as Claire Trent joked, to be her new number two at MIT. After John Gorman and Charlie Whitworth retired, she concentrated on moving MIT into the twenty-first century, improving its capabilities: liaison with other forces, digital detection, surveillance, interviewing, CCTV analysis and even offender profiling. It was a far cry from just 'nicking the bad guys.'

For her, he was the last piece in the puzzle; somebody who could bring all the new elements of policing together into one coherent investigation. He had a reputation for being a hard task master, but one who obtained results and was focussed on gathering evidence, exactly the sort of person Claire Trent thought she needed.

Ridpath asked himself where he would fit in to this new world order. Last week, he had even summoned up enough courage to ask Claire Trent.

'You're the grit in the oyster, Ridpath, the sand in the shoe. The one copper who looks at things differently. I've got a whole team who can follow the SIO's Handbook to the letter. I need someone who doesn't. Someone who works from his gut and makes those leaps of insight that solve cases. You're my bit of Northern grit, Ridpath, my bit of rough. You've postponed your decision long enough, are you joining the team or not?'

As ever Claire Trent was as blunt as a pickaxe in the head.

So he'd finally said yes. Only two more weeks working with the coroner and he would move over, spending his time permanently at Police HQ. For some reason, he wasn't sure whether he had made the right decision.

Paul Turnbull's voice brought him right back to the present.

'Right, the Russell case. Have all the evidence docs gone to the CPS?'

Detective Inspector Harry Makepeace answered quickly. 'They went off last night, guvnor, the trial's in two weeks at Manchester Crown Court.'

'I want no cock-ups on this one, Harry,' Claire Trent interrupted, 'this bastard managed to get off two years ago on a technicality and his brief is as sharp as a scalpel. I want him nailed this time.'

'CPS are happy with everything, boss,' said Paul Turnbull, 'I checked the submission before it went out, and Harry has done a great job.'

Makepeace smiled at Turnbull like a spaniel who'd just brought his master's slippers. Somebody was already brushing the man's teeth from the inside.

Claire Trent stayed quiet as Turnbull moved onto the next topic. 'The drugs and county lines investigation with South Yorkshire in Doncaster, how's it going?'

As he said this, her phone rang. She checked the number. 'I have to take this.' She stood up and left the room.

Turnbull nodded and looked back to the detectives. 'As I was saying, the county lines investigation...'

Ridpath listened for a minute as Alan Jones described tracking drug movements from Manchester across the Pennines. Apparently, the business had been taken over by two women while their respective husbands were banged up.

'Keeping it in the family, hey?' said Rob Allenby, another of the new detectives brought in to join the team. Ridpath caught a whiff of the man's breath as he leant over to whisper in his ear.

Ridpath didn't answer, zoning out as Alan Jones continued detailing the minutiae of tracking mobile phones and ANPR. He stared out the window at the February day outside. Somehow Manchester managed to look pretty in the soft morning light of a winter's day. Like an old man wearing a track suit and a baseball cap back to front. In the distance, a blanket of snow carpeted the tops of the Pennine hills, glistening in the sunshine.

'Ridpath...'

He turned around as he heard his name.

'...Anything from the coroner?'

He looked down to check his notes. 'One hundred and fifty-three deaths in Manchester last week. The coroner has decided to look into forty-four of them but nothing seems out of the ordinary. Everything is running smoothly.'

'Not digging up any more coffins, then?' said Turnbull. The rest of the detectives laughed, all understanding the reference to the Beast of Manchester case which Ridpath had helped to solve after exhuming the body of one of the victims.

'No, no more empty coffins. But we did have seventeen suicides. One man drank sulphuric acid.'

'Did he want to wash the taste of the canteen's tea out of his mouth?' joked Harry Makepeace.

'Or maybe the curry from Rusholme had been a bit hot,' said another.

'Does sulphuric acid burn at both ends too?'

More handclaps from the front. 'Quieten down, people,' said Turnbull.

Claire Trent re-entered the room, her face dark.

'Finally, a couple of housekeeping jobs. There's a new stack of MG5F forms with Chrissy.' The civilian research officer raised her right hand. 'Make sure you complete them correctly. Also CPS is being stringent on paperwork at the moment. Everything must go out in one bundle, clear?'

Again, he stared at the detectives, receiving a few mumbled 'yeses' in reply.

'Next the deputy chief has said the recent glitches in the IOPS management system have been solved. Everything should be working as planned from now on.'

Rob Allenby leant over to Ridpath again and whispered, 'I'll believe it when I see it.'

Another detective had raised his hand. 'I had a chat with a mate at Cheetham Hill last night. He said it was still screwed up and they are entering addresses by hand onto the files.'

'Look I'm just relaying what I've been told...'

'I heard two poor coppers from Stretford went to a house on a domestic – a step-father beating up his wife.'

'I'd teach the bastard what to do with his fists,' whispered Emily Parkinson, a DS sitting behind Ridpath.

'Turns out the man had form for domestic abuse, but nothing came up on the system.'

There was a collective shake of the head.

'Look people, that's not our problem. We're MIT, we concentrate on our job which is to prevent serious crime in the City, understand. No more, no less,' said Claire Trent. She held up her phone. 'The chief constable just called me. Apparently, somebody has killed John Gorman's dogs...'

'Isn't that a job for the RSPCA, boss?' said Paul Turnbull.

'Not according to the chief constable, he wants us on it. An attack on one of us is an attack on all of us. Ridpath, as you're re-joining and you know John Gorman, this can be your first job.'

'But I've still got a lot of work with the coroner, boss.'

'You said everything was running smoothly,' smirked Turnbull.

'You're on it, I'll brief you now. Meeting over, people. Stay safe out there.'

As the detectives filed out past Ridpath, he heard a few comments.

'Don't go barking up the wrong tree, Ridpath.'

'Pack it in, Rob, stop hounding him.'

'Where should a dog never go shopping, Rob?'

'Haven't a clue.'

'A flea market. Boom boom, tish...'

Ridpath could hear the laughter of his fellow detectives as he walked towards Claire Trent. Sometimes, he missed the banter... sometimes.

Had he made the right choice to come back?

Chapter 7

'Sit down,' ordered Paul Turnbull.

Ridpath took a seat opposite them both as the rest of the team filed out of the room behind him. He could hear a few dog howls from outside in the corridor.

Claire Trent spoke first. 'Like I just said, I want you to work on John Gorman's case.'

'Can't the local plod handle it? I've still got a lot to finish up with the coroner and she hasn't found my replacement yet.'

'That's her problem, not ours,' snapped Turnbull.

'I saw the names. You offered her one ageing detective three months away from retirement and another famous for his attraction to the snug at the Horse and Jockey. They've even got a seat with his name on it.'

'Still we made the offer, if she wants to turn them down, that's her business.'

Claire Trent's hand touched the sleeve of her DCI's jacket to quieten him. 'I think you'd be best on the Gorman case for a number of reasons…'

'Which are?' asked Ridpath.

'You know the man.'

'He was my boss.'

'Only Harry Makepeace worked under him too and Harry's stuck on the Russell case.'

Ridpath thought for a moment. 'You said reasons?'

Claire Trent smiled. 'Let's say it will be a soft introduction back into MIT…'

'We changed a lot of the systems and approach around here since your day,' added Turnbull.

'Investigating the murder of some dogs—' interrupted Ridpath. '—Will be a way of integrating you back on the team. Besides it's important to the chief constable.'

'And if he's worried about it, so are we.'

'It's a case that would suit your undoubted talents.'

It was like a Morecambe and Wise double act. Each finishing the other's sentences. Ridpath recognised he had hardly any choice in the matter. 'I still have to do all my work for the coroner...'

'You'll just have to work a bit harder. You've had a cushy number for the last two years, Ridpath, about time you put some hours in.'

Again, Claire Trent's hand touched her DCI's arm. 'Do you want me to call Mrs Challinor?' she asked.

Ridpath shook his head. 'I'll let her know. Who'll be on my team?'

'We thought you could handle this on your own.'

'I'll need somebody else to help. To show me the new systems,' he said looking at Turnbull.

The DCI glanced across at Claire Trent. 'We could give you DS Parkinson. She's free at the moment.'

'Anybody else?'

'What's wrong with her?'

Ridpath wondered if it was time to tell them they didn't get on. Emily Parkinson was still smarting about his investigation of Ronald Barnes and Rowley Police station, her ex-nick. 'Nothing. I just wondered if there was anybody else...'

Turnbull shook his head. 'It's her or nobody.'

Claire Trent stood up. 'Sort it out and quickly, Ridpath. I don't want any more calls from the chief constable or from John Gorman.'

Ridpath stood up too. 'What's the case name?'

Without missing a beat, Turnbull said. 'Operation Rover.'

Chapter 8

When Ridpath had closed the door, Paul Turnbull turned to his boss. 'I know you asked him to return before I arrived, but having met him, I don't know what you see in the man.'

'He's a good copper.'

The DCI scowled. 'He's not a team player.'

'Sometimes you need someone who thinks out of the box. We've got lots of team players, but not many who can think for themselves.'

'Let me rephrase it then. I'm not sure I want him on my team.'

Claire Trent made a moue with her mouth. 'That's your call. As I said when I hired you, create your own team and I'll back every decision. But if I were you, I would wait to see what Ridpath can do before you move him on somewhere else. You want results? He gets them. He did well in providing a link between the Coroner's Office and MIT, helping us get a handle on the Gangland killings and the Barnes case as well as discovering the identity of the real Beast of Manchester.'

'Wasn't that why Gorman retired?'

'The ex-head of MIT twisted a few arms and took a few short cuts when he put away James Dalbey for those killings. It always comes back to bite your arse.'

'So why have you got him on the death of Gorman's dogs?'

'I don't like it when the chief constable tells me to investigate a case. The death of a few dogs is not a major investigation in my book. The local plod could have handled it, not MIT.'

'I'm sure Gorman asked the chief constable for his old team.'

She stared at him. 'You may think that, but I couldn't possibly say.'

Turnbull chuckled to himself. 'Gorman's not going to be too chuffed when Ridpath turns up on his doorstep, is he?'

'He'll be spitting blood. But if he complains to the chief constable, my answer will be he's the only resource available.'

'And if the chief wants somebody different?'

'He's going to have to give us more resources.'

'Ach, you're a canny woman, Claire Trent. Remind me not to cross you.'

'You'll do well to remember it, DCI Turnbull. And give Ridpath a chance, he might well surprise you.'

'That's what I'm frightened of.'

Chapter 9

And so it begins. Not with a bang but with a Wimpy.

He remembered the joke from his childhood and laughed to himself.

It was time.

He had been planning this for the last year, ever since he had received the news, going over it again and again in his mind like a terrier worrying a rat.

The plan was ready. The details discussed and determined. The i's dotted, the t's crossed and the orders written. Every last sentence and instruction pored over until it was exactly right.

He was ready. They were ready.

The first two phases had gone exactly as they had been designed. Now it was time to ramp it further, turn up the pressure on the bastards.

There was an end target but they didn't need to know yet.

Nobody needed to know.

Except him, of course. And he would be leading them by the nose to their final destination.

Hell. Or as near as he could make it.

He remembered reading somewhere that hell was other people. In his world, it wasn't that complicated.

In this brave new world, hell was going to be never-ending pain.

The pain he was going to inflict to pay them back for what they had done.

The weird thing was he expected killing the dogs would be easy, but it wasn't. The way they had looked at him with their mournful eyes as he hoisted them up to the rafters, had surprised him.

He hadn't expected it to hurt.

Killing people was going to be easier.

Chapter 10

As he left the conference room Ridpath was handed a file by Chrissy Wright. 'I hear the country bumpkin from Cheshire has made you the lead on the killing of John Gorman's dogs?' she said smirking.

'Is that what they are calling him? Country bumpkin?'

She leant in closer. 'He's not the most sophisticated copper I've ever met.'

'He's still our boss Chrissy and you would do well to remember that.'

She sniffed twice. 'He should treat people with a little more respect.'

Ridpath glanced down at the file. The name of the investigation was printed in big, bold, black letters on the cover.

OPERATION ROVER.

'See what I mean? His idea not mine.'

Ridpath shrugged his shoulders. 'He's the boss. And this is an investigation like any other. We're going to do it properly. Understand?'

'Yes, Detective Inspector Ridpath.' She saluted him ironically.

'Talking about doing things properly, I see City lost again last week. Relegation looming?'

'Still higher in the league than United.' She tightened the City scarf around her neck, turned on her heel and walked away.

People seemed very touchy today. Ridpath wondered if Paul Turnbull had been throwing his weight around, showing the team who was the big new dog in town. He looked down at the file again. Operation Rover was still printed on the cover. Not the best introduction to life back at MIT.

Emily Parkinson was sitting at her desk, staring at her computer.

Ridpath caught her eye. 'You're with me, Emily. We're going to interview John Gorman.'

'What?'

'I said we're going to meet John Gorman.'

'The dogs case? But I was supposed to be working with Alan Jones on the county lines investigation. Why have I been moved?'

'I don't know. Take it up with Turnbull, but you're with me today.'

She looked around at her fellow detectives for support. They all kept their heads down or carried on staring at their computers as if the most important information in the world was on their screens.

'Come on, we'd better get a move on.'

Reluctantly, Emily Parkinson stood up and put her jacket on. 'Do you mind if I check? I was looking forward to working with South Yorkshire not looking into the death of some dogs.'

Ridpath shrugged his shoulders. 'Be my guest, I'll be in the car out front.'

Ridpath took the lift to the exit. He hoped this wasn't a harbinger of his new life at MIT; a dodgy case and a DS who was reluctant to work with him.

Emily Parkinson came out of Police HQ five minutes later and got into the car without saying a word.

'John Gorman lives over in Didsbury, posh end of town.'

No answer.

Ridpath put the car in gear and drove down to Princess Parkway in silence. They stopped at a red light. 'Listen, Emily, do we have a problem? If we do let's sort it out now.'

For the first time, she turned to face him. 'Look, Ridpath, we've been put together. You're my boss, let's leave it at that.'

The lights turned green and Ridpath accelerated away. 'What's going on? Why is everybody so touchy all of a sudden.'

'Everybody isn't "so touchy" as you put it.' She sighed. 'Look, we're supposedly short of staff and resources but Turnbull has been giving me the shit jobs or nothing at all.'

'So this is a shit job?'

'Investigating the death of a couple of dogs? It's hardly a major crime is it? Now if somebody had shot Goofy...?'

They both laughed.

'We don't get to choose the work we're given but we'll investigate this case as we would any other. Because it's John Gorman, the high-ups will be taking a personal interest. The man was an ex-chief super and still has many close friends in the Force.'

'The funny handshakes mob?'

'I don't know and I'm not a Mason if you are asking.'

'I wasn't but it's good to know. It's still a couple of dead dogs though, isn't it? Hardly Major Investigation Team work?'

'We still do our jobs. We gather evidence and work the case. Whether it's a dog or a stabbing, I don't work any differently.'

She was quiet for a moment as a February shower suddenly came from nowhere and pelted the windscreen with hailstones. 'You know you have a reputation as a bit of a maverick?'

'People have been talking have they? You don't want to listen to gossip.'

'Is it true you were one of the reasons for Gorman's retirement?'

Ridpath sighed. 'Not really. There were some inconsistencies in the evidence on the Beast of Manchester case, Gorman was in charge and, when they came to light, he decided to retire early rather than face a prolonged investigation of his conduct.'

'But didn't you discover the mistakes?'

'I was the coroner's officer who discovered Alice Seagram's body was missing. There were other mistakes in the investigation leading to the arrest of James Dalbey rather than the real killer, Harold Lardner.'

'Concealing evidence, pressuring witnesses, changed testimony from the pathologist?'

'That was some of it.'

'So where's Dalbey now?'

Ridpath shrugged his shoulders. 'I dunno. He got a large payoff from the government for his ten years inside. I suppose he's living off the money somewhere.'

'Ten years inside. How can anyone be compensated for the loss of ten years?'

'I don't know, but he was. Anyway, we're here.'

Here was a large detached house in a quiet road in Didsbury, not far from Fletcher Moss gardens.

'Not a bad place to retire,' said Emily Parkinson, getting out of the car. 'Worth a few bob is our ex-Detective Chief Superintendent.'

John Gorman was waiting for them at his front door. 'I might have guessed they would send you, Ridpath, rubbing my nose in it, are they?'

'No, sir. I was available.'

'You're back with MIT now?'

Ridpath didn't know how to answer. 'Nearly, sir. Another couple of weeks and I'll be back full-time.'

'And you are?'

'DS Emily Parkinson... sir.'

John Gorman looked her up and down. 'I've heard about you too. Got a bit of a mouth on you, apparently.'

Emily glanced across at Ridpath. 'I wouldn't know about that... sir.'

'No, you wouldn't.'

Ridpath decided this was going nowhere. 'Can you tell us what happened, sir?'

'Come in. I won't be offering you tea, you won't be staying long.' He turned and headed back to the rear. The kitchen was neat and tidy with nothing out of place. John Gorman sat on a bar stool, leaving the other two detectives standing.

'As usual, I let the dogs out when I woke up.'

'What time was that?' asked Ridpath.

'Around eight o'clock. I do the same thing every morning. I let the dogs into the garden so they can pee and have a bit of a run around before I make them breakfast.'

'So you opened the door to let them out?'

'Right. I came back in here to make myself a pot of tea, like I always do. It's my favourite time of the day. Hearing the dogs run around, snapping at each other's heels while I listen to the news on the radio.'

'When did you notice they were missing?'

'Well, it must have been about ten past eight. I heard a car engine start up. It sounded like it was the neighbour going off to work. I couldn't hear the dogs, so I went to the front garden and they weren't there.' John Gorman's voice began to break.

'What did you do then?'

'I noticed the gate was open, I thought I must have forgotten to close it last night and I decided to go up to my allotment.'

The man looked down and Ridpath could see there were tears forming in his eyes. he pushed on with his questions. 'Why did you decide to go there?'

The answer was stumbling, the man's voice cracking. 'It's happened before. If the dogs get out, that's where they go.'

'So you walked up to the allotment?'

'Did your wife go with you, sir?' said Emily Parkinson looking at a family picture on the wall.

The ex-chief superintendent raised his head. 'My wife has been dead for two years, DS Parkinson. She died just after I retired.'

'I'm sorry, sir.'

'So am I.'

42

'You walked up to the allotment.' Ridpath was trying to keep the interview on track.

There was a long pause before the answer finally came. 'I got there and found the dogs, Cora and Big Charlie, hanging from the roof of the shed. Somebody had tied a rope round their necks and strangled them.' John Gorman's voice broke again. 'Once my wife died, they were the only things I cared about. Myself and Annie, we couldn't have kids so...' His voice trailed off.

'Have you had any threats recently? Anybody with a motive for the attack?'

'Listen, DS Parkinson, you can't be a copper for over thirty years without making a few enemies. But, to answer your question, there have been no threats recently, nothing.'

'No local kids you've annoyed?'

'I don't annoy local kids, DS Parkinson, they annoy me. But look around you, this area doesn't have any kids, it's all old people like myself.'

'Good,' said Ridpath closing his notebook. 'We'll go up to the allotment and take a look around.'

John Gorman nodded slowly, his eyes glistening. 'I won't come with you, I can't come with you. The place is tainted for me now. You know there were only two things I enjoyed in my life since leaving the Force; my dogs and the allotment. Both have been taken from me.'

'I'm sorry to ask this but what happened to the dogs?' As he asked this, Ridpath noticed a solitary mug sitting unwashed in the sink. On the drainer next to it, a single bowl and spoon.

'The RSPCA took the bodies away. Poor Cora and Big Charlie.'

'We'll go and take a look, see if we can spot anything.'

John Gorman stood up. 'When you find the bastards who did this, let me know before you arrest them, Ridpath. I want to be there.'

'If I can, sir.'

'That's an order. Understand?'

Ridpath was about to explain to John Gorman he didn't give orders any more, but stayed silent. What was the point? 'I understand, sir,' he finally said. 'I'll go and check out the allotment, now.'

Gorman's voice changed. Once again, he was a detective superintendent giving a command. 'Do it now, Ridpath. I want whoever did this caught and taught a lesson, you understand me? And if you don't do it, I'll find somebody who will.'

This had gone far enough. 'Please leave it to us, sir. Don't take the law into your own hands. This is a police matter and you are retired.'

For a second, it looked like John Gorman was going to punch him in the face, but, in a long moment, the man shrivelled before his eyes like a balloon being punctured, sitting down heavily on the chair.

The ex-chief superintendent, once feared throughout Greater Manchester Police for being able to cow criminals with one look, covered his face with his hands and began to cry.

Ridpath glanced towards Emily Parkinson and indicated they should leave quietly. She headed for the door. He stepped forward and said, 'We'll find out who did this, sir.'

There was no answer. Nothing save the sound of his ex-boss sobbing.

Ridpath touched him on the shoulder and then followed Emily Parkinson out of the door.

He couldn't bear to see his ex-boss reduced to this.

Chapter 11

At the allotment, nobody would have guessed this was a spot where two dogs had been murdered just a few hours before.

The place was quiet with only two people, both old men, preparing seed beds. Ridpath had always loved allotments ever since he was a kid. His dad had one before he died and Ridpath had a fond memory of being carried home after a day digging and sowing, the smell of the earth and sweat buried deep in his father's shirt.

That was before the cancer took hold, before his dad coughed himself to death. The disease ran in his family. Another thing he had inherited as well as his big ears.

'I always hate the smells of these places, don't you?' said Emily Parkinson. 'Too much manure and rotting vegetables.'

Ridpath didn't answer, staring out across the separate plots, each as individual as the owner. Some were neat and well ordered; beds planted in straight lines, precise sections for the different plants. Others were more chaotic with old pea canes leaning at jaunty angles like drunken sailors after a few too many.

Ridpath spotted a stretch of police tape waving in the breeze. 'Gorman's plot is over there.'

They walked slowly towards the shed. The land was open here, the view blocked only by the occasional bush or large plant. 'Whoever did it wasn't afraid of being seen.'

'At eight in the morning, I don't suppose there were a lot of people working up here.'

'We should check it out though.'

They reached the shed. Other than the strip of police tape flapping in the wind, there was nothing to suggest the dogs had been killed. Emily Parkinson looked around before finally saying, 'So the dogs were either taken and driven up here or they came on their own and somebody attacked them.'

'My vote is for the first. This was a deliberate attack, not something random.'

'So how did he get them up here?'

'My bet is meat laced with a sedative. Either knock them out or make them docile enough to carry them here. Gorman said he heard the sound of a car or van outside his house.'

'I don't think we'll be doing a post mortem on the dogs or checking the toxicology. I can't see the Manchester tax payer paying even if it is John Gorman.'

Ridpath wandered around the shed, staring at the ground.

'What are you doing?'

'Checking for footprints in the soft earth, but there's lots of them.'

'The local plod and the RSPCA were up here.'

He knelt down. 'Hmm, that's interesting.' Next to the door, a piece of paper was wedged under a broken half brick.

'What is it?'

Ridpath pulled a pair of bright purple plastic gloves from his pocket and put them on. Picking up the paper by the corner, he began to read. 'It's a flyer for a local undertaker, but it's been torn in half and the name is missing. Why would John Gorman have this here?'

'Perhaps it's been there for a couple of years. Remember he said his wife died two years ago.'

'I don't think so. The paper is still white, not faded in the sun.'

'It's Manchester not the south of France.'

'Still, it looks and feels like it was placed there.' Ridpath checked the flyer again. 'The "something" Undertakers. All your funeral needs.'

Somewhere inside his head, alarm bells were going off. Which undertakers? Perhaps somebody back at the Coroner's Office would recognise it. He took out an evidence bag from his other pocket and placed the paper carefully in it.

'You got a rabbit in there too?'

He looked at her quizzically.

'Your pockets…'

'Always be prepared, saves trudging all the way back to the car.' He stood up. 'Right, we're done here.' Ridpath checked his watch. 'I need to get back to my other job.'

'With the Coroner?'

He nodded. 'Can you follow up here? Do a local canvas and see if anybody saw anything this morning. Check if other dogs have been killed in the area?'

'You want to know if this was a random attack or if John Gorman was targeted?'

'Exactly. But it feels planned to me, not random. Also see if there's any CCTV anywhere?'

'Out here, doubtful. And there's not a lot of cameras in suburbia.'

'Check it anyway, we may get lucky.'

'What are you going to do?'

Ridpath held up the flyer from the undertaker. 'I'm going to look into this. For some reason, I feel it shouldn't be here.'

Chapter 12

He watched from behind a tree on the golf course. He'd already been home to change his clothes, getting rid of them on his way here. The bloody dogs had covered him in saliva.

There was Detective Inspector Ridpath looking as officious as usual and now with a young assistant. He had come up in the world. He must have been assigned to the case.

Good. It was early but it had to happen eventually.

He knew Gorman would go squealing to the chief constable as soon as he found the bodies of his precious dogs. It had been planned for MIT to be the investigators rather than the local nick but having Ridpath involved from the start was an added bonus.

This was going to be fun.

He continued watching until Ridpath and his woman had finished walking around the shed and the surrounding area. Then Ridpath left, leaving the woman on her own.

Should he give her a little surprise?

Slit her throat? Knock her over the head with a hammer?

No. Keep to the plan. Always keep to the plan.

He couldn't resist getting closer though. He walked down the path near the Mersey and around the back of the allotment, occasionally stopping to check on the woman.

She was going around to the few allotment owners who were working on their vegetable patches and talking to them.

He couldn't resist it.

He walked into the allotment and right past her.

'Excuse me.'

He pretended not to hear.

'Excuse me,' she said in a louder voice, running after him. 'Could I ask you a few questions?'

He turned to face her. She was quite pretty in a dowdy sort of way, but not his type. Not that he had a type any more. He'd lost all interest in the opposite sex a long time ago. They only mattered when they were useful to him. When they helped the plan.

'I'm off to my allotment, love.' He waved vaguely towards the far corner.

'It won't take long.' She took out her notebook. 'My name is Detective Sergeant Parkinson, we're looking into an incident that happened this morning. Were you here?'

'What time?'

'Around 8.10 am.'

He smiled. 'No, too early, love, I was still making zeds.'

She looked at him quizzically.

'Still asleep love, in the land of nod. Don't wake up till well past nine. Mornings don't agree with me.'

She laughed. 'I know how you feel. So you didn't see anything at that time.'

'Just you in my dreams, love.'

She started to blush. She really was quite innocent. Coppers were getting younger and younger.

'Thank you for your time, sir.'

'No worries.'

He turned to walk away, he had been reckless coming here. He should have stayed on the golf course, watching from a distance.

'Before you go, sir,' she called after him.

His hand went to the knife he kept in his jacket pocket. What had she spotted? What mistake had he made?

'Could I get your name and address for our records?'

He smiled. 'It's George, George Charlton. I live at 7 Aylesbury Street.' He quickly invented a name and address. She might checkup later but if she did he would be long gone.

'How do you spell that sir? Charlton as in Sir Bobby?'

'That's right, but he's a bit before your time, love.'

'Nah, United's the best team with him in it. 1968 European Cup.'

'Stepney, Brennan, Dunne, Foulkes, Nobby Stiles, Paddy Crerand, Best, Sadler, Aston and, of course, Bobby Charlton.'

She laughed. 'You know them well, sir, but do you know who was the man of the match?'

He thought for a moment, then held his hands up in mock surrender. 'You got me.'

'John Aston. Not many people know that.'

'I didn't. You know United.'

'Been a fan since I was seven.'

'But you're not from round here?'

'How do you know?'

'The accent, love, there's something about Manchester that puts a whine into the voice.'

'You're right, Preston originally.'

'Still from the North though.' He moved slightly closer and lowered his voice. 'What happened here?'

She smiled, stepping back. 'I'm sorry, sir, I'm unable to disclose information concerning an ongoing investigation. Have a nice day.' She turned and walked away.

She really was quite sweet. He would hate killing her.

But he would do it anyway.

They all had to die some time.

Chapter 13

When Ridpath returned to the Coroner's Office, Sophia was hovering over his desk like a kestrel waiting to pounce. 'Mrs Challinor has finished her inquest for the day and wants to see you.'

'What about?'

'She didn't tell me. Beneath my pay grade, but...'

'But what?'

'But I worked it out.'

Ridpath stood there, jacket still on, waiting for her to continue. Of course she didn't. She was too well versed in the idea that knowledge equals power to ever let an opportunity like this slip from her grasp.

Finally, Ridpath gave in. 'What did you find out?' With Sophia's ability to use silence, she would make a great interrogator one day. God forbid if she ever joined the secret police.

'She's got a job for you. An interesting job.' She leant in closer to whisper something.

Before she could speak, a commanding voice stopped her. 'Ah, Ridpath, you're back.'

The coroner appeared in front of them as quietly as a cat in slippers.

'I am indeed, Mrs Challinor.'

'Good, can you come into my office for a moment, I need a chat.'

The coroner turned and went back to her office. Ridpath raised his eyebrows at Sophia and was rewarded with a mouthed, 'Told you.'

He put the flyer in its plastic bag on the table. 'Ok, clever clogs, ask the others about this. See if anybody recognises it.'

'Will do,' he heard her say as he followed the coroner, closing the door behind him.

'You wanted to see me?'

'I did, didn't I?' She passed a piece of paper folded in half across the table. 'I received this in the post this morning.'

Ridpath opened the letter. 'Dear Coroner,' he read aloud. 'He's out and he's ready to kill.' Ridpath frowned, turning over the paper to see if anything was written on the back. 'Who's it from? It isn't signed.'

'I'm not certain but the postmark says Ashworth Hospital.'

'The high-security psychiatric hospital in Liverpool?'

'The one and only. It has two claims to fame. Ian Brady, the Moors Murderer, was kept there for thirty years until he died in 2017.'

'And our ex-pathologist, Harold Lardner, otherwise known as the Beast of Manchester, is still there. You think this is from him?'

The coroner shrugged her elegant shoulders and handed him the envelope.

He examined it carefully. 'All letters from a prison should be given to the wing office unsealed and the envelope should have the name, wing and cell number, along with the prison number of the sender.'

'There's nothing on this one, only the postmark.'

'Since year zero, prisoners have worked out ways to beat the system.' He put the envelope back on her desk and picked up the letter again. 'Who's the "he" in this? Could be anybody.'

'Actually, it couldn't be a woman.'

Ridpath smiled. Mrs Challinor was a member of the self-help organisation Women in Law, along with his boss Detective Superintendent Claire Trent. A group known as 'The Muffia' by some of the detectives.

'Probably just a crank trying to wind you up,' he finally said handing the letter back, 'Ashworth Hospital is full of nutters.'

'The psychiatric profession would love your classification of mental illness, Ridpath.' She glanced over it once more. 'It's the "ready to kill" sentence I don't like. For some reason, it sends shivers down my spine.'

'Somebody dancing on your grave, my mum used to say, when she got that feeling.'

'Well, it feels like somebody is doing the Charleston and I don't like it.'

Ridpath shuffled his feet. 'Do you want me to look into it? See if I can find out who was the sender?'

'If you would, Ridpath. The idea of Lardner communicating with me directly...'

There was a gentle knock at the door before she could finish.

'Come in,' shouted Mrs Challinor.

The door opened to reveal Sophia standing in the entrance. 'There was a phone call from a DS Parkinson. She wants you to call her back. Apparently some sports club has CCTV footage of something.' Sophia's forehead creased in a frown. 'Something about dogs.'

Chapter 14

Emily Parkinson was standing directly behind DC Phil Reynolds when Ridpath arrived back at MIT. Reynolds was the team's dedicated CCTV officer, one of the new posts instituted by Claire Trent since she had been in charge.

Ridpath was glad this time he didn't have to rely on Sophia and her trusty laptop.

'The footage is pretty murky, but I'm cleaning it up, won't be a minute,' said Reynolds twiddling some knobs on his console. It all looked far too hi-tech for Ridpath. He had only just learnt how to programme the timer on his VHS before they became obsolete. Now he didn't bother to learn any of these new skills, reasoning there was always going to be somebody better at them than him.

'This was taken from the sports club next to the allotment. Lucky for us, they were having problems with people nicking stuff from cars so they installed the CCTV. It's a bit far away, but it gives us a view of the allotment's car park and the plots,' explained Parkinson.

'Any eye witnesses this morning?'

'Nobody saw nothing – as usual.'

Ridpath did a double take for a moment before realising his DS was joking.

'Nobody was around that early in the morning,' she clarified, 'but I've put a note on the gate in case I missed somebody.'

'Good, well done.'

She returned back to staring at the screen without acknowledging the compliment.

'Do you want the good news or the bad news?'

'Both,' said Ridpath.

'Well, it's a dome camera using a digital system not the old VHS tape, and quite modern. This model was manufactured in 2015.'

'And the bad news?'

'It's a pretty cheap camera, using a CMOS sensor rather than CCD. They've compressed the footage before saving it. It looks like they haven't cleaned the lens since it was installed and, of course, it's actually focussed on their car park not the allotment.'

'Can we see anything?'

'It's the best I can do, I'm afraid. You need to watch the top left of the picture.'

Phil Reynolds rolled the picture and a time code in the corner ticked over to 8:08:13. A white van appeared and parked in the allotment's car park and just sat there for a few moments. A man dressed in what looked like a boiler suit wearing something dark over his head stepped out from the car and unlocked the rear doors. He reached inside and two dogs, one small and one large, jumped out from the back as he held their leads.

'The dogs weren't drugged,' whispered Emily Parkinson.

'Can we zoom in closer to catch the man's face?'

'I'll have a try but the image is too far away for this lens and it looks like he's wearing some sort of balaclava.'

Phil Reynolds tapped a few keys and the camera zoomed in, the image starting to break up before freeze framing. 'Sorry, I may be able to clean it up a bit more but this is close to the best you'll get.'

On the freeze frame, Ridpath saw the image of a man in a blue boiler suit.

'We're looking at a Caucasian male, probably aged over forty,' guessed Emily Parkinson. 'But we can't see his face.'

'Roll it forward, Phil.'

The freeze frame began to move. The man walked away from the camera with the dogs towards the allotments, before vanishing out of frame.

'Can we watch it again without the zoom.'

'No problem.'

The image reversed back to the arrival of the van and the dogs being removed from the back.

'There. Did you see it?' said Ridpath.

'See what?'

'Movement in the front seat. There's somebody else there. They just put something on the dashboard.'

Phil Reynolds reversed the footage again, this time playing it back in slow motion.

'You're right,' said Parkinson, 'there is somebody there, see how the light changes? But they don't get out of the car.'

'So we're looking for two people. Also the dogs look like they know him. They don't seem to be struggling or fighting.'

'Dogs like that are easy to make friends with. A few meaty treats and they'd walk off with anybody,' said Reynolds.

They both looked at him.

'I used to be a dog handler before I retrained in CCTV.'

'Ok, can you print me off the copy of the picture of the man. We'll show it to Gorman and see if he recognises him.'

'It'll be more of a blur than an image.'

'Print it anyway. Any chance of getting a shot of the number plate of the van?'

Reynolds shook his head. 'I doubt it, but I'll have a try. It's too far away and the definition on this camera is shite.'

'Is that the technical term?'

'Yeah.'

'Have a go anyway. Can you find out the make and maker of the van?'

'Now, that I can do. Give me a second.'

Reynolds pulled up some pictures of white vans taken from a variety of angles and compared them with the model used by the man who had killed the dogs. 'Looks like a Ford Transit Custom, built before 2018. Also happens to be the most popular van in the UK.'

'Thanks, Phil.' He turned to his detective sergeant. 'Was there any more CCTV in the area?'

'That's it. We could check the local traffic cams but without a registration number, it's going to be like looking for a City fan in the Stretford end.'

'Any witnesses?'

Emily Parkinson shook her head. 'I also checked with the local nick. There have been no reports of kidnapping or killing dogs or any other animals in the area. HOLMES has nothing either.'

Ridpath nodded. She had been thorough, even checking the national police data base. 'What about the neighbours? Did they see anything?'

Another shake of the head. 'Not a sausage. It's a quiet area, everybody keeps themselves to themselves.'

'Looks like we've run out of leads,' said Reynolds smirking.

'Ha, bloody, ha, everybody is a joker these days.'

Chapter 15

After briefing Claire Trent and Paul Turnbull on the progress of the case, Ridpath decided to go home. Turnbull had been scowling throughout the briefing as if he'd eaten something rotten for lunch, while Trent had been silent, merely asking one question at the end. A killer question.

'What are your next steps?'

The truth was Ridpath had exhausted most of the obvious lines of enquiry already, but he wasn't going to let them know.

'We know he used a white Ford Transit Custom. I'm going to get the data for sales in the North West since it was launched in 2012.'

'How many vans are we talking about?' asked Turnbull.

'Possibly a thousand.'

'You're going to check up on a thousand vans? Do you know how long that's going to take you?'

'We can probably narrow it down pretty quickly but it's still a lot of work. The other option is to go through the ANPR footage from the area. The van must have been caught on one of the traffic cameras.'

'Without knowing the number plate or the direction it came from, it would be like looking for a stem of straw in a haystack. Whoever did it could have taken back roads to avoid the traffic cameras.'

'That's true, boss.' Ridpath continued. 'Emily is looking at the angle that it might be somebody Gorman arrested who held a grudge against him, but there have been no threats issued.'

Turnbull sighed. 'The man was a copper for over thirty years. Do you know how many convictions he was involved in?'

'A lot, but it's the most plausible explanation for the killing of the dogs.'

'A revenge attack?'

'It's the likeliest explanation. I want to go back and talk to the neighbours. Somebody must have seen something that morning or on previous mornings.'

Claire Trent lifted her eyebrow. 'Previous mornings?'

'The dogs didn't struggle or make a fuss. My feeling is they already knew their killer or had at least met him before.'

'You're clutching at straws, Ridpath, from your bloody haystack.' Paul Turnbull sat forward. 'Are we going to waste resources on this, Claire? Investigating the death of a couple of dogs when we've got a county lines case with South Yorkshire, a series of post office robberies to look into and, just a minute ago, I had to send a team out to a stabbing in Longsight?'

'The chief constable is on my case. John Gorman is demanding action. He's already rung to complain.'

'But we can't justify it, guvnor. It's two dogs, for God's sake,' pleaded Turnbull.

Claire Trent looked down and touched the file in front of her. Her bottom lip came up and her mouth formed a tight line. 'Give it one more day, Ridpath. After that I'll go to the chief constable.'

'But boss—'

'That's my decision, Paul,' she said curtly. 'Make it happen, Ridpath. I want to show John Gorman we've done due diligence.'

'He won't be happy if we halt the investigation, boss.'

'We won't halt the investigation, we just won't put any more resource behind it.'

So Ridpath had left the room and briefed Emily Parkinson on what to do. He would go back himself tomorrow morning to talk to the neighbours. Perhaps she had missed something or asked the wrong questions. Either way, it would be useful to quiz John Gorman again. This was a targeted attack not some random nutter killing dogs because he felt like it.

Ridpath had a strange feeling about this case. Why did he keep thinking it was going to bite him on the arse? Was it just a bit of nervousness about returning to MIT full time? After all, he had been away for nearly two years now and the place had changed from before. Was he as good as he used to be? Claire Trent seemed to think so, but he wasn't sure. Two years was a long time in anybody's career.

He tapped the side of his head. What was it Charlie Whitworth used to say? 'Don't overthink it, son. K.I.S.S. Keep It Simple Stupid. Just follow the evidence, let it tell you what to think, not the other way round.'

God, he missed Charlie.

Chapter 16

'Hiya, I'm home.'

Ridpath furled the umbrella, took off his jacket and hung it over the bannister in the hallway. Outside the skies were dark and it was pouring down in a way that was normal for a February in Manchester. After the beautiful start to the day, it was as if the gods were wringing out a particularly wet dishcloth all over the city.

He could hear music coming from the kitchen. Inside both Polly and Eve were sitting at the table whilst a saucepan of something bubbled away happily on the stove.

'Did you get the milk?' asked his wife.

Ridpath palmed his forehead. 'Sorry, I forgot.'

'Looks like it's going to be water on the cornflakes tomorrow, Eve.'

'Again, Mum, but I had water last week.'

'Don't worry, I'll nip down to the offie, they're bound to have some.' He turned to put on his jacket again and face the floods.

'Dad, don't go,' Eve shouted, 'Mum knew you'd forget so she bought some herself. Two pints.'

'If I had to rely on your memory, we'd both starve.'

'Yeah, sorry, busy day.' He rubbed his eyes, 'I'm beginning to wonder if I made the right decision in moving.'

After being wary for a long time, Polly had finally come round to the idea of him rejoining MIT. She still wasn't happy about it, worrying about his health and the stress, but she wasn't actively opposed. 'If you don't do it now, you'll always wonder if you'd made the right choice.'

'Thanks, Poll.'

'But if I see you suffering or becoming ill again, I'll be down in that woman's office demanding a change.'

'Don't worry, Poll. What do the Chinese say, "Suffer a moat, grow in wisdom."'

'Well, if you want to be strict about it, we actually say, "*Chi yiqian, zhang yizhi.*" The idea only works if you learn from your setbacks, Ridpath. Remember, "*Chong dao fu zhe.*"'

'I'm sure you're going to tell me what that means.'

'Don't follow the track of an overturned cart.'

'Something I will avoid like the plague. Even in my police Vauxhall—'

Polly changed the subject. 'How is Claire Trent?'

'You're the second person to ask me. She's fine, political as ever. She gave me a case to handle today. John Gorman's dogs were killed this morning. Hung from the rafters of a shed.'

'Your ex-boss? How did he take it?'

'Badly at the time, he was distraught, but he'd recovered enough this afternoon to ring Claire Trent and complain about me.'

'Oh, Dad that's awful,' said Eve. For a moment, Ridpath thought he was going to get some sympathy from his daughter, but she added. 'Why would anybody kill dogs?'

He had forgotten Eve was listening. 'Sorry, love, too much information for an eleven-year-old.'

Polly was thinking. 'Isn't that one of the signs of a possible serial killer?'

'What?'

'Killing or torturing animals. That and being abused as a child.'

'Listening to this conversation is abusing me. Can we eat yet, Mum?'

Ridpath lifted the lid of the bubbling pan. 'What is it?'

'Chicken and corn soup.'

'Why is it green?'

'I didn't have any corn so I used peas. Same thing really.'

Despite having a father and mother who owned a Chinese restaurant, Polly had never learnt to cook. As she said, 'My job was to eat the stuff or serve it, not make it.' Ridpath and Polly had met in her dad's Chinese restaurant one evening and hit it off immediately. It wasn't long before he was going back for the chicken and corn soup virtually every night. Her father's soup was the right colour though; a fluorescent yellow.

'Shall we try it?' said Polly hopefully. 'There's pizza in the freezer if it's not great but it should be okay. I followed my mum's recipe.'

In the end, the soup was vaguely edible. They heated up the pizza anyway because Eve was a growing girl and she needed her carbs.

That night in bed, as Ridpath lay awake staring at the ceiling, Polly softly snoring at his shoulder, her words came back to him. Torturing animals was one of the first signs of nascent psychopathic or sociopathic behaviour.

Had he missed something this morning?

Had John Gorman's old job blinded him to another motive?

He replayed the images from the CCTV in his head. The man in the boiler suit wasn't some kid. He was at least forty and probably older. The motive must be revenge, mustn't it? Somebody who John Gorman had put away in the past and now held a grudge.

Ridpath was still asking himself questions as his eyes closed and he drifted into a shallow and troubled sleep.

Chapter 17

It wasn't how he imagined at all.

He thought it was going to be like sleep. Dark, uncontrollable, unaware of anything but the dreams drifting past like freshly blown soap bubbles on the air.

But it wasn't like that at all.

It felt more like a deep well, with him at the bottom, looking up and listening to the world above. A fuzzy and grainy world, just out of reach, like an old black and white film rescued from a junk yard.

He always thought he would be able to control it. Decide to surface when he wanted, pop up suddenly like a jack-in-the-box, shout 'Ta-da' and stare at the stupid looks on their faces.

But he didn't have any control at all, his mind floating and drifting, going where it wanted to go without any rhyme or reason.

He was sure he would eventually regain control, as he always did. He would manage it when he was ready. In the future when the dreams stopped and the world came into clearer focus.

But not yet.

There was a reason he was here.

It was the best reason of all.

He wanted to stay free.

He'd thought about it for a long time, read all the literature, worked it out properly.

He knew it was the only solution that would keep him safe and get what he wanted. He had no desire to go back into the four walls with their smells and noise and illness and hatred.

Here he was safe.

Here he was free.

Here he could kill.

Chapter 18

Don Brown hung his overalls in his locker and closed the door. Outside the window of the changing room, the sky was still pitch black despite it being the dawn of a new day. God, he hated February.

'Thank God, another shift is over, mate. Did you see the state of the woman in number three? Covered in vomit. Her friends said she'd had twelve tequila shots.'

He shook his head. 'Some people, hey? Can't take their booze.'

'Enough to put you off drink for life, ain't it?'

'Not really.'

The man shrugged 'Nah, I suppose not. I'm off home. You on nights again?'

'All week, but I've got the weekend off.'

'Same here. See you later this evening.'

His friend left in a hurry, the door banging loudly behind him.

The changing room was empty now, he was the last one there. Moving the old man up to the surgery ward had taken longer than he planned and put him behind time. Never mind, the NHS could have the extra fifteen minutes on him.

He washed his hands before he put on his jacket. He was always punctilious about having clean hands. One of the doctors had even called him a germaphobe, whatever one of those was. But he didn't care. Working in the mortuary had taught him cleanliness was far more important than godliness. Hospitals were breeding grounds for all sorts of bugs and germs. Why would he be wanting to take them home with him?

At least he was on days next week, the nights were beginning to get to him. He would go to work when it was dark and come home when it was dark, sleeping through the daylight.

Sometimes, he felt like one of those pit ponies who spent years underground never seeing the light of day. That was him, the human hospital porter pit pony.

He dried his hands on a clean towel and put on his jacket. If he rushed, he could catch the bus and be home in time to spend a few minutes with the kids before he went to bed. A time he loved more than anything else. As he drank his tea and they ate the breakfast his missus had made for them, sitting in their high chairs and gurgling away.

He checked his watch. Time to get a move on; he could catch the 6.23 bus. The bus stop was only 200 yards away and the one good thing about being a hospital porter is it gave you legs of steel from all the walking and lifting.

He ran out of the door and past the security guard on the gate. 'Morning, Norman, see you tomorrow.'

'No you won't. I'm on holiday. Off to Ibiza tomorrow morning.'

'Lucky bugger.'

Despite the dark of the morning, he could see his breath frost in the air in front of him as he strode towards the bus stop along the deserted road. Underneath his feet the ground was covered in a dusting of white. When he got home, a nice hot cuppa and three rounds of toast would set him right for a good sleep before his shift tonight.

He couldn't remember the last time he'd taken a holiday. After the rent, there wasn't much left over for holidays. Since the wife had lost her job, all the money went on the kids; they both understood it was the priority. Later there would be plenty of time for holidays.

Some days he missed the time before he was married; working at the mortuary, making a little on the side with the backhanders from the undertakers and not having a care in the world. But that all stopped when he was caught. Luckily, the police were more interested in the pathologist than him and he was let off with a caution. It was frightening though, a message from on high he needed to change. He met Hilary and before he knew it, Rosie was part of the family followed pretty quickly by Tracy.

He was a dad now, time to put his head down and work.

In front of him, a white van pulled up, a man stumbled out and nearly fell on a patch of ice, putting his hand out to steady himself on a low brick wall.

'Are you alright, mate?'

A cough, clearing the throat. 'I'm fine, just a bit of a turn. Thought I'd better stop driving. Pain in my chest.' His breathing was heavy and his face flushed.

'Are you sure you're ok?' He glanced back at the hospital, before checking along the road to the bus stop. The bus would be here any minute now. 'Emergency is back there. You could be having a heart attack. I can take you if you want?'

A cough again. 'Would you? That's so kind, I feel a little unsteady on my feet, I don't know what it is.'

As he moved to help the man, he didn't see the hand come round with a cloth to cover his face. He didn't smell the sweet fumes of the chloroform, nor did he feel the needle as it pierced his neck.

By then, the man had him in a vice-like grip and the world went black.

His last thoughts before he lost consciousness were who was going to read to the kids tonight?

Chapter 19

Ridpath was up bright and early that morning, before either Polly or Eve had even thought about coming down from their dreams. Outside, the light was just piercing the sadness of a Manchester morning. The sunlight and bright blue of yesterday replaced by a blanket of grey cloud just aching to rain.

He left a large pot of coffee for his wife and instructions for making cornflakes for his daughter. He remembered these from his youth on the side panels of the packets. It would at least help Eve make her own breakfast as she stared out at the world through the tangled forest of her hair.

He was now parked outside John Gorman's house, the remains of last night's frost riming the lawn. He had come up here to get a feel for the sort of activity he could expect early in the morning. But the place was as quiet as a bookie's on Christmas Day. Not one car passed him as he sat there, not a curtain twitched or a front door opened. It was like a scene from *28 Days Later*, and he had just woken up to be faced with a zombie apocalypse.

The problem was all the zombies were still asleep.

Finally, one old woman passed him dragging a shopping trolley behind her.

'Excuse me, madam,' he said stepping out of the car.

She almost jumped out of her skin at the sound of his voice as it competed with the rustle of the wind in the trees.

He took out his ID. 'Detective Inspector Ridpath, I'm making enquiries regarding the theft of two dogs in the area yesterday.'

She patted her chest. 'You frightened the life out of me. You shouldn't sneak up on people.'

His mouth opened to explain he hadn't sneaked up on her, but before he had time to respond, she continued speaking.

'You're looking into the death of Mr Gorman's dogs? I thought you would have better things to do. You lot are supposed to be short of resources but you still find time to investigate two dogs?'

The voice was as sharp as her tongue. Again, Ridpath considered responding but there was no point. Instead he asked, 'Did you see anything unusual yesterday at this time?'

She shook her head. 'A female policewoman asked me the same question. A nice girl, at least she didn't sneak up on people.'

He didn't need this at such an early hour. 'I'll take that as a no. You come by at the same time every day?'

'I do. Have to go and make my mum's breakfast. Same time every day.'

The woman looked far too old to still have a mum. She tried to edge past him. 'Can I ask you one more question? Did you see a white van, a Ford Transit parked in the area recently?'

She stopped for a moment. 'Yes. You can ask me one more question. And no, I didn't see a Ford Transit parked here recently. This is a nice area, we don't have many Ford Transits on this street.' She pointed along the road.

He could see her point. All the cars except his were what was euphemistically known as 'executive models'; BMWs, Mercedes, Jaguars and one solitary Vauxhall.

His car.

She sniffed twice and walked past him.

'Thank you for your help,' he shouted after her.

He thought about knocking on John Gorman's door, but what could he tell him? We're looking for a white van with two people? Gorman would chew his ear off. He would save the pleasure for later.

Instead, he drove up to the allotments. Here it was even quieter if that was humanly possible. The gates were still closed and nobody was working on their plots.

He had forgotten places like this still existed in Manchester: oases of calm, peace and quiet in a sea of change. Perhaps he should get an allotment, but he dismissed the idea as quickly as he thought it. He had yellow fingers. Every plant he touched died a painful death.

But listening to the starlings in the trees and smelling the scent of manure on the wind, he understood the attraction of growing things for yourself. It just wasn't for him. Tesco was more his style, everything the same size and wrapped in plastic.

After checking the allotment out once more and walking to the sports club to see the angle of the CCTV camera, he decided to go back to see John Gorman.

He couldn't put it off any more. Time to let John Gorman know the details of their progress.

Or, in this case, lack of progress.

He'd show him the footage Phil Reynolds had sent him last night to see if he recognised the man. But Ridpath doubted if he would. The image was too far away and the face covered in a balaclava. Plus he had to ask him about the undertaker's flyer. Why had he kept it in the shed?

He might get lucky but he probably would get a bollocking. And because of who the man was or, more correctly, who he had been, Ridpath would have to stand there and take it.

Sometimes he hated being a copper.

Chapter 20

He laid Don Brown down, making sure the man was comfortable. He wasn't as heavy as he had expected; carrying him downstairs had been easy.

As he looked down at the man's face, he wondered whether they had started to work it out yet.

Probably.

Ridpath must have noticed the undertaker's flyer at the shed. He'd made it so obvious even a Manchester copper couldn't miss it. Placing another on top of the cairn of Charlie Whitworth's gravestone was obvious, perhaps too obvious, but he had to be sure they made the connection.

He'd read somewhere that everything was linked. The paper the flyer was printed on came from a forest planted thirty years ago by a man in Scandinavia working hard to buy the Ford Capri built by a worker in Dagenham who'd just decided to go on strike after reading a flyer printed on the same press, using the same black ink.

And the world went around. And around. And around.

Cause and effect.

All one had to do was find the connections to understand the world.

All modern detection was about looking at an effect and trying to find the cause. A dead body would have a murderer. A burglary would have a burglar. A fingerprint at a scene would have a finger somewhere that laid it down.

The evidence would lead them to the cause.

But what if he messed with their heads?

What if, this time, the plan was to cause an effect. To lead them to a series of conclusions and then blow all of it up?

The plan was brilliant. All he had to do was follow it to the letter. That was his job now. He checked the details on the plan, so painstakingly typed out. This was version seven, and the instructions were clear.

Now was the time to extract some blood.

He reached for his medical case and selected a syringe. Tapping the inside of Don Brown's elbow, he found the vein and took a good sample. He would use this before he left to lay a trail.

Sometimes they needed to be led by the nose.

He looked at the next procedure.

Check the restraints are secure and padlock the freezer.

Done.

Time to wait now. In about an hour the man would wake and the fun could begin.

Until then, he would read and check what he had to do next one more time.

There was still work to do and the plan told him exactly when to do it.

Stick to the plan.

Chapter 21

Back at Police HQ, Ridpath took the lift up to MIT's floor.

John Gorman had been remarkably restrained in his bollocking. The word incompetent was only used twice and there was only one threat to ring the chief constable. He supposed that was a result. Gorman didn't know anything about any 'bloody undertaker and his bloody flyer'.

Nor had his ex-boss ever seen the perp. The man had gone silent at seeing his beloved dogs jumping out of the white van before finally answering, 'Never seen him before.'

'Are you sure?'

'Listen, Ridpath, I know how to ID somebody. Spent thirty-three years doing it while you were still sucking your mother's tit. Is this all you've got? Some ropey CCTV footage? What about the car number plate? What about ANPR? What about witnesses?'

'We're working on it.'

'Well, work quicker, work smarter, work like a copper not like a navvy.'

And he was off, the hairdryer in full, blasphemous flow.

Eventually, Ridpath had managed to escape but not before one last threat. 'Find out who killed my dogs or I'm going to kill your career. Understand?'

Ridpath doubted whether Gorman had that sort of power any more, but he didn't underestimate the man's connections. Why had Claire Trent given him this case?

As the lift doors opened on the MIT floor, Harry Makepeace rushed out of the office.

'What's going on?' he asked as he stepped out.

'Some bastard's gone and desecrated Charlie's grave.'

'What?'

'Smashed the marble gravestone into little pieces and spray-painted the word "Scum" on the fragments. One of the grave diggers spotted it and called it in. Worst thing is, the place stinks of ammonia.'

'Ammonia?'

'Looks like somebody poured bleach or something like it all over the place. They're going to have to dig him up.'

'Why would anybody do such a thing?'

Harry Makepeace shrugged his shoulders. 'Beats me. There's some sick fucks out there. Now I have to go and tell his widow.'

'Shit.'

'Dead right. Sometimes I hate being a copper.' He shook his head and wandered past Ridpath.

'Harry, when did this happen?'

'Must have been the night before last if the grave digger reported it yesterday. Nobody let us know until a sergeant at the local nick recognised Charlie's name and made the connection.'

'Were any other graves touched?'

'That's the weird thing. It was only Charlie's. None of the rest were damaged in any way. The bastard even left a flyer for an undertaker next to the grave.'

Makepeace wandered off to pick up his coat. Ridpath stood there for a moment.

It was too much of a coincidence, wasn't it?

Emily Parkinson approached him. 'Was it any help this morning?'

Ridpath stared at her uncomprehending.

'Going back to John Gorman's house,' she added.

He brushed his hair off his eye to cover his confusion. 'Not much use. Nobody had seen a white van and the allotment was deserted.'

'The man who killed the dogs must have used a different car when he was casing the scene.'

'Yeah, must have.'

'Speaks of planning and pre-meditation, doesn't it?'

'What?'

'He's been planning this for a while. It's not something he did on the spur of the moment.' She stared at him. 'Excuse me, Ridpath but you seem to be distracted.'

'Yes, planning. Of course, he planned it. He had to know John Gorman released his dogs every morning. What worries me more is the desecration of Charlie Whitworth's grave.'

'I heard about it, pretty sick.'

'Charlie used to work for John Gorman at MIT.'

Her forehead creased. 'You think the two are linked?'

'I don't know but you'd better grab your coat.'

'What? Where are we going?'

'To the dead centre of Manchester, where else?'

'But I have training with Paul Turnbull.'

'This is more important. Come on.'

Chapter 22

By the time they found somewhere to park next to the lodge at Southern Cemetery, it was nearly lunchtime. A police constable from the local nick was waiting for them.

'Morning, sir.'

Ridpath checked his watch. 'Actually, it's afternoon. Never mind, show us where it is.'

'This way, sir.'

'You can nip off for a break afterwards.'

'Can't, sir. The family will be here soon. I should be around in case they have any questions.'

Ridpath stared at the young man, he couldn't have been more than twenty years old. 'You still on probation?'

'I am, sir.'

'It's Ridpath, Constable?'

'Allchurch, sir, I mean Mr Ridpath.'

'And this is DS Parkinson.'

Parkinson grunted hello.

'Don't worry about her, she just looks mean.'

They walked along a path shaded by trees. On either side, large Victorian monuments to long dead and long forgotten Mancunians lined the way.

'We think whoever did it came over the fence near the bus stop, sir.'

'Why?'

'I found shoe prints in the earth near the wall. They were still fresh after all the rain we had yesterday, sir.'

'That was diligent of you.'

'A CSI has taken a cast of the shoe and dusted the gravestone, or what remains of it, for prints.'

'Did he get any?'

'No, sir. Clean.'

'More's the pity.'

'And it must have been after ten o'clock at night. The security guard did his rounds at that time and the grave was untouched.'

'Who discovered it?'

'The same security guard. Did his morning round just before the gates opened at eight a.m. yesterday.'

'Pretty big time window,' said Parkinson.

'It's over there, sir.' The young constable paused for a moment. 'Was he a good copper, sir?'

'Who?'

'Charles Whitworth.'

'Charlie, he was the best.' For a brief moment, Ridpath flashed back to Charlie Whitworth, hitching up his trousers, his bottom lip coming to cover the ends of his moustache and the famously gravelly voice intoning. 'Evidence, Ridpath, collect the bloody evidence and the crime solves itself.'

'It's where the small black pile of stones is sir.'

Ridpath stared where the constable was pointing. 'It's a cairn, not a pile of stones. At least it's an attempt at one.'

The constable was staring at the shattered gravestone three rows in from the path. 'Someone must have hated him pretty badly.'

'Not someone, half of Manchester, PC Allchurch. He was good at the job was Charlie.'

'The CSIs have laid down blocks to walk on, sir.' The constable pointed to a path between the graves.

'Where are they?'

'Having a break in their van.'

'Do me a favour and ask one to come out, will you, and tell him to bring the flyer they found.'

'Will do, sir.'

The constable ran off in the direction of a wider road threading its way through the cemetery.

Ridpath watched him go. 'Probationers always get the worst jobs.'

'This one's not so bad. I had to stand guard over a house fire once when I was on probation, three people burnt to death. The smell... last time I ever had a Sunday roast.'

Ridpath looked around. He had attended the service for Charlie but not the interment. He couldn't stand the idea of putting Charlie into the ground. Burying him forever in the black earth.

As they got closer, the smell of ammonia became stronger, coming from the soil in the grave, suffusing everything around it. It was a smell he always associated with death and hospitals. In this location, it just reminded him of death.

Parkinson covered her mouth and nose. Ridpath coughed. It was as if the essence of the soil had risen up from the grave to assault his nose and shrivel the back of his throat.

He put on a pair of plastic gloves he always kept in his pocket and he noticed Parkinson follow suit. She was a quick learner.

Bending down, he examined the fragments carefully, trying not to breathe in.

'The gravestone was trashed pretty well.'

'But why bother to build a cairn?'

She didn't answer.

'He must have used a fairly heavy hammer. Brought it with him, with a can of paint too.' The word 'scum' was stark against the black marble. He stood up and looked around at the nearby burial plots. 'None of the other graves have been touched. Charlie's grave was the only one targeted.'

A CSI came running up from the direction of the van carrying an evidence bag with her.

'Hiya, Helen, good to see you again.'

'Wouldn't have thought this was a job for the coroner, Ridpath.'

79

'It's not, I'm transitioning back to MIT.' Emily Parkinson glanced at him. 'Besides, it's Charlie and it might be linked to something else. So we've left the cold comfort of Police HQ.'

'Mrs Challinor will miss you. She holds you in high regard.'

'Didn't know you knew each other so well.'

'She's part of the women's business group I'm in. Bit of a star is Mrs Challinor.'

'Anyway, Helen, we heard you found a flyer on top of this cairn.'

'More of a pile of stones actually, but someone has arranged them. They didn't just fall here naturally. We found this pinned under a stone on top.'

She held up a clear evidence bag for Ridpath to see. 'Sorry, can't give it to you, chain of custody and all that.'

'No worries.' Ridpath bent down to look at it. It was exactly the same as the one found in John Gorman's shed, except it hadn't been torn in half. The name of the undertakers was now clear to see.

The O'Shaughnessy Undertakers. All your funeral needs.

He glanced across at Emily Parkinson and, in a moment, it came back to him. A shiver went down his spine as he stood there, facing his detective sergeant.

'I think we've got a problem, Emily. A big problem.'

Chapter 23

It had been over two years since Ridpath had been here but nothing had changed.

O'Shaughnessy Funeral Directors was still situated in an imposing detached building set back from the road in the suburb of Northenden, a place of terraced streets, old-fashioned chippies, a Jehovah's Witness temple and local butchers. Old Manchester rather than the glass and tiled facades of the new monstrosities the council was creating.

There was a sense of community here and not a single artisan cafe or sourdough bakery in sight.

'What are we doing here, Ridpath?' asked Emily Parkinson.

'Two years ago I investigated the Beast of Manchester case.'

'I heard about it. There was a miscarriage of justice and the real killer, a man called Harold Lardner, was caught and jailed.'

He pointed to the sign over the entrance. 'This was the undertaker involved in the burial of one of the victims, Alice Seagram.' The images came back to him quickly; wandering through the frozen animals hanging from the ceiling at the body farm. Opening the long white freezer. Peeling back the body bag. Seeing her face frozen in time.

The memories would stay with Ridpath for the rest of his life. The nightmares even longer.

'So you think the flyers are pointing us back to that case?'

'An innocent man, James Dalbey, was imprisoned for ten years for the murder. Guess who the two lead detectives were on the case.'

'John Gorman and Charlie Whitworth.'

'Got it in one.'

'Is this James Dalbey linked to the attacks on the dogs and the grave?'

He opened the car door and stepped out. 'Let's go and find out.'

They stepped into the reception area, styled to look like any modern office with blonde woods, muted pastel colours and comfortable armchairs. Somewhere a medley of Beatles hits was playing softly. Ridpath could just hear the first chords of 'Let it be.'

There was one incongruous exception to the modern office design. A coffin complete with open top, and a mannequin reposing inside, along the left-hand wall.

A pretty girl sat behind the desk. 'How may I help you?' she asked.

'We'd like to see Padraig Daly?'

Before the girl could pick up the phone, a large florid man wearing a golf sweater and checked trousers stepped out from behind a hidden door. 'Well, if it isn't Inspector Ridpath. And how could I be helping the Inspector and his good wife on such a fine February day as this?'

The voice was Irish and the man behind it looked the polar opposite of the traditional image of an undertaker. He was bright, friendly and loud. But behind the back slapping and the bonhomie, Ridpath knew there was a lot more going on with this man. Some of it not altogether on the straight and narrow.

'Looking for something, Mr Ridpath? We have a special on the Everlasting Repose line at the moment. It's got everything you'd need for a comfortable interment; a cushioned mattress, Chinese silk lining in thirty-three different colours, a matching linen head pillow, all in an American cedar casket guaranteed for 100 years. Money back if you're not happy. There's even a panic button.'

'Panic button?' asked DS Parkinson.

82

'You'd be surprised at the number of people who have a morbid fear of being buried alive. For an additional payment spread over five years, this panic button gives them and their relatives the peace of mind they seek.'

'Where does the panic button link to?'

'My office. Between you and me, I haven't heard a peep so far from any of the clients who've used this service.' He leant in close, lowering his voice. 'To be honest, I wouldn't know what to do if I ever heard an alarm go off.'

'Mr Daly,' Ridpath interrupted, 'this isn't my wife, it's Detective Sergeant Parkinson.'

'So I'm guessing this isn't a social visit.'

'Right again.'

'What a shame, Inspector, I would have done you a wonderful deal. You'd better come through to the conference room, we can talk there.'

They followed the undertaker as he led them down a short corridor to a large, airy conference room complex with flat screen TV, designed in the same style as the reception, but without the open coffin.

'Since I last saw you, we've expanded to Wakefield, Leeds and even back home to Dublin. Business has been good and the publicity from the case helped us immensely.' He pointed to the seats on the opposite side of the fake walnut centre table. 'As my old da used to say "There's a good living in dying." Now what is it you wanted to see me about?'

Ridpath pulled out his phone and pulled up the picture of the flyer. 'Is this one of yours?'

Daly took one look at the image and shook his head. 'Definitely not, Inspector,' he said with distaste. 'It has our name on it but we wouldn't produce something so lacking in finesse. Our customers expect a quality service from us and that extends from our flyers to our embalming. And we would never describe ourself as an undertaker. We are funeral directors and proud of it. This is what our brochure looks like.' He leant back and opened a drawer, pulling out a glossy, magazine-like book with full colour pictures and images of happy families. 'We offer a lifestyle not a death, Inspector.' He looked at the phone again. The avuncular man about town disappeared and the angry businessman took his place. 'This looks like something from a morgue. Who produced it, Inspector? I've a mind to sue them. That piece of rubbish could affect my brand and my business if people saw it.'

'We found one in an allotment and the other in a cemetery.'

'There's more than one? Jaysus, I will sue. Are they after destroying my business?'

'I don't believe you are the direct target, Mr Daly.'

'Who is then?'

'We're not at liberty to say.'

'Well, that's no use to me. There could be thousands of these around town.'

'We don't believe there are, Mr Daly. But you confirm these flyers were not produced by your company?'

'I wouldn't be seen dead doing something so awful.'

Ridpath stood up. 'Thank you, you've been a great help.' He passed over his card and began to walk towards the door. 'Call me if you find any more of these.'

'That's it? You're not going to investigate these bloody flyers? Why even the telephone number's wrong on them.'

Ridpath stopped in his tracks and slowly turned back. 'What did you say?'

'The telephone number's wrong. It's not even bloody close.'

'Call it, Emily,' ordered Ridpath.

The detective sergeant pulled out her phone and dialled the number on the flyer, putting the phone on speaker as the ringtone trilled. Finally, there was a squeak and an answering machine cut in and a voice intoned. '*This is James Dalbey. It's time for the past to come alive.*'

There was a long beep and silence.

'What the hell was that?' asked Emily Parkinson.

Another shiver went down Ridpath's spine. He hadn't heard that voice in a long time.

Chapter 24

'We have a problem, boss.'

Ridpath was standing in front of Claire Trent's desk, next to him sat Paul Turnbull in the only chair.

Her eyes drifted away from the computer and up to him. 'I've told you before to bring me solutions not problems.'

He played the voice recording. '*This is James Dalbey. It's time for the past to come alive.*' Then, he sat back and waited.

'How did you get this recording?' she asked eventually.

'The telephone number was on a flyer for an undertaker's found at the shed where John Gorman's dogs were killed and at Charlie Whitworth's grave. We rang it and heard this message.'

'Is it Dalbey?'

'It sounds like him. I only met him once but the voice is similar. I remember there was a precision to it.'

Claire Trent and Paul Turnbull were both silent.

'What does it mean?' the Detective Chief Inspector finally asked.

Ridpath took a deep breath and plunged forward. 'I have reason to believe James Dalbey is behind the attacks on John Gorman's dogs and Charlie Whitworth's grave.'

'You think the two are linked?' asked Paul Turnbull.

Before Ridpath could answer, Claire Trent asked another question. '"It's time for the past to come alive." What the hell does that mean?'

Ridpath scratched his head. 'I don't know at the moment, boss. Plus Mrs Challinor received this letter yesterday.' He placed a copy on the table.

86

Claire Trent read it before passing it over to Paul Turnbull. '"Dear Coroner,"' he read aloud. '"He's out and he's ready to kill." Sounds like a nutter.'

'Who's it from?'

'Mrs Challinor doesn't know but she thinks it could be Harold Lardner.'

'The Beast of Manchester? Isn't he in Ashworth? Why would Lardner be warning the coroner about an upcoming murder? And how did he know about it in the first place?' Turnbull rattled off the questions.

'I don't know, but we need to find out.'

Claire Trent stared directly at him. 'If this letter is from Harold Lardner and if it is a warning, how do we know he's talking about James Dalbey? He could be referring to somebody else. Lardner was famous for grooming people to do his killing for him.'

'We don't, boss.'

'And what about the undertaker, what was his name?'

'Padraig Daly. He would prefer to be called a "funeral director".'

'Is this undertaker straight? Could he be involved with Lardner or Dalbey?'

'I don't know. It's possible I suppose.'

'There are an awful lot of suppositions here, Ridpath. Too many for me. But then again I'm just a country bumpkin from Cheshire.'

The DCI stared directly at him, daring him to say something. Ridpath, for once, had the sense to keep quiet.

'Hmm. You are right, Paul, too many unknowns.' Claire Trent stroked the side of her face. 'But we have to take anything involving Harold Lardner seriously. The press could have a field day if we ignored it. What are your next steps, Ridpath?'

'DS Parkinson is tracing the number as we speak boss. But my bet is it will lead us nowhere. There are two things we have to do. First, is find out what's happened to James Dalbey since he left prison.'

'He's probably on a tropical island surrounded with beautiful women with the money he received in compensation from the British taxpayer.'

'Your fantasy, not his Paul,' said Claire Trent.

'Too bloody right. Better than being in Manchester surrounded by coppers.'

Claire Trent ignored him. 'And what's your second step, Ridpath?'

'To go and see Harold Lardner. It's time we had a chat with the Beast.'

Chapter 25

Don Brown opened his eyes.

For a moment the world was dark, then he noticed a small yellow light off to his left piercing the gloom. A pin prick of light.

He tried to move but couldn't. His hands and feet were gripped tightly. He tried kicking out, but his legs wouldn't move.

Where was he?

What had happened?

He remembered the unsteady man and a hand coming over his mouth.

Then nothing.

He tried to scream but his mouth couldn't move. A pain shot though his lips as he tried to force his jaws open. Something was holding his lips together.

A wave of panic surged through his body as the elemental urge of flight or fight sent a cascade of adrenalin into his brain.

Where was he?

Why couldn't he move?

Stay calm, Don, stay calm. He closed his eyes, concentrating on his breathing.

In.

Out.

In.

Out.

In.

He felt the warm air fill his chest.

Better, Don, stay calm.

He wriggled his body, feeling his shoulders hit smooth walls. He was in some sort of box. Why was he in a box?

And then it hit him. Was he in a coffin? Had somebody buried him alive?

Once more, panic surged through his body. He rocked from side to side, feeling the smooth walls and the ropes holding his hands strain and tighten.

He stopped, panting. Got to control yourself. Think!

He tried lifting his head but it only rose three inches before touching a solid surface. The material was smooth, plasticky to touch, not made from wood.

Where was he?

He tried to kick out with his legs, rocking his body from side to side. He felt the box move a little.

Perhaps if he rocked it harder he could push it on to its side?

He threw his body against one side, feeling it rock slightly but not move too much.

He was sweating now and breathing heavily. Was the box airtight? Would he run out of air? He didn't want to run out of air.

Maybe he should kick against the lid?

He lifted his knees and tried to push them against the lid, feeling the strain on his upper thighs.

The lid wouldn't budge.

He pushed harder, feeling the sweat run from his brow and drip down his face. His breathing became more ragged now and he was panting harder. A cloud of hot, damp air seemed to hang over him, his shirt clammy against his skin.

He relaxed his body. He had to conserve his energy.

They would let him out soon, wouldn't they? It was just somebody's idea of a joke, but this time they'd gone too far.

What was that?

It sounded like a cough or somebody clearing their throat before they spoke.

He heard a voice.

'Mr Brown, I wouldn't struggle too much if I were you.'

A muffled voice talking to him. Was somebody out there?

He tried to answer but his jaws still wouldn't move.

Another cough. 'You may have realised by now, you are in a box. I have taken the precaution of tying your hands and feet together as well as wrapping your mouth in duct tape. We wouldn't want the neighbours to hear, would we?'

There are neighbours? He must be in a house.

'You have oxygen and if you look to the top right, you will see a small hole which allows a limited amount of air in. We don't want you to suffocate. But, as you will have worked out by now, the more you move, the more oxygen you consume.'

The voice was warm and almost friendly, like a beloved uncle talking to an errant child.

He tried to shout again. *Please release me, let me go.* But his jaws were clamped tightly by the tape.

He stopped and waited, listening for the man and his voice. In the silence, his breathing sounded short and wheezy.

Another cough, and the voice began speaking again. 'You may be wondering what we want and why we have locked you in here. But we're not going to tell you. Perhaps in a few moments you might guess the truth or you may continue in a state of ignorance. It is a state most human beings happily live in for most of their lives. You can enjoy it for the few moments you have left in yours.'

What was that? What was he saying?

'But what I will tell you is you are presently lying in an ice box. A floor standing freezer might be a better name for it. Just an ordinary home variety, nothing fancy I'm afraid. In a few moments, I'm going to switch it on. You'll hear a motor start up and perhaps you will feel the vibrations through the fabric of the freezer. I've also arranged for a light to come on. We wouldn't want you to die in the dark, would we?'

Die? Was he going to die? He didn't want to die. Not now, not when there was so much to live for.

'You might see the delicious irony of your death. Or you might not. But as the cold increases and your bodily functions begin to shut down, I'd like you to think of this. Alice Seagram spent ten years in such a box. I hope you enjoy the rest of your life there.'

What? What did he say?

He kicked and wriggled and rocked his body against the side wall again and again and again, until he was exhausted, lying there, panting, desperately trying to catch his breath.

'Good bye, Mr Brown.'

A loud click and a motor hummed into life. He could feel the vibrations through the walls of the freezer. A light came on, flooding the interior with an intense, brain-shattering brightness.

He shut his eyes, forcing his eyelids together to cut out the bright light, still seeing bright spots imprinted on his retina.

When the spots had vanished, he slowly opened his eyes again.

He raised his head three inches until it touched the lid and looked down past his chest. He was in a white, ridged box slightly longer than his body. His hands were tied together in front of him and his legs were bound at the knees and ankles with tape.

Perhaps, if he bent slightly, he could use his fingers to undo the tape around his legs. He scrunched up his body, trying to reach down to his knees. He felt his fingers crawl over the fabric of his trousers and touch the edge of the tape.

A bit further and he could undo it.

He pressed his body against the side, trying to reach further but his fingers just touched the tape, sliding over the edge of it, but unable to pull it apart.

Scrunching his body up even more, he extended his fingers another inch. If he could only reach a little further, perhaps…

As he exhaled and stretched his fingers out for one last try, he noticed his breath frosting the air. A cold wind swept across the skin of his hand and up towards his chest.

Fear, along with the sharpness of the cold air, crept into the marrow of his bones.

Chapter 26

Detective Sergeant Emily Parkinson was not a happy camper. She had just spent most of the last two hours staring at a list of telephone numbers.

Next to her, Chrissy Wright was also going through a reverse directory looking for the number used by Dalbey on the undertaker's flyer. It was grunt work, the sort given to police civilian workers like Chrissy, not to detective sergeants. But Ridpath had insisted she handled this personally.

She didn't enjoy working with the detective inspector. He kept far too much to himself, not sharing his thoughts on the investigation or the case. She felt like she was becoming his dogsbody, his gopher.

Go for this, Emily. Get that, Emily. When the grunt work had to be done for the Gorman case, it was her who had to do all the house-to-house interviews and check up on the CCTV while he swanned off to the coroner doing God knows what. If he ever did come back to MIT, she would make sure she was as far away as possible from his team.

'This could be it.' Chrissy Wright's high-pitched shout interrupted her thoughts.

'You're not at a City game now, Chrissy. No need to shout, I'm sitting right next you.'

'Sorry, Emily. The numbers match. It's one of those business offices. You know the ones who provide services for companies. Do you want me to ring it?'

'No, I'll do it.' She picked up the phone, checking the number pointed out by Chrissy as she dialled. The call was answered in two rings by a woman's voice.

'Telford Business Services, how can I help you?'

'This is DS Parkinson of the Greater Manchester Police, one of your numbers has come up as part of our investigation.'

'Oh, I hope we haven't done anything wrong.'

'We don't know yet. The number is 0333 8693 5277.'

'It's one of our business reply numbers served by our answering machines.'

'Who rented the service?'

'Just a minute.' Emily heard the sound of steps and the opening and closing of a filing cabinet.

'It was rented two weeks ago by a Mr D Brown. He paid in cash.'

'Do you have an address?'

Emily nudged Chrissy Wright.

'The address is 212 Barlow Moor Rd, Manchester M21 7GL.'

Chrissy typed it quickly into Google Maps. The image focussed and the red marker entered itself in the middle of Southern Cemetery.

Emily Parkinson rolled her eyes. 'You know that's the address of a cemetery. Apparently, your renter was a dead man.'

'Well, we don't check every address. As long as the punter pays on time.'

'Did you meet with him when he placed the order?'

'No definitely not. It's all done over the phone. We never see the punters.'

'Well,' Emily tried a different tack, 'do you remember speaking with him?'

There was a long silence. 'Truth is, I can't remember. We get so many enquiries and I handle them all. I'm the only person here. All the punters end up sounding the same.'

'One final question. Did you check the answering machine message?'

'Nah, no point. They're all the same. It's all done remotely once the punter pays his bill. No need for me to get involved, I'm far too busy.'

'Thank you, you've been a great help.' She put down the phone pulling a long face towards Chrissy Wright.

'What's next, Emily?'

The detective sergeant sighed. 'I don't know. You should ask his highness when he deigns to come back. And right on cue, here he is.'

Ridpath had exited Claire Trent's room and was putting on his coat.

'The answering machine belonged to a business service company, the client paid in cash and the address given was at Southern Cemetery,' said Chrissy Wright as Emily Parkinson sat back with her arms folded.

'Doesn't surprise me. What was the client's name?'

Chrissy checked her notes. 'The name wasn't Dalbey, it was a Mr D Brown.'

Ridpath's eyes narrowed. 'D Brown? Was it Don Brown?'

She checked her notes again. 'Don't know, the woman didn't say. All she had was a Mr D Brown.' Emily Parkinson sat forward. 'Who's Don Brown when he's at home?'

'If it's the same man, he was the mortuary attendant in the Beast of Manchester case. He was the one who removed Alice Seagram's body.'

'Is there a connection?'

'I don't know. It's a bit of a bloody coincidence though isn't it?'

Chapter 27

'We need to find Don Brown urgently. Chrissy, can you check the electoral lists for all the people with that name?'

'In Manchester? Or anywhere else?'

'Start with Manchester and expand outwards. From what I remember of him, he won't have moved far from his home town.'

'Brown is a common name, Ridpath, there'll be thousands of entries.'

'Better start right away then.'

'And how will I know if I find the right Don Brown?'

'We'll have to call each name to check. We're looking for a former mortuary attendant who would now be in his mid-thirties.'

'That narrows it down – not.' Chrissy Wright went back to her desk, muttering to herself.

Emily Parkinson looked up at him. 'You really think we need to look for this man?'

'I'm certain of it. Don't you realise, if it is Dalbey who's attacking Gorman's dogs and Charlie Whitworth's grave, he's been leaving clues each time? The undertaker's flyer and now the name of the man who booked the answering machine.'

'It's a little far-fetched, isn't it? And one more thing, I might realise more if you kept me in the loop instead of making me your bloody gopher.'

Her voice had risen and some of the other MIT detectives looked up from the computers to see what all the fuss was about.

'Look, I'm sorry, ok. I'm sorting it all out in my own head. It's like we're being led by the nose by Dalbey or whoever is doing this, always one step behind. But everything you've done has been useful. I wanted to let you know.'

'They said you were a bit of a maverick, a loner.'

'Perhaps they're right. In the last two years with Mrs Challinor I've got out of the habit of telling people what I'm doing. She just lets me get on with it.'

'Yeah, well now you're part of a team and, if we're going to be effective, I need to know what's going on.'

Ridpath ran his fingers through his hair. 'I'm sorry, I'll communicate better, you need to know as much as I do.'

'Apology accepted. Talk to me, let me know what's going on.' She smiled. 'You can start now, if you want.'

'That's just it, I'm not certain what's going on.'

'Start from the beginning.'

'Ok. I arrested Dalbey when I was a probationary constable—'

'I heard the story, first day on the job, wasn't it?'

Ridpath nodded. 'First day and I caught a serial killer. Dalbey confessed to murdering three young women when John Gorman and Charlie interviewed him.'

'The Beast of Manchester was caught.'

'And then two years ago, the murders began again.'

'But Dalbey was inside.'

'Right, we finally worked out Dalbey was innocent and we found the real killer.'

'The pathologist, Harold Lardner.'

'The man himself, now a resident of Ashworth High Security Prison in Liverpool. Dalbey was released and paid substantial compensation for his arrest and imprisonment. John Gorman led the team involved in securing his confession. He was allowed quietly to retire while Charlie Whitworth, his number two, was passed over for promotion and killed in the line of duty later in the year.'

'So what has Don Brown got to do with all this?'

'The body of one of the Beast of Manchester's victims, Alice Seagram, went missing. Don Brown was paid by the undertaker to dispose of it at a research facility near Preston. The discovery of the body helped us secure the conviction of Harold Lardner.'

Emily Parkinson stared into mid-air for a few seconds. 'So you believe Dalbey may be taking revenge against those who put him inside? Bit of a stretch isn't it? He was well compensated. If I were him, I'd take the money and enjoy myself.'

'But you're not Dalbey. I interviewed him in Belmarsh prison. He was a bitter man, blaming GMP for his years inside. Even worse, his mother died while he was there. We refused to let him out for the funeral on the grounds he was a risk to the community.'

'A pretty good motive. Shouldn't we be looking for Dalbey?'

'The short answer is yes and we need to find him quickly.'

'Why?'

'Because if it is him behind all this, he's not going to stop at killing dogs or destroying graves. Everybody who was involved in the case could be in trouble.'

'Including you?'

'Including me.'

Chapter 28

Don Brown shivered uncontrollably, his teeth chattering loudly despite the tight grip of the duct tape.

He had tried everything. Blocking the pipe where the cold air came in with his foot. Rocking the freezer back and forth. Pushing with his knees braced against the lid.

Nothing had worked.

The voice had spoken to him once more before going silent.

'We believe you will last two hours before your organs shut down and your heart gives out.'

He had tried to kick through the bottom of the freezer but only succeeded in exhausting himself, finally stopping, watching his breath mist in the cold air.

'As you lie there dying, please think of Alice. Her body lay in a freezer like this for ten years. Cold, forgotten, unwanted. The same fate now awaits you.'

Don Brown banged his forehead on the lid of the freezer again and again and again, only stopping when he realised the futility of it all.

He thought of his wife and children. He longed to hug them just one more time, to hold them in his arms, feeling their small bodies next to his.

And then he saw his wife.

She was wearing her yellow summer dress, the one she wore when they went to the beach. She was saying something to him but he couldn't make out the words.

He tried to ask her what she was saying but for some reason he couldn't move his lips. Why couldn't he move his lips?

She was beckoning him forward now. Behind her was a pool and the children were already swimming there, wearing their orange water wings, also waving for him to join them.

The sun was beating down and the water looked so cool and inviting. His wife was calling him to join her in the pool. He lifted his hands and tried to take off his shirt.

But he couldn't do it.

He clawed at the shirt with the ends of his fingers but still the fabric clung to his body. Why was the cloth so cold? Why couldn't he move his arms? Why couldn't he take it off?

His wife vanished.

The children vanished.

The pool vanished.

He opened his eyes and stared up at the white plastic surface above his head.

And he felt cold. So cold…

Chapter 29

'I think I've found him.' Chrissy came running towards Ridpath and Emily Parkinson waving a printout in the air.

Ridpath stood up as she handed him the paper.

'He's working as a hospital porter in Tameside.'

He checked the clock; it was less than thirty minutes since she'd started to look. 'Great work, how did you find him so quickly?'

'Stroke of luck. I was looking in the electoral register and getting nowhere. You realise there are seventy-nine Don or Donald Browns in Greater Manchester? And then there's another sixty-three D Browns. I was just about to start ringing them one by one, when I checked the wire. As I was looking, an alert came up about a missing hospital porter called Don Brown. I rang the local nick and they said his wife reported he didn't come home from his shift at the hospital this morning.'

'Could've gone for a drink or a walk,' said Emily.

'Not him, always comes home after work. And get this, he must be our man because he used to work at the mortuary. That's how they met. She was visiting her dad who'd just died from a heart attack.'

'Romantic,' said Parkinson.

'He's missing?'

'That's what I just said.'

'Come on, Emily.' Ridpath moved quickly to get his coat.

'Where are we going?'

'To see the wife,' he shouted over his shoulder.

'Why?'

'Because I think we've found Dalbey's next victim.'

Chapter 30

His face looked almost peaceful in repose, with a few flecks of white at the flare of the nose and in the eyebrows. An enigmatic smile on the blue-grey lips reinforced the impression. Like a male Mona Lisa caught admiring himself in a mirror.

The expected curling of the body in a futile effort to keep warm had not happened. Instead, the body was stretched out, filling the length of the freezer, the hands folded serenely across the chest as if it had been professionally posed by an embalmer.

Death always comes as the end.

Don Brown's death had taken less than the time allotted. The frenzied rocking and banging on the freezer had died down after a couple of minutes. Occasionally over the next hour it started up again, becoming shorter and weaker each time until finally there was silence.

That wasn't true.

There was still the sound of the motor of the freezer as it pushed ever harder to reach the desired internal temperature.

Minus ten.

Cold enough to kill but not cold enough to destroy.

Perfect.

An incredible beauty was born.

He stared at Don Brown's frozen face one last time and closed the lid, picking up his mobile to make the call.

'Emergency services, how may I help?'

A cough to clear his throat. He'd tried many times to cure himself of this habit but he couldn't stop. One day perhaps. It was one of the reasons why he had never made it as an actor. He remembered a theatre director criticising him during a casting. 'Listen, love, can you stop coughing before every line. Did the playwright write a cough in the script? No, well stop doing it. It's so irritating.'

He didn't get the part, or any others.

He coughed again. 'I've just seen a man breaking into my neighbour's house. They're away on a skiing holiday.'

'And your name is?'

'Brown, Donald Brown.'

'The address is?'

'10 Devonshire Avenue, Glossop.'

He heard voices in the background as the message was relayed.

'Thank you, Mr Brown, a response vehicle has been dispatched, they will be there in six minutes, please stay on—'

He switched off the phone, cutting the woman off mid-sentence. The next step in the plan would now be implemented – everything was right on schedule.

Using a syringe, he laid a trail of blood spots from the bottom of the stairs to the freezer. He closed the lid, pulling out a card he had written from his pocket, and placed it on top.

He checked his watch and set the timer which he placed behind the boxes at the back of the basement. One final look at the plans to see if he had forgotten any procedure and he was done.

He walked back to the stairs, taking in one last look at the basement. 'Time to turn up the heat,' he said out loud, smiling to himself at his little joke.

It was payback time.

Chapter 31

PC Amir Khan and PC Becky Donachey were having a quiet day.

They had taken a walk around Manor Park, checking for local truants, but the park was empty. Either it was too cold to wag off school or it was one of those days when lessons were more interesting.

Remembering his own school days, Amir knew it wasn't the latter.

Afterwards, they had parked up at Manor chippy. Haddock and chips for her and a meat and potato pie and chips for him. It wasn't halal but who gave a toss on a wet Wednesday in Glossop.

'You doing anything this weekend?'

'Nah, got a family dinner with the wife. Every Saturday, mum cooks for all of us. She spends years doing it and I always feel guilty if I don't go.' He stopped for a moment. 'Actually, I'm *made* to feel guilty if I don't go. Mums, especially Asian mums, all have Masters in guilt. You know, sometimes I think we should have my mum interview all the cons we nick. She'd have them pleading guilty in five minutes tops. You going walking again?'

'It's hiking and yes we are. As soon as the shift finishes on Friday, I'm off up to the Lakes.'

Amir took a large bite out of his pie and checked outside the window. 'You got amazing mountains around here and you go all the way to the Lakes to climb one? Mental.'

'Done all these and anyway we're collecting the Wainrights.'

'Sounds like a pub crawl.'

Becky sighed and went into lecture mode, something she often did with Amir. 'There are 214 Wainwrights, named after Alfred Wainwright, a walker in the Lake District who described the fells in his pictorial guides.'

Amir nodded pretending to listen as he bit a large chunk out of his meat and potato pie.

Becky carried on. 'They are hikes in the Lakes. We've done 79 so far. Should finish the rest by 2022 with a bit of luck. We're doing Scafell Pike this weekend, just over 3,000 feet straight up.'

It was Amir's turn to shake his head. 'Mental. I'll be scoffing a pakora, straight down.'

The Airwave squawked. 'Report of an attempted break in at 10 Devonshire Avenue. One intruder. Over.'

'That's close.' Becky picked up the receiver. '279 responding over. ETA six minutes. Over.'

'More cold food.' Amir put the Vauxhall into gear and activated the siren, turning the car 180 degrees so it raced down the High Street.

'Any information on the occupants, over?' asked Amir taking a sharp left at speed.

'According to the informant, occupants away on holiday. Over. Proceed with caution, over. Informant not answering his phone.'

Another sharp right and Becky was thrown against the door despite wearing a seat belt. 'Lewis Hamilton is it today?'

'I'd beat him easy. As long as we were both racing police Vauxhalls,' he added taking another corner.

Devonshire Avenue was up on the left. Becky turned off the siren before they turned into the road. 'We don't want them to do a runner.'

They glided to a stop outside a detached house, set back from the road. It was built from the local dark grey gritstone with overgrown gardens front and rear.

'Nice area if you can afford it. Shame they've let the house go to pot.'

They both stepped out of the car, putting their hats on, adjusting their stab jackets.

Amir surveyed the scene. 'Looks quiet. Perhaps our perp has scarpered.'

Becky opened the gate. 'Come on, he might still be inside.'

Amir looked over his shoulder. 'Shouldn't we wait for back up?'

'We should check it out.' She strode up the garden path, ducking beneath a tree branch. The large, etched glass front door was up a few steps, slightly above the gardens.

'Lovely house, must be four bedrooms at least,' said Amir staring up at the first floor. 'Big double bedrooms. With a bit of TLC, this would be a great place to live. I'll check round the back.'

He walked over to a high wooden fence at the side of the house. The door to the side entrance was locked so he jumped up and down a few times trying to check if there was a path leading round to the back.

Becky stared through the frosted glass of the front door. Accidentally she pressed too hard against the glass and the door swung slowly open, revealing a dark hallway. 'Amir, I'm going in.'

'Wait,' he shouted. But it was too late, his partner had already vanished inside. He ran back up the steps to the front door and strode through the entrance into the hallway.

No Becky.

His heart missed three beats.

Where was she? They should have waited for back up. 'Becky,' he shouted.

No answer.

'Becky, where are you?'

He felt a strong hand on his shoulder and he swung round ready to strike out.

'Calm down, Tiger, it's only me.' Becky stood in front of him, smiling. 'You make so much noise, you'd wake the dead.

The front parlour is empty. Nice room, but not my taste. Too old-fashioned.'

She brushed past him and walked towards the back. 'Kitchen and living room should be this way. We'll check here and then go upstairs. Looks like our perp has already done a runner.' She walked towards the kitchen past the stairs leading up to the first floor.

'Shouldn't we wait for back up?'

'The Sarge will be pissed with us if we haven't already checked the house before he gets here. I'll call it in anyway.' She adjusted the mouthpiece to her Airwave. 'Control, 279 here.'

'Come in 279.'

'Checking inside house for presence of the intruder. Front door open but... hello what's that?'

'What?' squawked the Airwave.

Becky stared at a small door on the left beneath the stairs. The white porcelain knob was covered in dark red smears. She pushed open the door, careful not to touch the doorknob. A flight of stairs led down to a basement.

On the left, a single old-fashioned light switch stuck out from the wall. She pressed it down with her elbow and the light from a single bulb illuminated the stairs. 'I'm going down.'

She began to descend into the gloom.

'We should wait!' Amir shouted, following her down the stairs, bumping into her back as they reached the bottom.

She had stopped to look around the basement. Two fan lights covered in dust and cobwebs gave a thin, diffused light across the whole whitewashed area. Blood-red footprints led straight to the single floor-standing freezer whilst, at the back, a pile of old boxes leant against another whitewashed wall.

In the half-gloom, she could just make out a note folded in two and standing up like a tiny roof on top of the freezer.

'What's that smell?' Amir's nosed sniffed twice. 'Like the stuff you use with windows. Or in a garage. An oily smell.'

'Yeah,' she muttered, striding across the basement avoiding what looked like blood spots on the floor, and pulling out a pair of plastic gloves from her pocket. The note was hand-written on card.

The man you're looking for is in here. Who's next?

She read the note again. Was the burglar inside the freezer? What was he doing there?

'Becky, we should wait for back up or the CSIs, we don't know if this is a crime scene.'

'And we won't know until we check inside. Imagine the bollocking we'd get if we called in a whole team and there was nothing in here but half a lamb bought from some farmer. Well?'

'But…' he protested half-heartedly.

She moved the card to one side and lifted the lid before he could finish. She leant over and stared inside.

'Jesus Christ,' she muttered softly before averting her eyes.

Chapter 32

Ridpath and DS Parkinson received the call when they were on the M67 racing to Glossop.

'It's Chrissy, Ridpath. Two constables have been called to a house in Glossop and they've found a body. It answers the description of Don Brown we circulated.'

'Shit.'

'I'll text you the address. It's not looking good.'

'Ok, Chrissy.'

Ten minutes later they were standing outside a large detached house interviewing the two police constables, having already navigated through the police cordon set up by the largest sergeant Ridpath had ever seen this side of a wrestling ring.

'We proceeded inside and...'

The shorter female constable was talking. 'Hang on, Constable Donachey, you're not in court. Just tell me what you saw.'

She shifted her position. 'Well, we got the call from control at 13:43 exactly, sir.'

'It's Ridpath not sir, and this is DS Parkinson. Where were you?'

She glanced across at Khan. 'We were parked up outside Manor Park, sir.'

'Why were you there?'

Donachey glanced at Khan again. This time, he spoke. 'We were eating, hadn't had any time for lunch.'

'No worries we were all uniforms once. There's never time to eat.'

Khan relaxed but PC Donachey was still standing at attention, shifting from foot to foot.

'So you got the call. What happened?'

'We arrived outside. It looked quiet so we checked the perimeter,' said Khan.

'And then I noticed the front door was open,' Donachey finished for him.

'So you went inside. What happened next?'

'The ground floor front room was empty.'

There was a squeal of brakes and a large transit van parked up behind them. 'Looks like the CSI team and the pathologist are here, Ridpath.'

'Can you brief them, Emily?'

She walked across to join the CSI team as they got out of the van and began to don their white suits.

'Carry on,' said Ridpath.

'We noticed what looked like blood on the door leading to the basement so we went down. And we found it.'

'Found what?'

PC Donachey blanched and looked down. 'A body in the freezer,' she whispered. 'There was a card on top of the freezer.'

'What was written on it?'

She thought for a moment, her eyes staring off to one side. 'Something like, "The man you're looking for is in here. Who's next?"'

'The man you're looking for is in here. Who's next?' repeated Ridpath.

She nodded. 'Those were the words, I'm certain.'

Ridpath ran his fingers through his thinning hair. 'Anything else you noticed, anything out of the ordinary?'

Becky Donachey shook her head.

Amir put his finger to his lips. 'There was a strong smell down there.'

'From the body? But I thought you said it was frozen.'

'No, not from the body, all around. Like the smell of the stuff you use when you put a window in.'

'Yeah, there was a strong smell,' echoed Becky Donachey.

Wearing bright white Tyvek suits with a blue line down the centre, the crime scene manager and the pathologist walked up to Ridpath. He didn't know either of them.

The smaller man put down his doctor's bag and spoke first. 'Are you from the Major Investigation Team?'

'DI Ridpath, and you are?'

He pointed to his chest. 'Dave Haslam, senior pathologist. This is Ann Summers from the Derbyshire CSI unit.'

'Hiya.' Her voice was muffled through her mask. 'Ridpath? I've heard about you from Margaret. You work with the coroner, too, don't you?'

Did Margaret Challinor know everybody? Ridpath wondered what she had said about him.

'That's me.'

'Busy man.'

'Have you seen the Derbyshire detectives?' interrupted the pathologist.

Ridpath pointed back to a pair of plain clothes coppers who were interviewing a pedestrian across the road.

'So who's running this investigation, MIT or Derbyshire? I need to know where to send my bill.'

'Not sure yet. We think the body in the freezer may be a man called Don Brown. He's involved in one of our cases.'

'Witness or suspect?'

'Neither and both,' answered Ridpath cryptically.

The pathologist frowned. 'Let me know which it is and who's running this case. Come on, Ann, I want to check out the body before it defrosts.'

The little man vaguely waved his hand and, taking his bag of tricks, opened the gate leading to the door. The CSI manager waved goodbye and followed the pathologist up the path.

Ridpath turned back to Khan. 'What was it you said?'

'The basement, it smelt strongly of the stuff you use to fix windows in their frames.'

'You mean putty? Soft, grey stuff like playdoh?'

'That's it. Putty. A sort of oily, sharp smell.'

Out of the corner of his eye, he watched as the pathologist and crime scene manager paused for a moment at the door before vanishing into the house.

'Putty? A sharp, oily smell? Like strong motor oil?' he asked.

The PC nodded. 'Yeah, could have been motor oil. It was coming from a stack of boxes in the back of the room.'

Ridpath glanced across at Emily Parkinson. Then he turned on his heels and started running towards the house, shouting 'Stop! Wait!' as loud as he could.

Chapter 33

He watched through the binoculars as the cavalry arrived. Did he have the timing right?

They set up the cordon and expanded it as more and more strobe-lit police cars parked at the side of the road.

The one thing about their behaviour was the total predictability of their actions. They all followed a process drilled into them from every crime scene they ever attended.

Secure the scene. Set up a perimeter. Clear the area. Wait for the detectives and the CSI team. Expand the perimeter.

It was all so predictable.

He spotted Ridpath striding towards the house with the detective from the allotment only a few strides behind him. They stopped in front of the two uniformed police and began to talk.

He focussed in on Ridpath. The man had aged in the years since they last met. He remembered sitting across a table as the man interviewed him.

But he was innocent then. He had always been innocent.

Until now.

He checked his watch. They were late but there was still time for them to arrive.

He spotted the CSI van as it edged towards the outer cordon. The police tape was removed and the vehicle edged its way slowly forward. He panned over Ridpath, still talking to the two police officers.

The van was three minutes late.

He had allowed them ten minutes to get ready and suit up before entering the building.

So far there was still time.

Perhaps, he wouldn't catch all of them as he had planned. He should have allowed more minutes for the traffic and their slowness.

No matter. It simply meant fewer people would be caught. This time.

The idea came from reading what the IRA had done to the British Army in Northern Ireland. The plan had simply replicated it. The irony wasn't lost on him. He didn't feel sorry for all the CSIs running around like headless chickens. Hadn't they all failed in their duty?

He could see two people in white suits emerging from the crowd. They would be the pathologist and the crime scene manager, the first to enter the building. One to assess the situation and the resources needed. The other to check out the body.

He glanced down at his watch again. The second hand was sweeping up to the twelve. Not long now.

The two people in white suits stopped for a moment to chat with Ridpath.

'Get a bloody move on!' he whispered under his breath.

As if they had heard him, they hurried off towards the house.

Finally. The last thing he needed at the moment was a long chat or briefing.

He lost them for a moment as the overgrown garden obscured his view. A second later they appeared again, mounting the stairs to the door, lumbering like two ungainly spacemen in their white suits and wellington boots.

Then they stopped.

What's holding them up?

They were examining the door. Why examine the door? Nothing to see there.

He checked his watch again. Only two minutes to go.

Get a move on.

Finally, one of them stood up straight and took the first step across the threshold, followed by the other, vanishing from view.

He could relax now. His work was done. The watch said just one minute to go.

He heard a faint shout, followed by another, louder this time.

He panned away from the door. Ridpath had broken away from the uniformed coppers and was running towards the house.

What are you doing? Stay away, it's too early.

The man was opening the gate and running down the path to the stairs in front of the door.

He checked his watch. Just thirty seconds to go.

Ridpath jumped up the stairs and vanished inside the house.

He was saving Ridpath for later, the main course in his menu of revenge. But no matter, if it happened now, it happened.

Now.

He looked at his watch. Only fifteen seconds to go.

He hoped they enjoyed the fireworks.

Chapter 34

Mrs Challinor had finished her third interview of the day. She was tired, grumpy and her back hurt. Even worse she hadn't found a replacement for Ridpath.

The first man had been fine on paper. She had found him through an advertisement in the Coroner's Office website: a degree in forensics from Leeds Uni, three years working in a lab followed by two years as a coroner's officer in the North East.

He sounded perfect on paper, but as soon as she met him, she knew he wasn't right. This was only confirmed when he stipulated he only wanted to work a thirty-seven-hour week as his wife didn't want to move from Sunderland. As an additional codicil to his interview, he stated he wouldn't be working weekends as he was going to commute back to the North East on Friday night.

She was polite and explained she expected more commitment from her officers. They both agreed he wasn't the right person for the job.

The second candidate was a woman who had done a biology and a forensic science degree but lacked any investigative or police experience. She would have been great as an officer in two years' time but not now unfortunately.

The third was a small man with greasy hands and a badly fitting suit. When she explained that a lot of the work involved dealing with grieving families, work requiring an understanding and empathy with the stages of grief, he asked her about his working conditions and holiday pay. When she asked him why he wanted the job, he answered because it was a pensionable career. And when she mentioned the sort of commitment she was looking for in terms of safeguarding and protecting the less fortunate in society, he stated there was too much mollycoddling of people these days.

He definitely wasn't right.

She sat back in her chair wondering what to do. She had only ten days left to find Ridpath's replacement. It wasn't going to be easy, they shared so much in common in their approach to the work and their attitudes to life and society. They had a mission to protect those who couldn't protect themselves. To be the voice for the dead in the world of the living.

'Damn the man, why doesn't he just stay?'

There was a knock at the door and she wondered if she had spoken too loudly.

Jenny, the office manager entered. She was wearing a bright purple skirt which flared out over her hips and her dyed blonde hair was held in place by a pink headscarf. 'Anything you need me to do before I leave?'

'Thank you, Jenny. Please check on the Garland case for me. I've set the inquest for a week on Tuesday.' The coroner paused for a moment before asking, 'Any more enquiries about Ridpath's replacement?'

'No additional CVs or enquiries, Coroner. I'll check once more before I leave this evening. I've empanelled the jury for the Robinson inquest tomorrow and all the witnesses have confirmed their attendance. Do you want me to give Ridpath a call? He was supposed to be in this afternoon.'

'No, I know he's on a case. I'll call him myself later.'

'Fine, I'll leave early tonight if that's ok?'

'Thanks, Jenny. Nice outfit by the way.'

'Do you like it? It's forties night at the community centre. I was wondering whether it was a little too purple. I mean, I don't want to look like a Tesco aubergine.'

'It's perfect.'

The office manager smiled broadly, the purple lipstick making her mouth seem wider than it was. 'I'll follow up on the Garland case before I leave.'

'Thank you, Jenny.'

The door closed in a swirl of petticoats and cheap perfume.

Margaret Challinor stared out of the large sash windows giving an expansive view over the modern wasteland that was Stockfield.

What was she going to do about Ridpath?

Chapter 35

Ridpath ran down to the gate and pushed it open, rushing up the path. 'Don't go in there,' he shouted.

The hallway was empty and dark.

He stood just inside and shouted again. 'Dr Haslam. Come out now.'

There was a muffled response from below his feet. They were in the basement.

He searched for the door to the cellar. There it was beneath the stairs. He pulled it open, hurrying down the stairs past a solitary light bulb hanging from a long brown flex, almost tripping at the bottom.

'What are you doing here, Inspector? We haven't cleared this crime scene yet.' The CSI tried to block his way into the basement. He caught a glimpse of the pathologist looking up from a freezer against the left-hand wall.

'You have to leave the basement.'

He tried to get round the CSI to talk directly to the pathologist. She blocked his way, shouting. 'You're not suited, you'll contaminate the scene.'

'I think there's a bomb here.'

'What?' He could see her eyes sandwiched between her face mask and the hood of the Tyvek suit over her head. There was now fear in them. 'What did you say?'

'There's a bomb. The smell. Linseed oil, like putty. It's classic C-4.'

She sniffed the air. 'I can't smell anything.'

The pathologist left the freezer and walked to the boxes at the back of the basement. 'The smell is stronger over here. Just as you said, smells like putty.'

The CSI looked back at Ridpath. 'Are you sure?'

'You need to get out now, both of you.'

The pathologist and the CSI glanced towards each other. At the same time, they began to run for the stairs leading up to safety.

Ridpath waited until they were both clear and followed them. What if he was wrong? What if the owners were just storing oil here rather than in their garage?

This could be the end of his police career. He had contaminated the crime scene of a major case.

He reached the top of the stairs. The CSI was already heading out the door, followed by the pathologist.

'Keep going, and get them to push the cordon back even further,' he shouted, running out of the door after them, stopping just for a second to look back at the dark house.

As he did so an enormous explosion ripped through the basement, shattering the glass windows and lifting the house from its foundations.

It was followed almost immediately afterwards by an earth-shattering noise like the thunder of a thousand storms. A whoosh echoed through his ears and it felt like the air was being sucked out from around his body.

Ridpath was thrown into the thick bushes on the right-hand side of the path. The undergrowth saved him as shards of exploded glass rained down from the sky, embedding themselves in the ground and branches of the trees.

He covered his face and hands, feeling the glass impact on his clothes. A large shard impaled itself in a tree trunk next to his head, its sharp point sticking horizontally out of the wood.

A plume of dense smoke rose up into the sky, followed by the sharp aroma of cordite, like the aftermath of Bonfire Night.

Ridpath lifted his head, shaking the leaves and dirt and glass fragments from his hair. His ears were ringing and his head felt light. He tried to sit up but collapsed to the ground again as his head spun. Blood dripped from a cut above his eye, down his face and onto the dirt at his feet.

He tried again to sit up. More slowly this time, making sure he didn't black out. His head was still spinning and his ears ringing. He felt woozy and rested on his right elbow shaking his head to clear it.

The first orange and blue flames begin to lick out from the windows of the basement and up the walls of the house.

He had to get out of here.

Slowly raising himself to a sitting position, he stopped for a moment to take three deep breaths and grabbed an overhanging branch to pull himself up.

The smell of burning was stronger now, the heat warm against his skin.

He levered himself upright, avoiding the larger shards of glass and stumbled back out onto the path.

Behind him, the house was fully ablaze, orange flames shooting out of the basement windows, stroking the granite walls.

On the first floor, another window shattered from the heat and exploded.

He stumbled down the path. The pathologist and the CSI were both being treated by paramedics on the ground. Blood was pouring out of the CSI's leg, staining the white Tyvek suit bright red. A medic was attempting to staunch the flow of blood.

'Lie back, let me handle it,' he shouted at her.

The CSI was struggling to get up, to run away, the fight or flight instinct deciding she had to get as far away from here as possible.

The medic pushed her back to the ground and shouted. 'Lie still, I need to stabilise your leg.'

Another medic appeared from nowhere, taking Ridpath's left arm as he staggered past the CSI. Emily Parkinson took hold of his other arm. She was saying something to him. Her lips were moving but he couldn't hear anything.

'What?' he shouted.

She put her mouth close to his ear and spoke loudly. 'Are you alright?'

He nodded. 'But hearing gone, the blast...' He shouted again.

They led him to an ambulance parked at the edge of the cordon. The medic sat him down and began examining him.

He stared out at the ground as the ringing in his ears lessened in intensity. What had happened? Had somebody planted a bomb?

Why?

In the distance, he could hear the distinct sounds of sirens. Not police this time, the fire brigade.

Emily Parkinson stood nearby watching him as the medic went through his triage. 'Seems ok, no concussion, but the cut needs stitching. We'll take him to Tameside right away.'

'I'll come with you.'

They slotted the gurney into the back of the ambulance.

'The pathologist?' Ridpath asked, trying to get up.

'He'll be ok.' The medic pushed him gently down.

'I need to check the house, the crime scene.'

'You need to check nothing,' the medic insisted, fastening a strap across Ridpath's chest.

Then the detective's head became extremely heavy and the world went dark.

He was tired, so tired, too tired.

Chapter 36

Ridpath woke when he was being rolled in the gurney into A&E. A doctor with a strong Indian accent was giving orders, as others came in and out of view. All were dressed in green masks and gowns.

'Name?' a nurse asked.

'Thomas Ridpath.'

'Date of birth?'

'October 4th, 1982.'

The nurse rushed off and the doctor began to examine his chest and mouth as he was rolled into a curtained area.

'You were involved in the explosion?'

Ridpath nodded.

'Can you please answer me? Any pain in your chest or throat?'

'No. A little tightness but that's all.'

The doctor examined the cut above his eye, removing the emergency dressing applied in the ambulance.

A light was shone in his eyes and his eyesight was checked. 'Any aches in your head or pain?'

'The cut above my eye stings like hell.'

The doctor performed an examination of the rest of his body, checking for any other cuts or broken bones.

The nurse returned and passed the doctor a folder. The doctor began reading. 'Mr Ridpath, you were a patient at Christie's, myeloma wasn't it?'

'Yes, but I'm in remission now.'

'No worries. We'll need to perform a precautionary x-ray but it looks like you were lucky Mr Ridpath. Just a few stitches above the eye and a couple of colourful bruises to show for your adventures. You'll be out of here this evening. No need to stay overnight.'

'How about the others?'

'I'm sorry I can't discuss other patients… Julie, please arrange a chest and head x-ray just to be on the safe side.' He turned back to Ridpath. 'I'll inform your consultant at Christie's, they may want you in for a check-up earlier than usual. Nurse, remove his clothes for the x-ray.'

After two hours, and three stitches over his left eye, he was allowed to leave the hospital. As he was exiting the front door, Eve and Polly came rushing in.

'Are you alright?'

'What happened?'

'We got a phone call…'

The questions and statements came thick and fast, as his daughter hugged him.

'I'm alright, just a couple of stitches.'

Polly lent in to check the wound. 'It's so close to your eye, you could have been blinded.'

'I'm fine, but I could murder a cup of tea.'

Polly glanced around looking for a cafe. 'You want one here or at home?'

'Home.' Ridpath and Eve spoke at the same time.

Polly drove them both and half an hour later, Ridpath and his wife were sat around the kitchen table drinking the finest cup of tea he'd ever tasted. Eve had already been ushered up to bed but not before giving her father another long hug.

'Were you involved in the gas leak explosion in Glossop?'

'Is that what they are saying it was?'

'We were watching the news when we got the call from a DS Emily Parkinson.'

Ridpath wondered where she had found his home number. He should ring her to check what was happening.

'It wasn't a gas leak. Somebody planted a bomb.'

'Somebody?'

'Somebody we were investigating.'

'I thought you weren't moving back to MIT for two weeks?'

'I'm not.'

'So why were you investigating a bomber?'

'I wasn't. I was looking into a case and it happened.'

'Ridpath, you told the hospital about your cancer?'

He stayed quiet.

'You didn't?'

'I didn't have to. I must be on their bloody computer, they knew already. For the rest of my life, I'm going to be the man with cancer.'

Now it was Polly's turn to stay quiet.

Her voice when it came was emotionless. She spoke without looking at him. 'For the two years you've been working with the coroner, I haven't worried. I see you more often, Eve loves the time you spend together at weekends—'

'Poll—'

'Let me finish.' She took a deep breath. 'When you said you wanted to return to MIT, I thought it was too early, but I kept quiet, thinking it was what you wanted, that it would make you happy, doing what you love.' She looked up at him finally. 'Now I'm not so sure.'

'It was a one-off, Poll, it won't happen again.'

'Ridpath, you know I love you. Eve loves you. How would we manage if you weren't here any more? The cancer was bad enough, but working at MIT is dangerous.'

'It's what I love, Poll.'

She stood up. 'I'm going to bed now. You think about it. Is the job worth it? You can achieve so much with Mrs Challinor, perhaps even more than with MIT.'

She walked to the kitchen door. 'I don't want to spend my life waiting to receive another call like tonight, Ridpath. You can't expect me to live like that. You can't expect Eve to wait for the call saying her dad isn't coming home.'

She looked him straight in the eye for a moment and then walked out into the hallway.

Ridpath listened to her going up the stairs. He knew she was right but what could he do? It was the job, the life he had chosen. It wasn't working in an insurance office, it was the life of a policeman.

For a second, he sat alone in the kitchen, swaying slightly. It suddenly came to him he loved the adrenalin, the surge of energy as action, not thought, was required. He loved that he could do something, not just sit back and watch.

He could understand how Polly felt though. It was always hardest for those not involved, the ones who had to sit on the side-lines unable to do anything except wait for the phone call. It was they who had to pick up the pieces.

A wave of anger shook Ridpath's frame. Had somebody tried to kill him? Had Dalbey tried to blow him up?

'Sod it,' he said out loud, walking into the living room and fixing himself a glass of Lagavulin.

As the golden liquid slipped down his throat, he selected a number on his mobile.

'Hi Ridpath, how are you feeling?' DS Parkinson's voice came through loud and clear. Behind her he could hear a hubbub of activity.

The cut above his eye throbbed slightly but, other than that, he felt fine. 'You still at work?'

'We all are. If you're up to it, the boss would like you to come in for a briefing tomorrow at 10 a.m. Don't worry if you're not, we'll come to you.'

Ridpath thought for a moment. He would go to see Mrs Challinor first and attend the briefing afterwards. 'No need,' he answered, 'I'll be there.'

'The manhunt is on for Dalbey, an APB has gone out. We've tracked down his last known address and sent an armed team there, but the house was empty. He's vanished.'

'Why am I not surprised? You could track his movements through his mobile?'

'Already done, but BT says his number hasn't been used for a year.'

'Shit. Shit. Shit.'

'Those were Claire Trent's exact words. Anyway, I need to go, Harry is asking for help. See you tomorrow, Ridpath.'

'How's the CSI?'

'We think she's going to lose the leg. The pathologist was shaken up but otherwise fine.'

'Thanks for looking after me, Emily.'

'No worries, you'd have done the same for me. I've gotta go.'

'See you tomorrow—' But the connection had already been cut.

Ridpath picked up his glass of whisky. He should go over the events of the day, get them clear in his mind. There must have been something which would help him solve this.

His head began to throb around the cut above his eye. Think, Ridpath! But his mind refused to focus. Perhaps he shouldn't have had the glass of whisky. He glanced down at the half inch of golden liquid still in the glass. 'Sod it,' he said once again and finished it in one swallow.

As he climbed the stairs to bed, a memory from before the explosion rattled around in his head.

What had the woman PC said was written on the card? 'Who's next?'

A shiver of fear rattled down Ridpath's spine.

Chapter 37

Harry Makepeace had already started briefing the team when Emily Parkinson entered. Outside, the night was as dark as a witch's soul and the window was soaked with rain, each drop sparkling in the light from the situation room.

At the front, Claire Trent and Paul Turnbull stood next to the whiteboards. Whilst on one side Alan Jones wrote action steps on a chalkboard as he was instructed by the senior investigating officers.

'We canvassed the local area, knocking on seventy-two doors and receiving fifty-four responses. We'll return to the rest tomorrow morning. The area is quiet and residential, with large houses set back from the road. Only one resident, a woman, reported anything unusual; a man sitting in a car about seventy yards away from the incident. She noticed him on her way to the shops.'

'Any description?' asked Turnbull.

The detective read from his notes. 'Nothing concrete, boss. Middle aged, white male. The car was grey or white, she couldn't be sure. And she didn't have a clue what make it was. I've asked for the dash cam footage from the responding vehicles to see if it appeared on any of those.'

'Could it have been James Dalbey? Did you show her a photo?'

'Didn't have one.'

'Go back tomorrow. She might recognise him.'

'Will do.'

Alan Jones wrote the action step on his board, adding Harry Makepeace's name at the end of the line.

'Anything else?'

'I checked where the car was parked. It gives a view of both the house and the area around it.'

'So Dalbey could have been watching?'

'Possibly, boss.'

'Well done, Harry. Finish the other houses tomorrow.'

Harry Makepeace nodded and stood down.

'Chrissy, what about the call to the emergency services?'

'The name given was Don Brown. We traced the number. A pre-paid phone, no longer active.'

'Can we have the tape of the call to Emergency Services for the meeting tomorrow? I'd like to listen to it.'

'On it, boss.'

'Emily, what's happening at the scene?'

'The fire has been extinguished and the bomb squad have declared the area safe. A CSI team are going through the house at the moment, but it's slow and the fire destroyed or damaged the living room, kitchen and basement.'

'So we can't expect too much from forensics?'

'I don't think so.'

'The bomb?'

'Still waiting on the report, boss. We should have the top-line for tomorrow's meeting.'

'Push them along, Emily. And the body?'

'It's the one piece of good news. The freezer protected it from the worst of the explosion. A pathologist will perform the post mortem tomorrow. We're just checking if Dr Schofield is free.'

'Why him?'

'He was recommended, and the Derbyshire pathologist is still in hospital with shock.'

'Push him to do it as quickly as possible, we can't lose a second.'

'It means transporting the freezer to Manchester.'

'Make it happen.'

Movement on the left as Alan Jones wrote once more on his chalkboard.

Claire Trent looked away from the detective sergeant and across at the crowded room. 'Right, people, this is the most important case we are working on at the moment. Our main suspect is James Dalbey.' She tapped a large picture of the man, posted on one of the whiteboards, taken on his release from prison. 'Finding him is going to be our main focus. Understand? Here is a video of an interview done with him by ITV when he was released eighteen months ago.' Claire Trent pressed a key on her laptop and an image appeared on the television to the left.

For a second, the face of James Dalbey was frozen on the screen before the picture started running. He was sitting on a couch. Behind his head, net curtains wafted in a slight breeze.

'Well, Mr Dalbey, you must be delighted to finally have left prison,' an off-screen interviewer asked.

'I am, but I should never have been there in the first place.'

'Your conviction for the torture, rape and murder of Alice Seagram has been quashed by the High Court, how do you feel?'

The face, placid before, suddenly screwed up with anger. 'How do you think I feel? I was locked up for ten years surrounded by convicted criminals; murderers and worse. Ten years of my life lost.'

'No doubt you will receive good compensation for the time you spent in jail.'

'Nothing can compensate me for the life lost. Nothing can soothe the anger I feel raging inside me. Nothing can stop the voices in my head when I'm alone at night. Nothing, absolutely nothing, can ever atone for never seeing my mother again.'

'Your mother died while you were in prison. The prison authorities refused you permission to go to her funeral, how do you feel?'

Dalbey clenched his jaw. 'Even before her passing, my mother never came to see me. She thought I was guilty you see. The police and the judges and the courts – everybody – had convinced her I was guilty.' A long pause. 'I never said goodbye to her before she died.'

'Have you been to her grave since?'

'It was the first thing I did when I came out. There was no headstone, just a patch of earth. There was nobody left to care for her once they put me away, nobody to mourn her...' Dalbey's voice trailed off without finishing the sentence.

The interviewer tried to end on a more positive tone. 'What are you going to do now? The government will pay you compensation for your time inside. Four hundred thousand pounds is one figure being bandied about. How are you going to spend it?'

Dalbey stared into mid-air. 'I don't know. I just know it can't bring my mother back to life.' He snapped his head back to stare directly into the camera, his eyes unblinking. 'They are going to pay for what they did to me. They are all going to pay.'

'Finally, do you have a message for any of the people who made the mistake of putting you in jail.'

The man was silent for a long while, before he looked up and gazed directly into the camera. 'This is James Dalbey. It's time for the past to come alive.'

The camera cut to the interviewer for the first time. 'The first interview with James Dalbey on his release. As he says, the government are going to pay for what they did to him. And it looks like it is going to cost the taxpayer in the region of 400,000 pounds. Back to you in the studio, Kelly.'

Claire Trent paused the film. 'I don't know why this wasn't flagged and this man put on a watch list.' She shrugged her shoulders. 'I guess we'll never know, but it's what we have to deal with now. We've had a forensic psychiatrist look at this footage. I won't bore you with the psychological mumbo jumbo but here are his main conclusions.'

She pressed another key on her laptop and four bullet points appeared on the screen.

1. Possible Asperger's
2. Neurotic Anger and Hostility
3. PTSD?
4. Narcissism – inflated social confidence and sense of entitlement could produce a desire to retaliate against

Conclusion

Highly likely to seek revenge for his time in prison. Revenge seeks to have the transgressor suffer while punishment looks to improve the transgressor's behaviour or to deter future bad behaviour. In this case, 'making someone pay' is an emotional not a financial desire. He has a strong desire to seek retribution.

Harry Makepeace leant into Emily Parkinson and whispered. 'If someone banged me up for ten years, I'd make the bastards pay too.'

The detective sergeant ignored him as Paul Turnbull stepped forward.

'Despite all this we are not here to psychoanalyse this man. Our job is to find him and put him away. Clear?'

The assembled detectives nodded their heads.

Claire Trent continued. 'It's nearly midnight. Most of you need to go home and get some rest. I'll brief the night shift separately. The hunt begins in earnest for Dalbey now. We need to get the bastard and get him quick. The chief constable wants this sorted. An attack on a CSI is an attack on the police. Any questions?'

Linda Doran, GMP's head of PR, put up her hand. 'I'm getting questions from the papers regarding the gas explosion. It's gone national and they're smelling that something isn't right.'

'Stall them, Linda, we want to get out in front of this and them.'

'Right, Claire.'

Emily Parkinson put her hand up.

'Yes, Emily.'

'Shouldn't we be issuing Osman notices? I mean if Dalbey is the killer and the man who planted the bomb, he seems to be targeting people involved in his conviction ten years ago. Shouldn't we be warning the people involved?'

Claire Trent thought for a moment. 'Good question, Emily. Can you compile a list of possible targets for Dalbey? Anybody who was involved in his case ten years ago, even if it was at the periphery.'

'That could be a lot of people, boss.'

'It doesn't matter. Do it.' Claire Trent clapped her hands together. 'Get off home and I'll see you tomorrow at ten sharp. Night shift stay here, I'll brief you on follow up.'

The detectives began to funnel out of the room.

'We're gonna get this bastard and quickly,' shouted Claire Trent over the hubbub. 'Understand?'

Chapter 38

It had been planned down to the last detail.

First, a phone call from the gas board telling the former coroner to stay at home as there was a leak in the area. The police calling it a gas explosion in Glossop helped immensely. Thank you, coppers.

He turned up thirty minutes later in the white van, dressed as an engineer come to check the pipes.

Once inside the house the rest was easy. A few drops of chloroform on a pad to knock him out long enough to tie him up, before feeding him with a sleeping tablet dissolved in some water to keep him quiet while he set the scene.

The isolated eighteenth-century weaver's cottage where the man lived was perfect for what he had in mind.

The wooden panelling of the living room provided exactly the correct atmosphere whilst the beams across the ceiling made what he had to do easy.

The camera was set up and the man dressed and prepared for the show.

While all the preparations were being made, he felt like an actor in a dressing room putting on his make-up, waiting to go on and perform for his audience. He had written the script, constructed the *mise-en-scène* and given each person their roles and lines.

The words from *Titus Andronicus* came back to him. *Vengeance is in my heart, death in my hand, Blood and revenge are hammering in my head.*

How apt.

Everything was in place.

The death of Don Brown and the explosion had been a suitable curtain call to the first act, but now he was in the play proper. It was time to give them a thrilling spectacle, lead them on, before turning the tables.

It was time to pay them back for all the hurt they had caused.

Chapter 39

He tried not to drift too much, but his mind was like a ship-wrecked sailor at the mercy of the ocean currents; it went wherever the thoughts took it.

Memories flooded in.

Underneath a table playing with a next door neighbour during the funeral wake of his father. At least, he believed it was the wake. His mother said it was, but her memory could be trusted less than his. A tin police car whose lights flashed as you rubbed the wheels against the lino of the floor. All around him a forest of legs and skirts. There didn't seem to be men in trousers. Just long, flowing skirts he crawled under and hid, smelling the rich, earthy scent of unwashed underwear and unshaven legs.

Another memory elbowed its way into his dreams. The first day of school, the first day of many. A cold day in an old building, surrounded by baying hordes of monsters all calling his name and prodding and pushing him like a cow in the market, their country voices rough to his city ears.

And the nun, the warmth of her skin as she took his hand and led him to a seat in church. He always remembered her touch. As if he was branded that day by her.

Branded in a nice way, marked for life as hers.

And the day he found out she was gone. A dark black dog of despair, a sadness like a tight hard ball in the pit of his stomach, threatening to grow bigger and overwhelm him at any second.

Close by, a few whispered words.

He strained to listen to their meaning but couldn't quite understand. Were they talking about him?

Probably.

People had been talking for years.

One day they would stop.

Not yet though.

There was still work to be done.

Chapter 40

The next morning, Ridpath was up bright and early. Surprisingly, Polly joined him in the kitchen as he made coffee.

'Have you thought about what I said last night?' she asked immediately.

He put his arms around her. 'Don't worry, yesterday was a one-off. It won't happen again.'

'I wish it were true, Ridpath.' She took a deep breath. 'Myself and Eve care about you so much, we couldn't bear if you weren't—'

He placed his finger across her lips. 'Don't worry, it won't happen again. I'll be extra careful from now on, I promise. And see, I'm as fit as a butcher's dog this morning.'

'The plaster above your eye does give you a rakish charm.' She touched his forehead and he pulled back. 'Does it still hurt?'

'A little bit sore but nothing to worry about.'

'I'll book you a time at Christie's. They can look at it there. You're due your monthly cancer check-up anyway.'

'Time to give another armful of blood.'

'I wish you weren't so flippant, Ridpath. I'm worried about you and so is Eve.'

For a moment, he considered telling her about the return of James Dalbey and the possibility he could be a target. But he didn't. There was no point in alarming her unnecessarily. With a bit of luck, MIT had already found him. 'Don't worry,' he said finally, 'it's just a job. I'll take care of myself.'

'Says the man who has a track record for doing exactly the opposite.'

'Look, today I'm going to the Coroner's Office, and on to MIT for a meeting and afterwards back to work with the coroner. That's my schedule, I'll be home by six at the latest. Promise.'

'I'll hold you to it, Ridpath. Perhaps I can cook something for this evening.'

The prospect of Polly's spaghetti fish balls didn't appeal. 'Or we can get a pizza delivered and make a movie night of it.'

'Eve's been wanting to watch *Zombies 2* for ages.'

'Pizza, popcorn, zombies and a bottle of wine for the adults. Perfect.'

'It's a date, Mr Ridpath.'

'See you tonight, Mrs Ridpath.'

He left the house five minutes later, driving to meet the coroner at Stockfield. She was already waiting for him when he got there, her face buried in a file as usual.

'Morning, Ridpath, what have you done to your eye?'

'It's nothing, the blast yesterday.'

'It gives you a certain *je ne sais quoi*. You could be starting a new fashion trend.'

He sat down opposite her.

'I read the news. Gas explosion?'

'That's the story at the moment. But it wasn't. We're pretty certain it was James Dalbey. Remember the mortuary attendant in the inquest on Alice Seagram?'

'The one who switched the bodies for Harold Lardner?'

'That's him. We're pretty certain he was killed and stuffed in a freezer by Dalbey.'

'But why?'

'He was also behind the attacks on John Gorman's dogs and the desecration of Charlie Whitworth's grave.'

'All people involved in his case twelve years ago.'

'I've been thinking about it all night. It seems he's looking for revenge on those who put him away.'

'Weren't you involved?'

Ridpath nodded. 'Emily Parkinson told me this morning that they're drawing up a list of possible new targets. You could be on it too.'

'Why me? I ran the inquest that unveiled Lardner as the killer, so Dalbey could be freed from jail. It proved his innocence.' She stopped speaking for a second as a thought struck her. 'The letter from Lardner, he talked about "somebody starting to kill."'

'Exactly.'

'How did Lardner know Dalbey wanted to take revenge?'

'We don't know.'

'Are they working together?'

'We don't know that either. Why would Dalbey and the man who framed him for murder be working together? It doesn't make sense. And before you ask anything else. The answer is—'

'We don't know.' She finished his sentence for him. 'Sounds like there are too many unknowns at the moment.'

'I have a meeting at MIT at 10 a.m., with a bit of luck, they've already found him.' He stood up. 'I'll just get a bit of work done with Sophia before I leave.'

'Ridpath.' He stopped as she called to him on his way out of her office. 'Take care with this one, I don't have a good feeling about it.'

'Neither do I, Mrs Challinor, neither do I.'

Chapter 41

'Very dashing, Ridpath, the beaten-up look suits you.'

Sophia Rahman was already behind her desk when he entered their office.

'You're in early.'

'It's my mother, she's driving me crazy. Every day it's "when are you going to get married" or "we can introduce you to a nice boy from Karachi, he's a doctor" or "the matchmaker is waiting for you both to meet." My mother doesn't know she'll be waiting till hell freezes over.'

'Sounds like fun.'

'Not. This place is my refuge away from her. And she's now decided she doesn't want me to work any more.'

Ridpath's ears pricked up. Since her arrival, Sophia had become indispensable to him, conquering the bureaucracy of the job in a manner which had defeated him. Paperwork, even in the police, had never been his strong point.

'Sorry, I'm rambling about myself, what happened to you?'

'Nothing, the explosion last night.'

'You were involved? I saw it on the news. Biggest thing that's happened in Glossop since the Romans.'

'It was – different. I need to get back to MIT at ten, so can we go through the outstanding cases?'

'Sure.' She pulled up a file on her laptop. 'There are only two cases which need your involvement; a death by drowning in the canal near the Gay Village. It looks like an accident but Mrs Challinor wants you to check up the details. John, I mean Dr Schofield, has finished the post mortem. There was a wound

143

on the head but he's uncertain whether it came from an attack or the fall.'

'Witnesses?'

'The police haven't found any so far. The case isn't urgent but the family are asking for the body to be released.'

'Give me the file and I'll get to it today. Anything else?'

'The death of a pensioner, Mrs Andrews. The pathologist, a Dr Shah, pronounced it a heart attack but now the son has come forward admitting he killed her. Placed a pillow over her head.'

'Mrs Challinor is reopening the inquest?'

'Exactly, she wants you to check the case and the police investigation.'

'Great, pass me the file and—'

'You'll get onto it today. Nothing else is urgent. All the files are up to date and the families have been informed of the upcoming inquests—'

As Sophia was finishing her sentence, a scream came from the coroner's office.

Chapter 42

The scene had been set; the furniture moved to one side, clearing an open area. A single chair had been placed in the centre and a rope with a noose looped over one of the old beams.

The coroner had been difficult to rouse. Perhaps he had misjudged the strength of the sleeping pill. But eventually the man had come round and, after a coffee laced with a mild stimulant, was awake enough to stand on his own two feet.

He checked the hands were still securely tied and removed the gag from the man's mouth.

'What do you want with me?'

A nervous little cough to clear the throat. 'Do as I say and you will be ok.'

'What have I done wrong? Why are you doing this?'

He shoved the gun under the man's nose, enjoying the fear in his eyes as he flinched away from it. 'Do as I say or I will shoot. Do you understand?'

The coroner nodded quickly.

'We're going to give people a little show.' He pointed at the camera. 'The script is on the board over there. If you say the words exactly as I have written them, you will be released unharmed. If you don't, you die. Understand?'

All the time, the man listened with fear starkly apparent in his eyes. It was a lie but the coroner wasn't to know. He nodded quickly.

At gunpoint, he forced the man to climb onto the chair and placed the noose around his neck.

The camera was already set up, framing the image perfectly. Through the viewfinder, he made his final check, sharpening the focus. The coroner stood on a chair, the noose around his neck attached to a wooden beam.

He donned his costume, adjusting the mask over his face. He didn't want them to see who he was, not yet anyway.

The clock was approaching nine a.m. Just thirty seconds to go before it was time for the show to begin. He opened his laptop and sent the message. A green light would go on as soon as Mrs Challinor clicked the link and connected to the streaming site.

The man sat back and waited. All the time, the coroner was watching him, his eyes following every move. The fear apparent in the jerky movements and the flare of the nostrils. The hands tied behind his back fluttered ineffectually against the rope around his wrist.

He reframed the picture slightly. Not too close, a three-quarters shot would do. He still wanted them to see the man's legs kicking as he was slowly strangled. He had decided not to make the drop too long. He didn't want to break the man's neck.

Instead, he wanted to drag the man's death out, hang him properly and let them all see the nature of his justice.

They used to sell tickets to hangings in the past. Meat pies were sold. Lucky charms made from the hair of previous victims displayed. The best seats changing hands for vast amounts. It was seen as one of the liveliest entertainments, a bit like *Big Brother* except there was always a death at the end, rather than a release from a house.

For this man, he was going to revive the spectacle for a special audience.

He waited.

The man waited.

The world waited.

The tiny green light went on.

Chapter 43

Her computer pinged loudly.

Mrs Challinor put down the file she was reading and tapped a key. The screen lit up. There was a message from her daughter, Immy. Strange they had only spoken last night.

The coroner clicked the message and the short email revealed itself.

Take a look at this, Mum, it's funny.

Attached was a link. Another light-hearted video her daughter had found on the internet. They always made her laugh.

She clicked on it and the screen changed to show the inside of somebody's house. It seemed vaguely familiar as if she had visited it before. At the far end of the room, a man was standing on a chair.

She leant in closer realising she knew that man. Brian Conway, the former coroner. What was he doing in one of Immy's links?

Brian lifted his head. There was something around his neck. Was it a rope? Did Brian have a rope around his neck?

Another man stepped in front of the camera, blocking the view with his back.

What was going on?

The man turned around slowly to reveal himself. He had the face of a wolf.

Mrs Challinor screamed.

Chapter 44

Within seconds, Ridpath burst into the room without knocking.

'He's going to kill him.' The coroner pointed at the screen, her hand covering her mouth.

She stared at the screen. On the top left-hand corner, a timer ticked over remorselessly.

9:01:53.

9:01:54.

Suddenly, Ridpath was standing beside her.

The man with the wolf mask was reading from a sheet of paper.

'You have been charged and found guilty of the crime of negligence in public office. How do you plead?'

The old man on the chair slowly lifted his head. His eyes were glazed as if he didn't know where he was.

'It's Brian…' said Mrs Challinor.

'Brian?'

'The former coroner.'

Mrs Challinor noticed Jenny and Sophia had come into the room too. 'What's going on?' the office manager asked.

Mrs Challinor shook her head, unable to speak.

Staring at the screen, Jenny whispered, 'What's Brian doing?'

As if answering her, Brian's lips moved.

'Speak up please, for the court.' The man with his back to the camera ordered.

Brian spoke slightly louder. 'What do you want?' The voice was slurred and slow.

'That is not the correct answer. Guilty or not guilty?'

'What do you want?' Brian repeated.

'What the hell's going on?' Jenny asked looking across to the coroner.

'I don't know,' she answered without taking her eyes off the screen. 'I received an email and clicked on the link and this came up on my computer.'

9:02:12.

9:02:13.

9:02:14.

'Brian Conway, you have been accused of negligence in the execution of your duties as coroner. Are you sure you don't want to plead?'

The former coroner mumbled something and shook his head. The noose around his head writhed like a snake.

'In the absence of a plea, the sentence will be carried out.'

Without waiting any longer, the man stepped forward and kicked the chair on which Brian Conway was standing. For a second, the old coroner was frozen in mid-air, before gravity took hold and his body plummeted down, bouncing twice as it reached the end of the rope, then stopped, the toes of his shoes almost touching the carpet.

Brian Conway's eyes were bulging from his head as he kicked his feet and struggled to free his hands.

Mrs Challinor looked away. 'Do something, Ridpath!'

The man was still kicking his feet. The rope had pulled tight and twisted his neck to one side without breaking it. The tip of his tongue appeared between his teeth and his face grew larger, taking on a blue tone.

9:02:34.

9:02:35.

The coroner slowly looked back at the screen. 'It's his home. I recognise the painting on the wall.'

'Where is it?'

'Saddleworth somewhere, up on the moors... Do something, Ridpath!' the coroner screamed.

'Jenny, do you have his number and address?'

'I think so...'

'Get it!'

The officer manager ran out of the room.

Ridpath picked up his mobile and dialled 999. The phone rang and rang.

On the screen, Mrs Challinor could see Brian Conway was struggling less now. His movements becoming slower and smaller, his face turning a bright blue. After a minute, all movement stopped and he hung there, the rope swaying slightly under the weight of his body.

9:03:35.

9:03:36.

9:03:37.

Ridpath began speaking as the operator finally answered. 'Police and ambulance. This is Detective Inspector Thomas Ridpath. I'm looking at a crime being committed at—'

Jenny ran back into the room, a filing card in her hand.

Ridpath snatched it from her. '—At 10 Penfold Lane, Saddleworth.'

A slight pause as Ridpath listened and then he said sharply. 'It's murder, code red.'

On the screen, Brian Conway was still, his body hanging loosely from the end of the rope, a dark patch staining the crotch of his trousers, the upended chair lying a few feet away.

The man who had kicked the chair was standing, watching, doing nothing.

9:03:55.

9:03:56.

Mrs Challinor dragged her eyes away from the screen. 'Tell them to hurry, he's dying.'

'I'm not there,' Ridpath said into his mobile. 'I'm watching the murder on a computer screen. You need to get there quickly, a man is dying.'

Ridpath listened to the operator, staring at the screen all the time. 'What the...?' he shouted.

On screen, the man, still with his back to the camera, picked up the chair, placing it against the far wall, folded up the charge sheet and placed it in his pocket, then walked towards the door. Before he left the room, he turned back to camera, staring directly at it.

The face looked like a wolf.

9:04:19.

9:04:20.

Chapter 45

Mrs Challinor was still trembling when Claire Trent questioned her.

'Are you sure this was the only email you clicked?'

The coroner nodded.

Claire Trent, Paul Turnbull and Ridpath were crowded into the coroner's office, all circling Mrs Challinor and her laptop. The live feed had been killed and all that was left was a grey screen.

Harry Makepeace knocked and came into the room. 'We didn't get there in time, boss. Whoever it was had already scarpered. We've got a chopper out but I'm not hopeful. All we know is roughly the time he left but we don't know the make and model of the car. I've ordered up the ANPR files for the M62 anyway.'

'What if he didn't come back to Manchester? What if he went the other way to Yorkshire and doubled back?' asked Ridpath.

Claire Trent stared at him, not bothering to reply. 'When did you receive the file, Mrs Challinor?'

'It must have been around nine a.m. I was looking at a case and my inbox pinged.'

Turnbull was staring at the screen. 'The arrival time was 9.01 a.m.'

'Was it normal for your emails to make a sound as they come into your inbox?'

'No, that's what was so strange, I'd turned the function off.'

'So you opened the email?'

'I saw that it came from my daughter, I always open those.'

'It didn't Mrs Challinor,' said Turnbull looking at the URL. 'Your daughter's address is gmail, this is a hotmail account.'

'But the name is the same.'

'They've cloned your daughter's name from her gmail account.'

'But how? How did they do that?'

'Lots of ways. She could have put her email on her Facebook, Twitter or Instagram accounts. Or given it to a friend. Or they could have bought a list of emails from your daughter's university on the dark web. Or they simply could have gone phishing.'

'Phishing.'

'Log on to this site and get something free is the usual way. A trip, or even just a personality analysis. Lots of ways of collecting emails.'

'Our digital people will have to take your laptop, Mrs Challinor,' said Claire Trent.

'But I need it. There's confidential information stored inside.'

'We need to trace the source of the file sent to you.'

'I can't let it go. There are too many confidential files; ongoing investigations, personal details of deaths, my coroner's notes.'

'I'm sorry. A man has been murdered. We'll download the files you need onto a drive.'

'The information is confidential, Mrs Trent,' the coroner replied firmly.

'I can get a warrant if necessary.'

The two women were at a stand-off.

Finally Ridpath said, 'Why don't I take the laptop to the digital team and stay with it while they examine the source of the file?'

They both looked at him.

'Agreed,' Claire Trent finally said.

'Agreed.'

'In the meantime, I'll ask Jenny to download the files for the cases you need in the next couple of days onto a drive.'

Mrs Challinor nodded. 'What did the police find in Saddleworth?'

'The same scene as you watched on the screen,' replied DCS Trent. 'Brian Conway was hanging from the rafters. An emergency medical team tried to resuscitate him but he was pronounced dead at 9.42.'

'Who was the man in the wolf mask?'

'We don't know. Probably James Dalbey. An explosives team are checking out the house before the CSIs go in. With luck we'll find a fingerprint or some link back to Dalbey.'

Turnbull interrupted the conversation. 'But what did Brian Conway have to do with Dalbey? He was a retired coroner.'

Mrs Challinor lifted her head. 'I can answer that.'

Chapter 46

He was pleased with the morning's work. The plan was going exactly as designed. It was now time for the next phase; time to ratchet up the pressure even more.

No doubt the police would be combing through hours of CCTV footage of the area around the house. It was one of the reasons he had chosen the coroner for the first live performance. The man lived close to the M62, the main motorway leading into Manchester from the East. They would have to examine the footage from the motorway. At that time in the morning, over 5,000 vehicles an hour were heading into the city.

To make it a little more difficult, he had driven towards Yorkshire early in the morning, coming in from that side across the Pennines, rather than take the more direct route from Manchester. They would eventually spot the van but it would double the number of vehicles they had to examine with the traffic cameras as well as extend the length of footage they had to watch.

He already knew where he was going to dump the van afterwards and change to another vehicle. By the time they had isolated the new car, he would have finished.

He only needed three more days to complete his work.

A lot could happen in three days though. He had to be careful and vigilant.

No mistakes.

No lapses in concentration.

No deviation from the plan or the timetable.

Just stay the course. Everything had happened according to schedule. The only error being the survival of the pathologist and the CSI in Glossop.

Never mind.

He had made his point. The pathologist was now a wreck of a man and the CSI would never work again. More importantly, he had slowed down all their forensic work. From now on, they would have to let the bomb squad perform a sweep of each location before they could enter.

It was the plan.

It was perfect.

Time to use those bastards on the web. The people who preyed on the suffering of others like mosquitoes feeding on a warm body at dusk.

He watched the video from this morning, seeing Brian Conway's eyes as he kicked against the dying of the light. The man hadn't cared about Alice. He had just pronounced her dead without bothering to investigate properly. They had their suspect, their sacrificial lamb, and nothing else mattered.

He saved the video and uploaded it onto a 4chan site on the dark web. These people were nutters but they would serve his needs well. They were used to spreading conspiracy theories, dark state gossip, and ridiculous rumours.

Here was a murder in living colour. They would spread it around the internet world in minutes.

The police wouldn't know what hit them.

It was time to keep them busy, buy some time while he finished his work.

The plan must be carried out.

It was the only thing to satisfy her memory.

Chapter 47

The coroner ran her fingers through her spiralling grey curls. 'Brian Conway was the coroner in the original Seagram case. Along with his officer, Anthony Chettle, he held the inquest into the death of Alice Seagram after the trial of James Dalbey. Given the conviction during the criminal case, the inquest was a formality.'

'Did he also release the body back to the family?' asked Ridpath.

'He signed the papers but the actual work will have been done by the officer.'

Claire Trent leant forward. 'We have yet another link to Dalbey. So far he seems to have targeted the police officers in charge of the investigation that put him in jail, Gorman and Whitworth, the mortuary assistant who stole the body and now the coroner who ran the inquest. Who else would he target?'

'The coroner's officer, Chettle, is an obvious target,' said Ridpath.

'Anthony couldn't be a target any more,' said Mrs Challinor, 'he passed away six months ago.'

'We'd better check where he's buried.'

'I'll do it,' said Ridpath.

'What about the judge who ran the trial?' said Turnbull.

'Or the prosecuting barrister?' added Claire Trent. 'Emily Parkinson is supposed to be compiling a list of all possible people linked to the prosecution of the case. I want it sooner rather than later, Paul.'

'I'll get it to you, boss,' answered Turnbull.

'There's also the family involved, the Seagrams. Remember they gave him his initial alibi but rescinded it—' said Ridpath '—after Lardner, the pathologist, lied under oath. He was the killer and yet he managed to shift blame to Dalbey.' Mrs Challinor finished his sentence.

'You want me to send out Osman notices to these people, boss?'

Claire Trent stroked her jaw. 'Not yet, we don't have enough proof they are under threat. What are we going to tell them? A killer is on the prowl and he might be coming after you next? Lock your doors and stay alert? A message like that will scare the hell out of anybody. The tabloids would have a field day. But we don't have the resources to protect all of them. When will DS Parkinson complete her list?'

'I don't know, boss, I'll check,' answered Turnbull.

'Do that,' said Trent eyeing the DCI, 'I want to see a full list before we act. No point in scaring all those people unnecessarily.'

'But why boss?' asked Ridpath, frowning.

'Why what?'

'Why is Dalbey doing it now?'

Turnbull answered. 'Revenge for his lost years in jail. He's going after all those who put him inside.'

'But why now and why kill John Gorman's dog but not the man?'

'Maybe he intended to go back for Gorman, and was disturbed before he could kill him? This man is organised, everything is planned. Look at what happened this morning.'

'Why not go back another day? It doesn't make sense.'

'I don't know, Ridpath, I'm not the bloody killer,' Turnbull exploded. 'Come up with a better answer rather than making me look stupid.'

Claire Trent held up her hands. 'Enough you two, we have too much work for you to bicker.' She checked her watch. 'I have to brief the chief constable. Paul, can you organise a full briefing for the detectives at 3 p.m? We'll need to bring everybody up to speed.'

'Yes, boss,' grunted Turnbull still staring at Ridpath.

The coroner spoke up. 'There is of course one person who may be a target of the killer whom we haven't mentioned.'

'Who's that?' asked Claire Trent.

Mrs Challinor pointed directly at Ridpath. 'Didn't you arrest him?'

Ridpath was immediately catapulted back in time. One of his first days on patrol. Stopping the van with Sergeant Mungovan, the chase through the streets of Chorlton, finding Dalbey at the lock-up, a fight and looking up to see the woman chained to the wall, blood splattered across her face.

'You arrested him, Ridpath?' asked Turnbull.

'I did.'

'It was also Ridpath's work which cleared Dalbey and discovered the real killer, Lardner.'

'It doesn't matter, add Ridpath to the list, Paul.'

Ridpath stood there, staring at the monitor, with its last, blurred image of Brian Conway hanging by his neck from a rope.

Was Ridpath next?

Chapter 48

'Right, gather round people.' Paul Turnbull clapped his hands and the assembled detectives took their seats. Claire Trent looked up from her mobile phone. Yet another text from the chief constable.

Ridpath glanced over the room. They were taking this seriously now. Over thirty detectives and virtually every civilian resource available to MIT was gathered together. Alan Jones was standing next to the chalkboard as usual.

'Following this morning's incident, this briefing is to bring you up to date on the investigation. Let me remind you, given the media involvement, everything spoken about in this room, is confidential. I will personally break any detective who leaks to the press, is that clear?'

A few mumbled replies.

'IS THAT CLEAR?'

'Yes, boss,' was the strong response from the room.

The tabloids had been calling the PR department of GMP for the last couple of hours, all desperate to find out why the coroner had been killed and who had committed the outrage. The footage had already gone viral, with over 500,000 views and rising.

Suddenly, all eyes were focussed on MIT.

Paul Turnbull scratched the top of his balding pate. Ridpath could see livid red marks already etched into the skin.

'As you know, this morning the former coroner, Brian Conway, was murdered and the act live streamed on the internet. John from the digital team will explain.'

A bearded, pot-bellied man rose from his seat. 'It looks like somebody created a site on the dark web and sent the link to Mrs Challinor. As soon as she clicked it, the link went live.'

'Can we trace the IP address of whoever set it up?' asked Claire Trent.

'That's the point of the dark web. Nothing is traceable. It would be like looking for a black cat in a dark room which isn't even there.'

Claire Trent shook her head and stared at him.

'Who uploaded the video to Facebook?'

'There are multiple accounts who have posted it on their pages. Some are sock puppets, some bots, a few trolls. These lurkers and spammers exist for one purpose; to spread disinformation, to muddy the waters.'

Harry Makepeace leant closer to Ridpath. 'What's he talking about?'

'Beats me, my daughter is better with an iPad than I am.'

'I thought you were there when they went through the laptop?'

'I was, but I was about as useful as the Mayor of Manchester. I didn't know what the hell they were doing.'

A quick scowl from Claire Trent stopped Ridpath from speaking.

'Can't Facebook do something about the video? It shows the death of a man for God's sake.' Emily Parkinson addressed the digital expert directly.

'They are trying but it's like playing whack-a-mole. As soon as you knock one out, another pops up.'

'Do you think we'll be able to find the source of the video?'

'In a one-word answer: no.'

'Right. But keep monitoring John.' Turnbull turned to his right, searching the crowd for a particular face. He saw the Manchester City scarf first. 'Chrissy, how are we doing on the CCTV footage?'

'We're checking everything from the roads around the house, but there are not many cameras in those Pennine villages and we don't know what we're looking for.'

'Try a Ford Transit Custom built before 2018.'

'Are you psychic, Ridpath, or do you know something we don't?'

'It's the van used to kidnap John Gorman's dogs. Emily found CCTV footage.'

'Shouldn't that be dognap?' Rob Allenby said from the back to laughter from the detectives.

Turnbull ignored them. 'And when were you planning to tell us?'

'It's in the Gorman case notes.'

Chrissy held them up.

'Along with a picture of the man who stole the dogs. The picture matches the man in the video for height and build but we can't see his face.'

Claire Trent smiled at Emily Parkinson. 'Well done. Put it on the wall. Knowing the area, he may have entered the M62 from Junction 21 or 22.'

'That's if he didn't use any of the A or B roads, boss, or went towards Yorkshire before doubling back,' interrupted Chrissy Wright as she put the picture of the van and the blurred close-up of the man on the wall.

'We have to focus now, Chrissy. We'll concentrate on the M62 first and shift to the other roads later.'

'Right, boss.'

'Look for a white Ford Transit on the ANPR cameras, using a window of eight a.m. to ten a.m.'

'In both directions? That could be over 10,000 cars during the rush hour, boss.'

'Could we cross reference ANPR numbers of cars in the Glossop area and at the M62 junctions?' asked Emily Parkinson.

'Too much information. Do you know how many number plates that is? It would take us years to go through all the footage.

And even then, perhaps the perp avoided using a road with an ANPR camera? Or maybe it wasn't functioning. Sometimes, too much information can be worse than too little.' Claire Trent answered, making sure everybody knew she was in charge. 'Let's focus first on a Ford Transit van on the M62 in this time frame. If we find number plates, we'll narrow the number of vehicles by cross referencing versus Glossop. With a bit of luck, we'll pick up one vehicle in both locations.'

'Right, boss.'

Paul Turnbull held both his hands up. 'People, let's concentrate on one incident at a time, otherwise we're going to be here for the next ten hours.'

Claire Trent looked at him like she had been stung by a bee. He moved to the left-hand side of the room next to a series of pictures of the Glossop incident. 'Any more news from the house-to-house survey?'

'Nothing we didn't already know, guvnor. Only one woman saw the man sitting in the car. The sketch we got from her is on the board,' said Harry Makepeace.

Turnbull pointed to a photo-composite of a nondescript man in his forties. 'It could be anybody. Anything from forensics?'

Chrissy stepped forward, leaving her Manchester City scarf on the table. 'They are still evaluating the scene. The explosion and subsequent fire destroyed everything.'

'When is the post mortem?'

'Dr Schofield is performing it as we speak.'

'As soon as this meeting is finished, I'll head over there.'

'Can I join you, sir?' asked Ridpath.

'You like post mortems Ridpath?'

'It's not about liking or disliking them, sir, they are the most useful tool for understanding our killer. And I find Dr Schofield's work to be particularly insightful.'

'We have our own resident ghoul in the office. You like looking at corpses, no wonder you enjoyed working with the coroner.' There were a few sycophantic laughs but most people stayed quiet. 'Of course you can come and watch a body being cut to pieces. Make sure you have your dinner first though. Wouldn't want you throwing up on an empty stomach.'

Claire Trent stepped in front of him. 'Remember people, James Dalbey is the most likely suspect for these murders. Any luck on finding him, Chrissy?'

'We found his address when he was first released from prison, boss. But after he received his compensation, he vanished.'

'I'd vanish too. To a tropical island with hot and cold running women.' As Harry Makepeace whispered in his ear, Ridpath caught a waft of his fetid breath. It was like standing in the mouth of an open sewer.

'Keep going Chrissy, he must have left a trace somewhere. Credit cards? Telephone records? Have you checked his bank account? Is somebody still withdrawing money?'

'Done, boss, there were four withdrawals in cash of 100,000 pounds each a year ago. It hasn't been touched since, the account has less than 20,000 pounds left.'

'Jesus,' Harry Makepeace whispered turning towards Ridpath. 'Can you imagine walking around with that much cash? Surprised he wasn't mugged.'

Emily Parkinson put her hand up, 'Given he's vanished, isn't it even more likely he is the perp?'

'Possibly, but we need to keep our minds open. Let's be guided by the evidence not guesswork,' said Paul Turnbull.

'But the evidence is pointing directly at Dalbey, isn't it?' she persisted.

Claire Trent stepped forward. 'It is, that's why we have to pull out all the stops to get the bastard. Right? Any thoughts? Ideas? Anything we're not doing that we should be doing?'

Emily Parkinson put her hand up. 'What about the forensics at the murder of the coroner?'

'First reports indicate the scene was as clean as a morgue. No fingerprints. No fibres. Nothing. They may find something but I'm not banking on it.'

'What about the camera?'

Claire Trent glanced across at Paul Turnbull. He answered. 'A common-or-garden Sony. Alan is following up on it.'

'Nothing so far boss, I'll push on.'

'Do that.'

It was Emily Parkinson who spoke again. 'Should we put out an appeal through the newspapers like the Manchester Evening News? They are desperate for information and somebody must have seen Dalbey?'

'We could, Emily, but I'd like to hold off for a day or two and see if we can find him ourselves. The problem with those appeals is we get swamped with information. All the nutters come out of the woodwork and we have to follow up the 'sightings'.' She formed quotation marks with her fingers. 'Anybody else?'

Ridpath put his hand up. 'The coroner received a letter from Harold Lardner. He talked about a man on a killing spree. Was he referring to Dalbey? Perhaps a visit to see him in Ashworth?'

'You volunteering?' sneered Turnbull.

'I could go if necessary.'

'It needs to be followed up and you know the ex-pathologist, Ridpath. Arrange to go and see what he has to say.'

'But Lardner has been locked up for over a year now, what help can he be?'

For a second Claire Trent's eyes rolled upwards before she regained control. 'I don't know, Paul, but we need to check it out. Wouldn't you agree?'

Put on the spot, Turnbull could only nod his head.

Ridpath spoke to ease the tension. 'I'll arrange it with the prison for tomorrow.'

'Take Emily with you.'

'I don't think it's a good idea, boss.'

'It's not an idea, Ridpath, it's an order, understand?' commanded Claire Trent.

Turnbull was now smirking.

'Yes, boss. We're off to Liverpool tomorrow, DS Parkinson.'

'Me and Scousers, we get on like that.' She brought her fists together.

Ridpath put his hand up again. 'One more thing, boss. Has anybody contacted the Seagram family? They should know what's going on if Dalbey is the killer.'

Turnbull stared at him. 'Why? Who are they?'

It was Claire Trent who explained. 'Alice Seagram was a victim of Harold Lardner. Unfortunately, we managed to put away Dalbey for her murder before the mistake was discovered ten years later.' She turned to Ridpath. 'You're worried he might attack them?'

He shrugged his shoulders in response. 'I think they should be informed, boss. It won't take the reporters long to find them. At least, if we let them know what's happening, they can tell the newspapers we have been in contact.'

Claire Trent narrowed her eyes. 'If I didn't know you better, Ridpath, I would have said that is a politically astute move to make.'

'It's just the right thing to do, boss.'

'Can you do it before you go to Liverpool?'

Ridpath nodded his head.

'Right, that's sorted. You all know what to do.' Claire Trent held up her arms as the detectives began to chat and move about. 'Listen, we have a dangerous killer out there. He's killed two people and attacked two others. We have to stop him quickly, understand?'

Chapter 49

He had moved quickly after killing the coroner, swapping the van for a car which he parked under a canopy of trees behind a pub.

He checked out the location well in advance. There were no CCTV cameras overlooking the car park, nor were there any other cameras nearby. The closest was 100 metres away in an ATM. That was the great advantage of operating in the countryside. Most of the cities were saturated with the bloody things. In the centre of Manchester, simply walking down the street meant you were going to be on a multitude of cameras from banks, shopping malls, shops, and traffic cameras at junctions. Nobody could move any more without being seen, watched, spied upon and possibly followed.

It was standard operating procedure for any investigation to do a search of all the local CCTV. More often than not, the criminal was picked up by some camera, somewhere.

But here he was safe from prying eyes.

They would eventually find the van, sooner rather than later, he imagined. The plods on the beat would notice it hadn't been moved within a couple of days. But he'd made sure it was forensically clean. He couldn't be certain of course, but he had taken all necessary precautions; made sure he wore gloves and taken everything with him. Even the clothes he'd worn were from Primark. A place that sold so many cheap clothes it would be impossible to isolate any fibres if he had left any behind.

Eventually though, they would make the connection. Perhaps the car had been spotted in Glossop and flagging the number plate up on ANPR in Saddleworth would immediately send a red flag to any half-decent copper.

But it would take them time to make the analysis.

Time they didn't have.

Because the next phase of the plan was about to be put into operation.

After that, there was only one more phase, then he would be done.

It had been planned perfectly.

All he had to do was execute the plan.

Chapter 50

Dr John Schofield stood over the naked corpse of the man lying on a clean white sheet on the mortuary table. He often waited for a few seconds before beginning his post mortem.

His assistant, the ever-dour Vera, had retreated to the back of the morgue, looking for some specimen slides and jars to place on the trolley next to the corpse's head. She understood him so well. Understood how important these few moments were before he began to slice into the body of the man.

A body that had once been a man.

He whispered a few words. 'Let me not miss anything and let me treat you with the respect you deserve.'

It was the closest John Schofield ever came to a prayer. Working with dead bodies had made him a convicted atheist. You were born, you lived, and you died. Ashes to ashes, dust to dust. Everything else was just a belief, a hope that there was something more.

But for him, there was nothing. A body lying on a stainless steel table, all life having departed long ago.

He paused for a moment. 'Vera, can you bring me the thermometer? I'd like to take this man's temperature again before we start.'

The measured tread of his assistant and the probe for measuring temperature appeared in front of his eyes.

He inserted it in the body and checked the reading. 89.2 degrees. Still way below any temperature that would sustain life.

He checked the time on the clock.

4.05 p.m.

Pulling the microphone down in front of him, he spoke softly.

'Initial examination of Donald Brown, date of birth 12 April 1988, a male Caucasian, aged thirty-one years old. This man has been frozen in a chest freezer. As such, the post mortem cannot be performed until the body has completely defrosted. According to the literature, this should take approximately forty-eight hours. A clean damp sheet will be placed across the body to aid the defrosting process.' He indicated Vera to come forward and assist him, before carrying on dictating. 'On an external examination, the man seems relatively healthy, if slightly overweight. No distinguishing marks or tattoos. An old scar on the stomach suggests this man had his appendix removed at some point in his life. We will ascertain if this is correct after opening the body.' He paused again, reaching over to open the eyelids with his gloved thumb. 'The corneas are cloudy. As this man was found in a freezer this confirms that at some point the body was frozen. Did the freezing occur before or after death? We shall determine the answer when we perform the post mortem.' He moved the angle poise lamp so it shone directly on the naked arms. 'I see contusions and bruising on either side of the mouth. This man has been gagged at some point. But the gag was removed after death. Moving to the arms, there are the marks of a thin rope around the wrists with similar scarring around the ankles. Fibres present in both locations and I will now take a sample of these and of the surrounding tissue.' He gestured for the assistant to move forward to collect the samples.

As he did so, Dr Schofield stopped her. 'Just a moment.'

The doctor moved round to the head of the man and stared downwards.

'What is that?' he said aloud, forgetting the microphone was recording for an instant. 'What the hell is that?'

Chapter 51

'Listen, Ridpath, I don't like you and, if it were my decision, you would be kicking your heels as a coroner's officer for the rest of your career.'

Ridpath concentrated on driving the car, not answering his gaffer.

'And you know why I don't like you?'

'I'm sure you're going to tell me.'

'Because you're not a team player. You're this little maverick copper who thinks he's smarter and better than everybody else. But you're not. Without everybody's work, you're just a nobody. If you return to MIT, you're going to knuckle under and follow the rules, ok? If you don't, you're out. I don't care what Claire Trent thinks. If it's a choice between me and you, I know which she would have to pick, don't you? What do you say to that?'

'I say we're here.' Ridpath pulled up the handbrake of the car and it squeaked like a strangled chicken.

Turnbull was in his face. 'Get with the programme, or get out, clear?'

Ridpath returned the gaze. 'Yes.'

'Yes *sir*.'

'Yes, sir.'

'Good, now we've cleared the air, let's get to work.' Turnbull got out of the car and walked through the main doors of the morgue. Ridpath locked the car and followed him.

'Jesus, I hate these places. Imagine what sort of nutter you must be to work here every day with these stiffs—'

'I imagine a nutter like me.' Dr Schofield's high voice echoed around the tiled reception area. 'Hello there, DI Ridpath, good to see you again. And you are?'

'Detective Chief Inspector Turnbull, the deputy head of MIT.' He stuck out his hand.

Schofield held up his gloved hands. They were covered in dried blood and assorted gore.

'You've finished the post mortem?'

'I haven't started yet. This is another customer.'

'What?'

'I said I hadn't started yet. I have done a preliminary external examination of the body but no post mortem has been performed.'

'I don't think you understand how urgently the post mortem information is needed doctor,' insisted Turnbull.

'And I don't think you understand, Detective Chief Inspector, you cannot perform a post mortem on a frozen body. It needs to defrost first. Imagine a Christmas butterball turkey freshly bought from Tesco's—'

Turnbull held up his hands. 'Enough, I get it.'

The image swirled around in Ridpath's brain and he shook his head to get rid of it. 'Did you discover anything on the external examination, doctor?'

'I did. I do understand the need for urgency, that's why I am talking to you before the post mortem has been completed. When you've suited up, come and join me in the morgue.'

He turned and walked through large double doors on the left.

'There's an invite I never thought I'd hear. Is this man for real?'

'Dr Schofield is the best pathologist I've ever worked with. If he says the body isn't ready for the post mortem yet, it isn't ready.'

Turnbull frowned. 'Is it necessary to get suited up? I never used to bother.'

'Dr Schofield insists on it if we want to enter his mortuary.'

'Never used to bother before,' muttered Turnbull again following Ridpath to the changing area. As they were putting on the green scrubs, he asked. 'What's with the voice? He looks like a thirteen-year-old. Are you sure he's the pathologist?'

'He suffers from Kallmann Syndrome, a form of congenital hypogonadotropic hypogonadism.'

'You trying to impress me with big words?'

'He told me so I looked it up. It's a disease stopping a person from starting or fully completing puberty, leaving him with a youthful appearance, despite being an adult.'

'So, he's a freak right?'

'No, just somebody with a genetic disorder.' Dr Schofield stood in the doorway. 'The good news is I never have to shave. The bad news is my sense of smell is severely diminished which is useful when cutting up a cadaver but not so useful when drinking wine. I also have a particularly short middle finger.' He held up his gloved hands, still covered in blood. 'Would you like to come this way?'

They followed him into a large white-tiled room with four stainless steel tables arranged in the centre. On one of the tables, an assistant was taking a sample from the stomach of a corpse. Above their heads, a large clock displayed the time. 4.30 p.m.

Ridpath shivered as the cold of the lab began to seep into his bones. He hadn't forgotten his appointment with Eve and Polly that evening. In fact, he would do almost anything to get away from this place.

The assistant made a cut with a scalpel across the stomach. Ridpath almost gagged as a smell like the abyss of hell rose from the body. Behind him, he heard Turnbull stop and take a step backwards.

Dr Schofield moved past his assistant and pointed to a corpse covered in a damp white sheet. 'This is Mr Donald Brown, a thirty-one-year-old hospital porter from Glossop. I believe you knew him Ridpath.'

The Detective Inspector focussed on the face of the body on the table. The man looked a little older than when Ridpath last saw him and he had lost weight. But it was Don Brown, the mortuary attendant he had interviewed two years ago.

'Can you confirm the identification for me, Detective Inspector Ridpath?'

Ridpath was surprised for a moment at the pathologist's use of his rank, and whispered, 'I can.'

'Can you speak louder, please?' The doctor pointed to the mike hanging down from the ceiling.

'I can. This is Donald Brown.'

The assistant moved away, carrying some petri dishes with slices of intestine.

'Good. You must understand these are preliminary findings only from an external examination. I still need to follow up with post mortem proper, the toxicology and the analysis of tissue samples.'

Turnbull finally joined Ridpath at the table. 'Understood doctor. Can we get on?'

'You mean there is someplace else you'd rather be, Detective Chief Inspector?'

'I can think of at least 2,000 places, doctor.'

'But you're here. The topline is you are looking at an adult male in the prime of his life. Slightly overweight, but otherwise quite fit.'

'Was he a druggie?'

'If you are asking if the man was addicted to any illegal substances, Chief Inspector, the answer is I don't think so. I can see no evidence of needle tracks or marks. The toxicology will discover if there are other substances in his body. I will have the results for this after the post mortem.'

'What was the cause of death then?' asked Turnbull.

'The *probable* cause of death was a myocardial infarction brought on by severe hypothermia.'

'What's that when it's at home?'

'In layman's terms, a heart attack brought about by a dangerous drop in body temperature. But once again, I will confirm this after post mortem. But I can see no signs of any external trauma or asphyxiation. Poison or drugs may have been used and I'll know after toxicology.'

Ridpath's eyes narrowed. 'Are you saying this man froze to death?'

'Exactly. The normal body temperature averages 98.6 degrees. With hypothermia, core temperature drops below 95 degrees. In severe hypothermia, core body temperature can drop to 82 degrees or lower. This corpse was removed from the freezer exactly five hours and seventeen minutes ago. Despite the freezer losing power during the explosion, the body's core temperature is still only...' he removed a probe from inside the chest cavity and consulted a display on his desk, '...still only 89 degrees. When we first inserted the thermometer five hours ago, the body temperature was 83 degrees. The power had been off since the explosion which was catalogued as happening at 5.17 p.m. yesterday.'

'So yesterday the body must have been much colder?'

'That is correct. He is gradually thawing out.'

'I don't understand, doctor, how did he die?' asked Turnbull.

'He froze to death. If I were to be a little more scientific, I would explain that during exposure to cold temperatures, most heat loss escapes through the skin; the rest, you exhale from your lungs. When this happens, the hypothalamus, the brain's temperature-control centre, works to raise body temperature by triggering processes to heat the body. Shivering for example or vasoconstriction; blood vessels temporarily narrowing.'

The doctor paused for a moment. 'If the core body temperature continues to fall, the organs begin to shut down to preserve heat and protect the brain. Breathing, heart rate and brain activity slows. Most people become confused and they have hallucinations. There is even evidence that some people rip off their clothes, even in the coldest conditions, believing they are too hot. I saw some evidence of that occurring in this case. His shirt was torn as if Mr Brown had tried to remove it.'

'What a way to die,' whispered Turnbull.

'Any estimate of the time of death?'

'You always ask the same question, Ridpath. This time, I can't offer you anything with any precision, I'm afraid, the cold slows down the normal process of decay. The microbiome may help but I doubt it in this case. When did he disappear?'

'Yesterday morning at approximately 6.20 a.m. He had clocked off from his shift at the hospital five minutes earlier.'

'Then the time of death is anywhere from 6.20 a.m. to 5.17 p.m. yesterday.'

'You can't be more precise?'

Dr Schofield shook his head. 'Anything else is sheer guess-work.'

'Thank you, Dr Schofield.'

Turnbull started ripping off his scrubs and walked towards the door. 'We're done here.'

Ridpath glanced at the clock. 'Was there anything else, doctor?'

'The nails.'

'What about them?'

Turnbull stopped and turned back.

'He'd ripped off his nails trying to claw his way out of the freezer.'

'And?'

'We found a thumbnail lodged in his clothing. I've checked under the microscope and there seems to be a blue fibre lodged beneath it. I've sent it over to forensics for analysis.'

'Did it come from his clothing or the freezer?'

'He was wearing a red Manchester United shirt when he was found so I don't believe it was from his clothing.'

'Locard's principle.'

'Exactly, Ridpath.'

'What are you two on about?'

The doctor answered. 'Locard's exchange principle holds that the perpetrator of a crime will bring something into the crime scene and leave with something from it, and that both can be used as forensic evidence.'

'The fibre may have come from the perpetrator.'

'Or perhaps from the vehicle in which he was transported. Thank you doctor, I'll follow up with forensics.'

'There's one more thing, Ridpath.'

'More?'

'I found this tucked into the top pocket of the t-shirt.' He held up a small piece of paper in an evidence bag.

'Any prints on it?' asked Turnbull.

'It's clean, Chief Inspector.'

Ridpath moved closer, staring at the evidence. 'What is it?'

'I've unfolded it, and it seems to be a game of hangman, with none of the letters filled in, but the game completed.'

Ridpath saw a spare drawing of a hanged man, drawn in a child's style. 'There are seven letters in the word.'

Both himself and Turnbull spoke at the same time. 'Coroner.'

'Let's go for a drink, Ridpath, I need to get the taste of the bloody morgue out of my mouth. Where's the nearest boozer?'

Ridpath checked the clock again. 5.45. He had promised Polly he would be back by six this evening. 'The Grafton is the closest, I reckon, down the street.'

'What beer is it?'

'Holt's, I think.'

'I'd love a pint of Holt's. Come on, my mouth's as dry as a kangaroo's jockstrap.' He marched down the street towards the pub.

While Turnbull was at the bar, getting the round, Ridpath messaged Polly. 'Back soon, stuck in a meeting.' A little white lie, but she was sure to understand.

Turnbull returned with a half for Ridpath and a pint and a chaser for himself. 'Here's the woman's drink.'

'I'm driving.'

'You think any cop is going to pull you over?'

'That's maybe how it was in Cheshire, but in Manchester, it's different. A bigger force, bigger responsibility.'

Turnbull took a large swallow of beer, wiping away the foam left on his top lip with his sleeve. 'Not a bad pint that. You trying to teach me my job, Ridpath?'

Ridpath could see this was becoming one of those conversations. So be it. The man's constant belligerence was starting to grate.

Turnbull took another swallow of beer. 'What was it with the double act with the pre-pube?'

This constant needling was deliberate. Ridpath was determined he wouldn't rise to the bait. 'Schofield is good. He's thorough, accurate and doesn't miss anything. If he says the fibre will be useful, it will.'

'You two know each other?'

'We've worked together before.' Ridpath flashed back to the Connolly case and the immolation of Samuel Sykes. 'Schofield was a great help.'

'Sure there isn't something more there.' Turnbull was leering as he picked up his chaser of whisky.

'What do you mean?'

'Nothing, I got the impression, you were more than colleagues. We're all open minded in the police now.'

The man was baiting him. Why?

Ridpath took a sip of his beer as Turnbull asked his next question. 'How's the coroner?'

'Mrs Challinor? Good at her job, never seen someone work harder.'

'You misunderstand me. I meant is she pro us? Or is she one of those coroners who sees it as her job to represent the victims in society? If there ever was a problem, would she be on our side?'

'Our side?'

'The police. The forces of law and order.'

'You'll have to ask her.'

'I will, next time I meet her.'

Ridpath decided to change the subject. 'The fibres may be the best lead we have so far.'

'How?'

'Well, if Schofield is right and the fibres do come from the carpet of a vehicle, it could help us isolate the make and model.'

'But we're looking for a white van, aren't we?'

'What if our perp used another vehicle? He must have known we would check CCTV around John Gorman's house?'

Suddenly, Turnbull's eyes narrowed. 'If it wasn't a white van, we'll have wasted our time.'

'But the fibre may help make the ANPR search easier by isolating the vehicle he did use; it may be the white van. We would no longer be looking for a needle in a haystack. Remember the woman said he was in a white or grey car?'

Turnbull thought for a moment before taking another swallow of beer. 'Why did you become a copper, Ridpath?'

Ridpath shrugged, 'Dunno, seemed like a good idea at the time.'

'I've checked your file. You were one of Charlie Whitworth's blue-eyed boys, being promoted rapidly despite not being one of the fast track mob with their university degrees and mouths full of long words. Then, it all fell apart, didn't it? The cancer was a bit of a kick in the teeth.'

'That's finished now, I'm in remission.'

'But is it ever finished? What if it comes back? What if you're in the middle of a case and you get ill again?'

Turnbull was staring at him, waiting for a reaction.

Ridpath smiled. 'Well, if it happens, I'll handle it, won't I? Cancer is an illness, not a permanent disability. I'm cured now and never felt better.' There was no need to tell Turnbull about the monthly check-ups or the procedures if he ever caught flu.

He finished his half and stood up. 'I'll be off now. I've got an early start tomorrow. You can get yourself home, can't you?' Ridpath was buggered if he was going to give the man a lift.

He walked out of the pub. Just before he left, Turnbull shouted across to him, 'Look after yourself, Ridpath, I wouldn't want you collapsing on the job again.'

Ridpath walked slowly back to him. He could see Turnbull brace himself, 'One last thing, boss. I'd check the coroner's body if I were you. So far, the killer, if it is Dalbey, has left a clue to his next murder on the body of each victim. It's almost as if he wants us to stop him.'

Ridpath turned and walked out of the front door, glancing back once. Turnbull was already on his phone.

He desperately needed a shower. Not to rid himself of the smell of the morgue, but to remove the stench of Detective Chief Inspector Turnbull.

Chapter 53

'Sorry, I'm late.' He bent down to kiss Polly on the forehead and wave to Eve.

They had already started watching the film. Eve had this strange obsession with creating 'movie nights'; pillows and blankets, snacks and drinks, blinds and curtains drawn, and lights off.

'Don't worry, we guessed you would be late,' said Eve, 'so we saved you some samosas, some bhajis and some onion rings.'

Polly paused the movie as the zombies were meeting the werewolves for the first time. 'We finished all the popcorn. Do you want a glass of wine? There's a Sauvignon Blanc in the fridge, but from the smell of your breath, you've already started.'

'I had to have a swift half with the new DCI.'

'How is he?'

'Honest?'

Polly nodded.

'A bit of a wanker.'

'Dad, you're not supposed to use language like that around me. Remember, duh, child present.' Eve pointed to herself, mimicking her mother's tone perfectly.

'You're old enough now to hear those words.'

'No, she isn't. I'll get you the glass of wine before you say something much worse.'

Ridpath sat down next to his daughter. She was covered by her favourite Disney blanket and was hugging her rabbit close to her. Still the child despite the desperate attempts of the internet and schooling to drag her kicking and screaming into being a teenager.

'How was *your* day?'

She shrugged her shoulders. 'Ok, Maisie Riley has been showing off her new choker from Claire's. Everyone is soooo jealous, even the teacher.'

'I thought you weren't supposed to wear jewellery to school?'

'A choker isn't jewellery, duh, it's fashion.'

When had 'duh' become a word? Obviously after his years at school. 'Anything interesting happening?'

'The choker is *the* interesting part of my day.'

'School work isn't?'

'School work is easy. Fashion is difficult.'

Polly came back carrying his glass of wine and a plateful of assorted samosas and spring rolls, but no popcorn.

He took the plate off her and asked, 'How was your day?'

She shrugged. 'Ok, but Maisie Riley has a new choker and it's totally rad, duh.'

Ridpath looked at both of them. They were both trying to suppress their giggles.

'This is a wind-up right? It's time to make fun of the dad?'

Eve snapped her fingers. 'Dad, is sooooo straight, duh.'

'Can we watch the movie so I can eat my samosas in peace?'

Polly leant over and gave him a hug. 'Bad day, lost your sense of humour?' She smelt his neck and recoiled. 'Sorry, Ridpath, you were at the morgue again, weren't you?'

Ridpath nodded. 'How did you know?'

'The smell, it's always the same when you've been to the morgue. It sort of clings to you.'

'Sorry, I'll go and shower.'

'No worries, it's not that bad, I just won't sit close to you. Eat your snacks first.' She sat down on the far end of the sofa. 'Eve, let's watch the movie while your dad eats.'

Eve pressed the remote and the movie began again. All three sat in silence, broken only by the crunch of a samosa between Ridpath's teeth.

His mouth may have been chewing but he wasn't watching the zombies dancing with the werewolves. Instead, his mind was full of questions about the day's events.

Had Dalbey returned?

Why was he taking revenge now?

Where was he?

And the worst question, the one that filled him with the most dread.

Who would be the next victim?

Chapter 54

Ian Stallard, the pathologist for Oldham and district, had received the call from DCI Turnbull just as he was about to start the post mortem.

He hated interruptions to his routine and this one annoyed him more than most.

'You need to check the body.'

The background sounds meant the man was calling from a pub. 'Which body?'

'The body of the coroner, Brian Conway.'

'I'm about to start the post mortem and, because of this interruption, I'm going to have to scrub up again.'

'You still need to check the body.'

'Why?'

'There may be a hidden message or something like that on it.'

'If there is anything, I will find it.'

He clicked off his mobile and began scrubbing his hands once more. After he finished, he walked over to the body on the slab. He had known Brian Conway for over twenty years. A good man was the coroner, a kind man, and not a bad golfer on a good day when the wind was blowing in the right direction.

Now here he was lying on a cold, stainless steel slab in an even colder morgue, ready to be cut open.

Stallard could have recused himself, asked somebody from Yorkshire to come and do the post mortem. But he felt that was a cop-out. And anyway, who could treat his friend better than himself?

He pulled down the mike and began speaking. 'Case number 179/20 is an adult male, Brian Conway, date of birth, 12.01.1951. From first appearances, the customer seems in good health, slightly overweight but nothing to worry about.' He checked the hands, arms and feet. 'Hands and feet clean, no sign of drug use or any external damage and no signs of any defensive wounds. Why didn't he put up a struggle?'

He often asked himself questions out loud as he performed his post mortems. Later, when he transcribed his notes they would help him form his conclusions.

He focussed for a minute on his friend's appearance. 'Ashen colour to the face, the nose, forehead and lips drained of colour. A coil of rope with which he was hanged is still around his neck. I am removing it now.'

After taking photographs, he cut through the rope with a sharp scalpel, before continuing to speak. 'The ligature shows discontinuity and an oblique shape above the level of the thyroid cartilage.' He measured the mark on the man's throat. 'With a depth of 2.3 centimetres. There are signs of abrasion, blackening of the skin through friction burns and a displacement of the skin around the ligature.' He angled his head slightly to get a better view. 'The displaced epithelium shows rightward displacement.'

He took a break, wiping his forehead, before returning to the body of his friend. He pulled the microphone down closer to his mouth and changed the angle of the light.

'There is contusion, damage to muscle fibres and haemor-rhage at the sternal end of the sternocleidomastoid muscle. The thyroid cartilage and the hyoid bone both seem to be intact as does the cricoid cartilage.' He moved the body to check the back of the neck. 'The cervical vertebrae are intact.'

He stood up again and stretched, his back was killing him. The classic pathologist injury; a bad back from stooping over bodies all day long. Still it had to be done.

He leant forward and gently opened the eyelids with his gloved hand. 'Petechiae are present in the eyes and on the cheeks. From initial examination, death was caused by brain ischaemia after compression on the airways and blood vessels of the neck. Did a reflex cardiac arrest occur due to vagal inhibition created by pressure on the carotid sinus?'

He moved his gaze down to the mouth. Saliva had dried on the left-hand side of the lips. 'What's that?'

As he leant closer, he could see an edge of something white peeping out from between the grey lips. He selected a clamp from the table. 'Sorry my old friend,' he said out loud, prizing open the man's jaws.

There was something there. He reached in with the tips of his fingers and slowly pulled out a sodden piece of paper folded into two. He opened it up.

'Is Justice blind?' he read the words printed on the paper out loud. 'What the?'

He placed the paper in an evidence bag and marked the time and place of discovery on the cover. He must remember to include it in his post mortem report when he sent it over to the police. DCI Turnbull could do with it what he wanted.

He returned back to the body.

How exactly had this man died?

Chapter 55

He had often wondered how this would feel.

Would it be dark or lonely? Would it be like a dream? Would he be able to feel anything at all?

The answer was it was none of these things.

It was heaven.

A time which he could spend in his own mind. He'd been there often enough. In prison, the only way to survive had been to go inside himself. To find a different place from the four walls, the guards, the rancid smell of too many human beings crammed together, and always the noise.

Nobody realises but prisons are never quiet. There is always noise somewhere. From the clanging of the closing gates on each corridor to the loud snores of the sleeping old con next door. The shouts of the lags playing table tennis to the radios blaring all kinds of music. The calls of the prisoners to each other in the middle of the night to the screams of the nightmares.

Noise all the time.

Some escaped it through drugs, the black hole of Spice. Some escaped through religion. Others went noisily insane.

Him, he went to two places.

He delved into the world of books, educating himself in a way which had been impossible when he wasn't incarcerated. A world where he could discover knowledge; it was all written down somewhere. All you had to do was know where to look.

The second place he went into was his own mind. Just like now.

He felt comfortable there. A place of solitude.

Not lonely just alone.

Away from the voice. Away from the nightmares. Away from the memories.

Just him.

Alone.

Occasionally though the world intruded.

As he lay there, he listened to the world outside. The regular beeping of the machine. The snuffles of the man next door. The soft tread of cushioned feet on the lino floor. The whispered conversations.

Some of them actually spoke to him. He could hear their voices but he didn't respond.

His mind wouldn't let him.

At times like this, he comforted himself everything was going according to plan.

They would turn up soon.

It was in the plan.

Chapter 56

The next morning Ridpath was up early and out of the house while Polly and Eve were still busy with their dreams.

He checked in on both of them before he left. Polly was gripping her pillow tightly as if hanging onto a life raft in a raging sea. Eve was the exact opposite; the bed clothes thrown off, her pyjamas creased, head at an awkward angle and her body stretched out diagonally over the bed.

He thought about waking them to ask if they wanted something for breakfast but decided against it. He brewed a pot of coffee for Polly when she woke and closed the door behind him as quietly as he could before he left.

He had arranged to meet Emily at a Costa in Didsbury before they visited the Seagram's after nine a.m.

She was already waiting for him when he arrived, two lattes sitting in front of her. 'Morning, Ridpath.'

'You're early,' he mumbled.

'Couldn't sleep. Too much going on in my head.'

He knew what she meant, he hadn't had the best night's sleep himself. Too many questions rushing round his brain like headless chickens on speed. 'Do you want anything to eat?'

'Nah, the only thing I can face in the morning is a ciggie, food is number thirty-six on my list of priorities.'

As she spoke, Ridpath realised he knew nothing about his Detective Sergeant. Where was she born? Why did she join the police? Was she in a relationship? What did she want out of life?

Did it matter? She was a good, efficient copper who did her job with the minimum of fuss. He thought back to Turnbull's questioning of him last night like he was some petty thief banged up in one of the interview rooms. It was just an exercise in power and control.

If he grilled her this morning like he had been questioned last night, was he any better than Turnbull?

'Sure you don't want anything?'

'Positive. Caffeine is perfect.'

He went off to get himself a sticky bun and when he returned she surprised him by saying. 'I just realised you know nothing about me.'

'You don't need to tell me.'

'I'm going to anyway. I grew up outside Preston, and moved to Manchester when I went to uni. Mum and dad still live there. Dad's a draughtsman for BAE and mum's a nursery nurse. I studied English at Manchester, don't know why, it seemed a good idea at the time. But when you've just read another Canterbury Tale for the nth time, followed by a slew of instantly forgettable Restoration comedies, you realise English should be read and enjoyed not studied. I got my degree through luck rather than hard work and I looked for a job. Ended up applying for the Force's fast track scheme and here I am.'

It was a potted history that left out a lot of details. In fact, the detective in Ridpath knew what she left out was far more important than anything she had told him.

'So you've heard about me, what about you?'

'No university, joined the police because I was bored and they paid well at that time. I realised on the second day of training that I loved it and, on the third day, I was actually quite good. After three years on the beat, passed my detective exams and ended at MIT under Charlie Whitworth.'

'The one and only.'

Ridpath nodded. 'He was a great boss and I learnt lots from him, but he was a bit old school.'

'The word on the street was he was born before the dinosaurs.'

Ridpath chuckled. 'That would probably be too late. Loved the work and moved up pretty quickly, even though I wasn't one of you fast trackers, to Detective Inspector, then…' Ridpath paused for a moment, shrugged his shoulders and said, '…then I discovered I had myeloma. I went through chemo and a bone marrow transplant, six months of hell, and I finally beat it. Rejoined the Force and was posted to the coroner as her officer.'

'I don't mean to be rude but it's a bit of a come-down from being a DI with MIT, isn't it? Usually reserved for those reaching down to put their slippers on.'

'I suppose it is. But I've enjoyed it immensely. Mrs Challinor has been great to work for; committed, honest and passionate about her job. It's given me a whole new perspective on policing. It's not only about catching the perps but also about the victims. The sort of people we're going to see today.'

Emily Parkinson gazed at him shrewdly. 'Word is you're coming back to run one of the teams?'

'There seems to be a lot of words floating around in the air. Enough for a bloody dictionary.' He glanced at the clock on the wall. 'Here's another few words for you: Drink your coffee, it's time to see the Seagrams.'

'That's a sentence not a few words.'

Ridpath stood up. 'You can't put anything past an English graduate, can you? I've got an idea to make your English degree useful.'

'What's that?'

'How about you take all the notes today, then you can put all the sentences together in coherent English, with no spelling or grammar mistakes, for the typed report.'

'I knew I shouldn't have told you about myself.'

'First rule of being a detective. Never let the bastards know anything about you.'

'Does that include my superiors?'

'Who do you think I was talking about?'

Chapter 57

The house was exactly how Ridpath remembered it. Still as neat as a new bed sheet, with the lawn beautifully manicured and the borders freshly dug.

Ridpath pressed the bell and stepped back.

The door was answered almost immediately by Mrs Seagram. She had aged considerably over the two years since Ridpath had last seen her. The same energy was still there but it was now clothed in skin that had wrinkled and a back which had begun to bow.

'I wondered when you lot would turn up.'

Ridpath raised an eyebrow quizzically.

Mrs Seagram reached behind her and showed them a morning newspaper. A blaring headline touted, 'THE RETURN OF THE BEAST OF MANCHESTER???'

Ridpath stared at the three question marks. Subtlety was not the *Sun*'s strength.

'You'd better come in rather than standin' there like last week's wet washin'.' The accent was strongly from Manchester with the lack of 'g's and the whine that nestled between the words. 'Neighbours will start to talk.'

They were shown into the same living room Ridpath had seen before. Pictures of Alice Seagram were still everywhere; in school uniform, laughing with friends, as a young girl, in a school photo. Unusually, the Seagrams had been instrumental in getting the government to reconsider the conviction of James Dalbey for the murder of their daughter. It was their persistence which led to the case being re-opened.

There was one picture of Mr Seagram in the centre of the mantlepiece. Ridpath remembered him as a man full of anger at the death of his daughter. 'Where is your husband?'

'He passed away eighteen months ago. Three months after we reburied Alice and just after James was released. We were married for thirty-seven years, met at a dance. He was dolled up in his uniform and I was on the prowl.'

'Uniform?'

'He was in the REME, an armourer, served in Northern Ireland, Cyprus, and the first Gulf War. A good man… but you lot killed him.' She stared out of the window. 'He had nothing left to live for,' she added quietly.

'Please accept my deepest condolences, Mrs Seagram, on the loss of your husband.'

'Aye, you're a bit late, Mr Ridpath.'

She remembered his name. 'I'm truly sorry. I should have checked the situation before coming here. My apologies.' He pointed to Emily. 'This is my colleague, DS Parkinson.'

'Are you still with the coroner?'

He nodded.

'Send my regards to Mrs Challinor. She was the only decent person in this whole mess. Without her…' The woman's voice began to break up and tears formed in her eyes. Emily Parkinson pulled a clean and pressed handkerchief from her pocket and gave it to Mrs Seagram.

Ridpath was always jealous of people who managed to have clean fabric handkerchiefs available. The most he ever carried was a miniature packet of Kleenex.

'Thank you, love,' Mrs Seagram whispered.

Ridpath decided to press on, to get this interview over as quickly as possible. 'Now you may wonder why we're here?'

'It had crossed my mind. You do seem to turn up when there's trouble, Mr Ridpath.'

'I need to ask if you have seen James Dalbey since his release from prison?'

She nodded her head slowly. 'Only once. He came to see us just after he got out. To thank us for everything we did on his behalf. He was always a nice, kind boy was James.'

'What was the exact date, do you remember?' Emily asked.

'Must have been the month after my husband died. We were still in mourning. So it will have been August 2018.'

Parkinson scribbled the answer in her pad. 'And you haven't seen him since?'

She shook her head. 'Why would I?'

Ridpath thought for a moment. 'You just said "us". "He came to see us after his release".'

'Myself and my son, Tony.'

There were no pictures to be seen of Tony anywhere. 'Where is he? Can we speak to him too?'

'I don't know.'

Ridpath frowned. 'You don't know?'

'He vanished about six months ago. Since his father died he's had some problems with drink, lost his job.'

Ridpath remembered an aggressive well-dressed and cultured man, even angrier than his father. 'He doesn't work with the television studios any more?'

'They sacked him. Turned up drunk too often. There were drugs involved too.'

'You haven't seen him for six months?'

'Roughly that. He came to see me and asked for money. I didn't have any so he took my husband's laptop. I haven't seen him since.' The woman pressed the handkerchief to her eyes. 'You see, I lost my whole family since our daughter was murdered. Alice, Harry, and now Tony. We were victims too but everybody forgets that after they caught Harold Lardner. You lot thought you'd finally brought him to justice. But where was the justice for my family? Where was the justice for me? I lost everything I loved...' Her voice trailed off.

Ridpath glanced at DS Parkinson. Nothing would be gained from interviewing this woman any further. 'I am truly sorry,

Mrs Seagram. If there is anything I can do, anything, please let me know.' He passed over his card.

The woman looked up for a moment. 'There is something you can do, Mr Ridpath.'

'Anything, Mrs Seagram.'

'Bring back my family.'

Chapter 58

He liked the dark.

Even as a child he had found comfort there: he wasn't scared.

One day his mother had caught him sitting alone in his bedroom, the curtains drawn. He must have been about six years old.

'You shouldn't sit here all alone in the dark.'

'But I like it, Mum.'

She bustled in, pulling open the curtains, letting the yellow light of the street lamps outside their house flood into his bedroom. 'It's not natural sitting in the dark.'

'It's safer in the dark.'

'Don't be silly, son. Now get beneath the covers, it's time for bed.'

Outside in the sitting room, he could hear a man's heavy feet clumping around. Who was it this time? He would never know, they would be gone by morning, vanishing as if they had never existed, never to return.

His mum often left him alone at weekends. Not her fault, she had to go to work and there was nobody to look after him.

The words as she left for work in the morning were always the same. 'Don't answer the door. Don't go out. Don't leave the house. There's a sandwich and some fruit in the fridge. I'll be back before seven.'

Sometimes she did come back and sometimes she didn't.

He didn't mind though because as soon as she left, he was in the cupboard under the stairs, the door closed, the safety of the dark swallowing him whole.

He stayed there all day.

His friend was the dark, he didn't have many others.

A hand touching his brow, forced his mind to drift closer to the surface.

Somebody was speaking to him. Was she singing? She had a rotten singing voice but he could hear the melody clearly.

Let it be.

Well he wasn't going to do that. The plan must have been moving forward now. He had spent months creating it, going over each and every detail until every eventuality was covered, every base checked, every possible action or reaction wargamed.

The plan was perfect.

Why was she telling him to let it be?

He was aware of a shadow over his head. The woman had stopped singing now. What was she doing?

A click of something being turned and a tidal wave of immense peace suffused his body and he drifted back down to the bottom of the well.

His memories were waiting for him there, calling him to come and play with them.

He'd done his job.

The plan was perfect.

Chapter 59

Ridpath and Emily Parkinson were sitting in a meeting room at Ashworth Hospital in Maghull near Liverpool. It was like any other hospital meeting room; posters advising against the spread of disease, furniture bought in some government job lot, green painted walls.

Except here, the furniture was bolted to the floor, some posters advised against ever being alone with patients and the green paint reminded Ridpath of a prison.

Despite the outside appearance of a hospital, Ashworth was in actuality a prison. Along with Rampton and Broadmoor, it was one of only three high security psychiatric hospitals in England, housing just over 200 of the most dangerous, and most disturbed, prisoners. Its inmates included Ian Brady, the Moors Murderer, Dale Cregan who gunned down two female police officers in Manchester, spree killer Robert Sartin, bank-robber-turned-film-star, Charles Salvador and, of course, Harold Lardner, the Beast of Manchester.

It had taken them both less than an hour to drive here from Manchester but it felt like a different world. They had been finger-printed, had their credentials checked three times, passed through two metal detectors and finally been escorted to this room and told to wait.

A key turning in the lock forced them to look up. The door slowly opened and a man dressed like a hospital orderly but with the voice of a prison guard announced. 'All clear. You can go in now Mr Lardner.'

There was a pause before an elderly man shuffled in. 'Thank you, Derek, you can leave us now.'

'You know that's not possible, Mr Lardner.'

He stayed where he was in the room as another guard closed the door.

'You can't get the staff these days.' The eyes looked up at Ridpath. 'I see you've brought somebody with you, aren't you going to introduce us?'

As Lardner moved to lift his arm to shake hands, the guard stepped forward. 'There will be no contact with the patient.'

Lardner put his hand down. 'They call me a patient but I'm actually a prisoner.'

Ridpath spoke for the first time. 'This is Detective Sergeant Parkinson.'

Emily nodded but didn't get up.

Lardner smiled. 'Detective sergeants are getting younger, aren't they? What are you Emily, twenty-eight? No, I'm wrong, twenty-seven. But it is a pleasure to meet you. We don't see many women in here and those that do visit, could probably spend more time with their razors, if you understand my drift. Do you mind?'

He pointed to the chair and sat down. 'Now to what do I owe this pleasure? Not that I have anything else more important to do. Today was the reading club. The doctors here are keen on reading clubs. Dostoevsky was their choice this week. *Crime and Punishment*—' He rolled his eyes, '—They do lack subtlety. I asked them to bring in a few cadavers for me to dissect. I do miss cutting up my bodies. But for some reason, they said no. I had to join a reading club instead. It's not the same, is it? Words rather than actions.'

'We're here about the letter you wrote to the coroner.'

'How is Mrs Challinor? Still trying to set the world to rights? I do so miss my interactions with her. I must admit she became a little devious towards the end. Trapping me to give evidence in an inquest was a cruel trick. Or was it your idea, Ridpath? Are you the one who loves deceptions and tricks?'

'About the letter you wrote…'

'Trying to stay on track? I do like a man who stays on the straight and narrow, don't you Emily? I can call you Emily, can I? I do like to be on first-name terms with my friends.'

DS Parkinson glared across at Ridpath.

'Ah, you're wondering how I know your Christian name?' He pointed back to the guard holding his clipboard. 'Sometimes, Derek is a little careless about security. He lets me read his notes over his shoulder.'

The guard blushed.

Ridpath stood up. 'It's time to leave DS Parkinson, we're wasting our time here.'

'Don't go yet, Ridpath, I'm having so much fun, enjoying our chat almost as much as when we met in the hospital, remember?'

Ridpath flashed back to the time he interviewed Lardner when he was still a senior pathologist. The doctor had hidden his double life for years, behind a mask of medical competency.

'You spent a long time staring at the magazines on my shelves. My pathology papers and journals. You have a certain attraction to death, Ridpath, a fascination maybe. Otherwise why do the job you do? In another life, it would be you sitting here with a chain around your waist not me.'

'I would never murder young women for pleasure, Lardner.'

'No, you would do it for pain. Don't you understand, Ridpath. It's all about pain. Yours and theirs.'

'For the last time, Lardner, why did you write the letter to Mrs Challinor?'

A fire came into Lardner's eyes. 'You are in no position to give me orders, Ridpath. An emotionally crippled detective whose remission from cancer could end at any moment?' Then he recovered his composure and smiled. 'How do you know I wrote the letter? Was there a signature?'

'You know there wasn't.'

'Do I? It would be a grave undertaking to write a letter bypassing the prison authorities in such a way, wouldn't it?'

'How do you know the letter bypassed the prison authorities if you didn't write it?'

Lardner laughed for a long time. 'You do amuse me, Ridpath. Would you be here asking these questions if the letter had passed through official channels?'

'Did you or did you not write it and what did you mean?' The exasperation in Ridpath's voice was obvious.

Lardner stood up and shuffled towards the door. The guard instantly became more alert. 'Can you escort me back to my room, Derek?'

The guard banged on the door and the sound of a key being turned in a lock echoed in the room. The door opened to reveal another guard. Lardner turned back to Ridpath. 'Remember it's about pain, he takes no pleasure in doing what he does. It's all about pain. His pain and theirs.'

'Who is killing, Lardner? Please tell me.'

The former pathologist smiled again. 'I don't know what you are talking about, Ridpath. But as a former pathologist, I can tell you one thing...'

'What's that?'

'For someone to kill is always a grave undertaking, both legally and medically, requiring organisational skills of the highest order.'

The prisoner shuffled out of the room, escorted by his guard. 'Please remain where you are. The deputy medical director will be along to escort you from the facility,' the guard said to Ridpath before closing the door.

'What was all that about?'

'I'm not certain, but I have a feeling Harold Lardner was trying to tell us something.'

Chapter 60

Outside the maximum security hospital, Ridpath stood by as Emily Parkinson smoked a cigarette before the journey home. She had offered him one but, surprising himself, he had refused.

The smell of the prison hospital still lurked in his nostrils; the combination of disinfectant, urine, human beings and fear saturated all places like this.

They had been escorted out of the facility by the deputy medical director, a Dr Halligan.

'Lardner is a classic narcissistic personality. He likes to control or seem to be in control, of people and of lives.'

'Is that why he killed all those young women?'

'Nothing can fully explain why a serial killer becomes the way he does. Look at Harold Shipman, even today we don't understand why he killed over 200 people. We can rationalise it in the usual way; a troubled childhood, the beginning of experimentation on animals, the escalation into humans, a delight in inflicting pain, in controlling the end of life. But all that is post rationalisation. Many people suffer those abuses without becoming serial killers. However, one thing is remarkable about Lardner.'

'What's that?' Ridpath was listening keenly.

'Throughout it all, Lardner maintained his professional life. He continued to function perfectly normally as a pathologist.'

'As did Shipman as a doctor.'

'That's correct. Most serial killers don't have such high profile positions. They are usually lorry drivers or soldiers or even policemen. Successful serial killers have an intelligence despite the job they perform. It's the ability to live a dual life that is key.'

They passed through a screening area.

'Successful?'

'Unfortunately, we measure serial killers in the number of their victims and their ability to remain undetected. It's not something I'm proud of.'

'Has Lardner received visitors, Dr Halligan?' asked Ridpath.

'He is allowed visitors. You'd be surprised at the number of people, particularly women, who request a meeting. Perhaps we have a morbid fascination for those who break the basic rules of society.'

'Could we get a list of those who have seen him? Plus we'd like to know who he has been calling.'

'Of course, I'll email it across to you, plus his telephone records.'

'Does he have any friends in the facility?'

They passed through the final security check and stopped in front of the main entrance.

'Me perhaps. He sees me as a friend who helps him.'

'Are there any others?'

'I'll ask the attendants who are closest to him.' The doctor waved at the guard in his booth. 'But people like Lardner do not have friends in the way you describe. Their narcissism prevents them from ever allowing others to come close. They have people they use or are useful to them. For example, with me he talks about the latest medical developments. I'm sure he sees it as useful to him because it means I allow the *Lancet*, *Scientific American* and other journals to be delivered. I am being used. Funnily enough, he knows I know but once again the narcissism convinces him he has me exactly where he wants me. A controlling personality never admits to being controlled even in a maximum security hospital. He thinks he controls me to get what he wants.'

'Thank you, doctor.' They shook hands.

'I hope your visit was useful.'

'I don't know if it was, but I'm convinced Lardner is involved in our case. Otherwise why send the letter?'

'Be careful, Inspector, is he really involved or is he simply diverting your attention to him? The narcissist who wants everybody to look at him.'

'But he knew a murder was about to take place.'

'Did he? There are always murders taking place somewhere, Inspector. Did he provide you with anything showing he knew more about your case?'

'The answer is – I don't know. I just feel he's involved.'

'Ah, feelings. Not something we're adept at understanding with science.'

'Thank you once again for your time, doctor.' Ridpath started to walk through the gate before stopping and looking back. 'One last question. Does he?'

'Does he what?'

'Does he control you to get what he wants. In the outside world, he was extremely effective at controlling and using people to help him kill.'

'I do not help him kill people, Inspector Ridpath, I simply facilitate his ability to stay up to date with the latest medical developments. One physician helping another.'

'But he does get special treatment here. Treatment that allows him to do things that an ordinary inmate would not be allowed to do. Like sending letters to a coroner that don't go through the normal channels?'

Dr Halligan pointed outside. 'I think it's time for you to go now, don't you, Inspector Ridpath. For security reasons we can't keep this gate open, I'm sure you understand.'

Outside in the car park, the smoke from Emily's cigarette drifted across to Ridpath. He inhaled, enjoying all the scent of secondary smoke.

'Lardner was playing with us,' he announced. 'He was having fun at our expense.'

'You think he knows more?'

'I'm sure he does. Despite what the doctor said.'

'How?'

'If I knew the answer, Emily, I would have solved this case.'

She crushed the cigarette under her heel. 'Let's be getting back, I should check in at MIT.'

'And I should see the coroner. Find out what's been happening to her. When you get back to MIT, do me a favour and check up on the good doctor, will you? Something about him worries me. Did he know Lardner before he was locked up in Ashworth?'

'What do you mean? Through the medical network?'

'Something like that.'

'You think he's not being straight with us?'

He shrugged his shoulders. 'Maybe I'm becoming a bit paranoid in my old age.' He glanced back at the looming red brick buildings of Ashworth Maximum Security Hospital. 'Perhaps, it's catching…'

Chapter 61

'How was Lardner?'

The coroner was seated behind her desk, an open file in front of her. She hadn't gone home after the events of the morning, preferring to bury herself in work.

'As usual. Manipulative, controlling and arrogant.'

'Did he tell you what he meant in the letter he sent to me?'

'No, but I'm convinced he's involved. He knows far more than he is telling us.' Ridpath moved from the door and sat down in front of the coroner. 'And you, how are you holding up?'

She held up the file. 'I've had better days but I still have my work, it keeps the terrors away.' She stared into mid-air. 'I can't stop seeing Brian Conway's face. It's like he was here in this room with me.'

'That's what he wants. Probably, why he sent you the video. He wants you to be afraid.'

'Who is he?'

'It has to be Dalbey.'

'Are you so sure?'

Before he could answer, there was a gentle knock on the wood. Sophia stood in the door frame. 'This email came through to you from Ashworth, I thought you'd want to see it straight away.' She handed over three sheets of paper to Ridpath.

The first was a covering note from Dr Halligan. It stated they had been through the logs of visitors and telephone records. Ridpath read the final line twice. 'But these are just the official records. You will appreciate our inmates often find ways around the system; smuggled letters, contraband mobile phones, verbal messages through day visitors or released inmates.'

'No shit Sherlock,' Ridpath said out loud.

'What was that?'

'The deputy medical director stating the obvious.'

Margaret Challinor looked at them quizzically.

'I asked the hospital for all their records. They've just pointed out they can't monitor everything.' He turned to the next sheet. It was a list of phone numbers Lardner had called in the last twelve months from the official telephone. There were over sixty-five records with some numbers appearing more than once. Somebody was going to have to go through each one checking the registered owner of the numbers with a reverse directory. Tedious work but indispensable in this investigation.

Finally, he turned over the final sheet.

'Bingo,' he said out loud.

Chapter 62

Back at MIT, Emily Parkinson quickly debriefed Turnbull on her visit to Ashworth. Despite the lateness, everybody was still at their desks; following up leads, typing reports or verifying witness statements.

'So it was a waste of time?'

She shrugged her shoulders. 'Not really, but we didn't discover anything of interest. Lardner is obviously a clever man.'

'So did he tell you why he sent the letter?'

'No.'

'Did he tell you who it referred to? Who was going to commit murder?'

'No.'

'Did he tell you anything of value?'

'Not really. He was obviously playing games. He kept hinting he knew more than he was saying. Ridpath wants me to check up on the man running the place, a Dr Halligan.'

'Why?'

'Ridpath didn't say. I got the impression he thought the man was giving Lardner preferential treatment and maybe even more.'

'A waste of time. Of course, Lardner is going to play games with you. He's a con. What else would he do? He's stuck in Ashworth on an indeterminate sentence, probably for the rest of his natural life. He craves the attention, the company.' He sat down on the edge of the desk, looming over her. 'And where is our Detective Inspector Ridpath now?'

'He went back to the Coroner's Court to brief Mrs Challinor.'

'Shouldn't his first job be to brief me?'

'He asked me to do it.'

Turnbull shook his head. 'Ridpath will have to be reminded of the chain of command.'

'I told him I would brief you.'

'Not good enough.'

From the far corner of the office, there rose a loud whoop of joy, followed by a shout of 'I got the bastard.'

Everybody looked up from their desks as Chrissy Wright stood up from behind her computer waving a printout.

Both Turnbull and Parkinson rushed over to her. 'What is it?'

A broad smile creased Chrissy's face. 'I couldn't work out how Dalbey seemed to drop off the planet eighteen months ago. He took out his money from the bank and there was no trace of him afterwards. No passport applications, no telephone contracts in his name, no rental agreements. Nothing.'

'We know all that, where is he?'

She frowned. 'I don't know yet, but at least I know the name he's living under.'

'What?'

'He changed his name. At first, I thought he may've used the old trick of wandering around a cemetery until he found a child who had died and was roughly the same age as him. Fairly easy to apply for a birth certificate in the child's name and using that document, get a passport, a bank account and rent an apartment.'

'Yes, yes, but where is he now?'

'Patience, Chief Inspector, I'm just explaining how I found him. It's important to know.' She sat quietly for a moment, obviously relishing the moment. The MIT room had gone quiet as all the detectives had stopped what they were doing and were listening to Chrissy.

'Go on,' Turnbull finally said.

'Well, if he used that method, it would be almost impossible to trace him. We would have to go through every request for a birth certificate at the Registry Office in the last couple of years. A nightmare. And even then, we might miss it. Too many applications you see. Or he could have gone to Scotland or Ireland.'

'Yes, yes, get on with it.'

'But I thought there would be the risk of getting caught. Having just come out of jail, why take the chance of going back in for misrepresentation and false impersonation?'

'What's the point, Chrissy?'

'So it struck me. There was a much easier way...'

Another pregnant pause as Chrissy relished the attention.

Turnbull sighed loudly. 'What was it, Chrissy?'

She smiled. 'Change your name by deed poll. Now you can do it yourself simply by making a statement and getting two witnesses to sign it. But this isn't usually accepted by banks.'

'The official way is to go through the courts, the Royal Court of Justice.'

'Exactly, Emily, fill in a couple of forms, pay them thirty-six quid and Bob's your uncle.'

'But there's one other thing you have to do, isn't there?'

'What?' interrupted Turnbull.

Emily Parkinson coughed. 'You have to place a notice in the *London Gazette*.'

Chrissy held up her printout. 'I have his new identity here.'

Chapter 63

Ridpath flicked back and forth through the printouts Sophia had given him. 'Lardner had two visits from Dalbey in the weeks after he was released. One on June 10, 2018 and another three weeks later.'

'Why? Why would James Dalbey visit the man who had put him inside for ten years? It was Lardner who set him up as the fall guy.'

'I love it when you use Americanisms, Mrs Challinor.'

'Too many American TV series. But you still haven't answered the question, Ridpath.'

Ridpath tapped the papers in front of him. 'I haven't answered because I don't know. Lardner, was, is, a manipulative person. He always controlled one person and let them do his work for him. Lesley Stone even went as far as to kill herself for him.'

'Are you suggesting Dalbey wasn't as innocent as he portrayed himself to get released?'

Ridpath shook his head. 'I don't know, Coroner. He said he knew nothing about Lardner's activities even though I caught him in the lock-up with a kidnapped woman.'

'From what I remember he admitted the crime when first questioned only to recant when he was in jail.'

'Precisely. Was he more guilty than he let on? Was he Lardner's accomplice and we let him go?'

'You mean me and you, Ridpath?'

Ridpath nodded his head.

'So you think Lardner may be using him to gain revenge on those who put him away?'

'At the moment, I don't know what to think, Coroner. But I do know this. Lardner is involved in what's going on in some way or form.' He glanced down at the printout. 'You know the man has had seventeen visitors over the last year.'

'What?'

'Despite being convicted of seven murders, locked up in a maximum security prison and being certified as insane, seventeen people still want to meet him.' He checked the printout of Lardner's telephone calls. 'Plus he's made over sixty-five calls and received eighty-three.'

'Popular, isn't he?'

'Do you want me to check up on his visitors?' Sophia asked.

Ridpath took one last look at the sheet before handing it back to his assistant. 'Luckily, their names, addresses and contact details are included before they can see him. Can you send a copy to Chrissy too?'

'I could ring those numbers?'

'No, it will be quicker for MIT to do it. I'm sorry Coroner, I have to get back there now.'

'Go, and I'll see you tomorrow.'

Ridpath stood up. 'You're sure you are ok, Coroner?'

'I'm fine. Get whoever did this, Ridpath.'

'I will, Mrs Challinor, I know we're close now.'

Chapter 64

The judge lived in a large arts and crafts house in Bowdon, with immaculately kept gardens to the front and rear. The house had the black and white solidity so representative of the period. The only feature out of place at the front was a large purple box with the words 'Total Security' printed in block white letters under the elegantly carved eaves.

He parked the van outside the gates and pressed the intercom.

A querulous voice answered almost immediately, 'Yes, what do you want?'

He pretended to stare at his clipboard and coughed to clear his throat before speaking. 'Mr Robert Brooking?'

'It's Sir Robert Brooking, and I will ask you again, what do you want?'

'My name's Matheson, from Total Security.' He pointed back to a new purple van, with its specially designed signage, even though the man probably couldn't see it. 'We have a booking to check the security.'

'No you don't.'

He tapped the clipboard. 'It's here in black and white. Mr Robert Brooking, 4 Ambrose Gardens, Bowden. Four p.m. Check security alarms. See.' He held the clipboard up to the camera on the intercom.

'I'll say it once again. I am a knight of the realm and my title is Sir Robert. You will address me properly. Thirty years as a judge earned me the title and I deserve it to be used.'

'I'm sorry, Sir Robert...'

'People these days have no respect, I'd have soon punished such behaviour when I was on the bench.'

'Yes, I'm sure you would, Sir Robert.'

'What? What did you say?' The voice was becoming increasingly querulous and tinny through the speaker.

'About the security check…'

'There must be a mistake. I made no booking for a security check. You only did one three months ago.'

'Perhaps, your wife made the booking.'

'Diana wouldn't normally involve herself in such mundane matters. And anyway, she's away at the moment, in our cottage in the Lakes.'

He already knew that. 'Maybe it was one of your servants?'

'Servants, we don't have servants any more. In my rooms at the High Court, but not here, not any more.'

'Well, I have a booking and if you want to miss out on the free safety check, I'll be on my way.' He pretended to leave.

'Free, you said?' came quickly from the speaker.

'There's been quite a few break-ins in the area recently and the company has been performing free checks on its equipment for its valued customers. Insurance, you know.'

'How long will it take?'

'Just ten minutes. We want to check the system's wiring.'

A long sigh from the speaker. 'Very well then, I'll be right out.'

Within thirty seconds a tall, ascetic looking man with a large nose came from a side door and marched down the driveway past the parked Jaguar.

'So sorry to bother you, Sir Robert.' He put on his most humble, contrite face. 'Perhaps they messed the dates up at the office.'

'Well, I suppose you're here now and it is free?'

'It is, Sir Robert.'

The old judge bent down to open the gate before quickly straightening up. 'Can I see some sort of identification?'

'Of course, Sir Robert.' He reached into his pocket and pulled out the laminated card, again created for this purpose.

The judge gave it a cursory glance, before handing it back and bending down to open the gate. 'You can't be too careful these days.'

'So true, Sir Robert, a lot of thieves and burglars wandering the streets.'

'The courts have become far too lenient.' The gates squeaked as they opened.

'I can put some oil on those if you want.'

'I would appreciate it.' The judge thought for a moment before asking. 'Since you are here, you could look at the side door. It makes an awful racket too. Diana is always complaining.'

The former judge was walking away, pointing to the side door.

He strode up behind him, wrapped his head in an arm lock and covered the nose and mouth with the pad soaked in chloroform. 'There, there,' he whispered feeling the man struggle against his grip, 'just take a few breaths, breathe deeply and it will soon be over.'

The former judge struggled feebly for a few more seconds, before his knees sagged, the weight of his body resting on the arm lock.

Glancing over his shoulder, he dragged the man to the rear of the van, dumping him in the back. He took the hypodermic and injected the Risperidone into the vein in the crook of the judge's elbow.

He laid him on the mattress, checking his airways were free, before closing and locking the back doors.

He ran quickly to the side door of the house, closed it and pulled the gate shut behind him.

It had all gone as had been planned.

It would soon be time for the judge to return to court.

This time though, he would be the one on trial.

Chapter 65

Chrissy read aloud from the notice in the *London Gazette*.

'Notice is hereby given that by a Deed Poll dated 12 January 2019 and enrolled in the Senior Courts of England and Wales on 12 March 2019, James Monroe, of 357a Lillie Road, Manchester M32 9GH, is single, a British Citizen, under section 11(1) of the British Nationality Act 1981, abandoned the name of James Dalbey and assumed the name of James Monroe. Any further communication on this matter should be addressed to Messrs Holbeck and Grimble, Two, St Peter's Square, Manchester.'

Turnbull pumped his fist. 'Get in.'

Emily Parkinson frowned. 'Why would he make the deed poll so official. People change their names all the time, you don't need to go to all the hassle of registering it officially.'

'Perhaps he needed to update his passport or open a new bank account,' suggested Chrissy Wright.

'It doesn't matter why he did it, we've got him now. Harry, check out the address. Find out if Dalbey, or Monroe as he is now calling himself, is still living there. But don't go anywhere near the address yet, I want it staked out and observed, nothing more. Understand?'

'Yes, guvnor.'

'Chrissy, get on to the Royal Courts of Justice. I want the original documents Dalbey submitted, they must have them on file.'

'Will do, boss.'

'And check out any bank accounts, telephone numbers, addresses registered to Dalbey's new name.'

'On it.'

Turnbull checked the clock. 4.45. 'Alan, you're with me.'

'Where we going, boss?'

'To visit the solicitors before they close this evening. Let's see if we can find out more about Dalbey. My bet is he's no longer living at the address, but they must know where he is.' Turnbull glanced around, looking for his jacket.

'What do you want me to do, boss?' asked Emily Parkinson.

Turnbull found his jacket and walked over to pick it up. 'You,' he said over his shoulder, 'you can brief the guvnor and Ridpath when he finally deigns to turn up.'

'Don't you want me to do anything more, boss?'

He smiled. 'I think it's enough to keep you busy, Emily, don't you?' He looked around for Alan. 'Come on, what are you waiting for? A bloody invitation?'

Chapter 66

'Ridpath, they're looking for you.' Emily Parkinson ran over to meet him as soon as he entered MIT.

'You told them where I was?'

She nodded. 'Seemed to piss Turnbull off even more.'

He looked towards the man's office, seeing it was empty. 'Where are they? I've got something on Dalbey.'

'So have we. DCS Trent is still at her meeting with the chief constable and DCI Turnbull has gone out.'

'Right, get the team together. Lardner met James Dalbey twice when he was first released from prison.'

Emily Parkinson's forehead creased. 'Really? Why?'

'I don't know, but we have work to do.' He started towards the incident room.

'Hang on, we've got news for you too. We can't find Dalbey because he's living under a different name. He changed it to James Monroe about eighteen months ago.'

Ridpath thought for a moment. 'I've seen the name before.' He took out the printout Sophia had given him. 'See it's here on the list. A James Monroe visited Lardner twice in the last three months. Once on December 16 and again on January 11. He used a driving licence as ID to gain entry to Ashworth.'

Emily Parkinson was looking over his shoulder. 'Plus he left an address in the visitors log. Chrissy, where's Fylde Terrace, Levenshulme?'

'Hang on, I'm just checking.' The civilian liaison officer quickly typed the address into Google Maps. The search engine was quicker than using the Force's latest computer programme,

IOPS. 'Nothing here, there's no such place in Levenshulme or anywhere else in Manchester.'

'A false address, not surprising when you think about it. The prison staff obviously didn't check.'

Chrissy stood up, her head appearing over the top of her computer. 'Did I hear something about a driving licence?'

'Yeah, he used one as proof of identity.'

'Give me the number and I'll check with DVLA in Swansea.'

Ridpath ran over to Chrissy's desk. Meanwhile the rest of the squad had stopped what they were doing again and were watching keenly.

'Here's the info he gave.' Ridpath pointed to the list of Lardner's visitors.

Chrissy accessed the police link to the DVLA website. She slowly typed in the long driving licence number and waited and waited. 'It's slow today.' Finally an image popped up on her screen.

'It's him,' said Ridpath looking at the picture.

'What's going on?' asked Claire Trent.

'We've found his address.'

'Who?'

'Dalbey, he's now known as James Monroe. Ridpath found his licence number when he visited Ashworth,' said Emily Parkinson.

Claire Trent looked at him coolly before walking round to stare at the screen. 'Longford Park? He's living in a park?'

'There are some old workers' houses in the centre, close to the pitch and putt course.'

'You know the area, Ridpath?'

'I grew up round there.'

'Right, Where's DCI Turnbull?'

'Out, boss.'

'Emily get onto the Police Tactical Unit, I want an armed squad at the address in fifteen minutes. Ridpath and Harry, you're with me.'

'Can I come too, boss?'

'No, Emily I want you to coordinate everything from here. Chrissy, send all the information you have to the PTU and get the officer on duty to contact me asap.'

'Where are we going, boss?'

Claire Trent tapped the screen. 'We're going to get this bastard.'

Chapter 67

Detective Chief Inspector Turnbull and Detective Sergeant Alan Jones took the lift up to the sixth floor offices in a new office building close to Oxford Road.

A map of the world in the elegant and tastefully furnished lobby proudly announced that Holbeck and Grimble had offices in London, Manchester, Glasgow, Belfast, Cardiff, Guernsey, Panama, the Cayman Islands and Gibraltar.

Alan Jones tapped the last name. 'Used to work in Gibraltar, boss. This lot are doing a lot of offshore work, tax havens. Nowadays, they don't even bother to hide it.'

'Nowt to do with us, Alan. We're here for one thing and one thing only; James Dalbey.'

A woman approached them. 'Can I help you, gentlemen?'

Turnbull produced his warrant card and explained what he wanted.

'You'll probably need to see Mr Collins, the partner in charge of our Criminal Law Division. If you would wait here for a moment, I'll see if he is free.'

She glided away across the thick carpet.

Jones looked around at the paintings on the walls and the minimalist Scandinavian furniture. 'A little bit different from HQ, boss.' He pointed to a Nespresso machine at one side. 'They even have free coffee.'

'A lot of cons have paid for this, Alan. Next time you're in an interview and some solicitor is being bolshie, remember this office. Remember how they earn their money. Reminds me of a joke. How does a copper save a solicitor from drowning?'

'Dunno, boss.'

'He doesn't.'

A discreet cough behind them. 'Mr Collins will see you now.' The same woman guided them down a long corridor to a large corner office. A small, scruffy man sat behind a large desk covered in empty coffee cups, papers and pink ribboned files. The man and his desk were in stark contrast to the rest of Holbeck and Grimble's office. As if an alien was suddenly playing for Manchester United.

He pointed to two seats in front of his desk. 'Please sit down, gentlemen. It's not often I get a visit from the police and certainly not one of the rank of chief inspector. Usually, I have to go to the station. How can I help you, Mr Turnbull?'

'I'll come straight to the point, Mr Collins, we're here to find out more about one of your clients, a Mr James Monroe, previously known as James Dalbey.'

Turnbull laid a copy of the *London Gazette* notice on top of a pile of files. Collins picked it up and read it, a small smile crossing his face as he did. 'Much as it would delight me to be of assistance to the Greater Manchester Police, I'm afraid paragraph 6.3 of the Code of Conduct for Solicitors requires me to keep the affairs of current and former clients confidential unless disclosure is required or permitted by law or the client consents. This obligation is also enshrined in common law under the data protection legislation.'

'But James Dalbey is one of your clients. It's says so on the notice.'

'It may be a philosophical point, but I'm sure you'll appreciate that simply disclosing whether or not Mr Dalbey may or may not be a client of this firm is a breach of the code.'

Turnbull waited for the man to continue, but he just sat there with his arms folded across his expansive belly.

'The notice states quite clearly Dalbey is or was a client of yours.'

Collins picked up the printout and read it again. 'No it doesn't, Chief Inspector. It states if anybody requires more

223

information on this notice, they are requested to ask at our offices. It does not state Mr Dalbey or Mr Monroe are our clients.' Again, a little smile of apology.

'Well, we're here now asking for more information.'

'What would you like to know, Chief Inspector?'

'We'd like know the whereabouts of your client, James Dalbey, also known as James Monroe.'

'I'm unable to give you the information without a client's express permission.'

Turnbull smiled triumphantly. 'So you admit Dalbey is a client.'

'I did no such thing, Chief Inspector, I was simply stating a general principle. The Courts have stated the duty to preserve confidentiality is unqualified. It is my duty as a solicitor to keep any client's information confidential, and that includes the information of whether somebody is a client or not.'

'That's just – words,' spluttered Turnbull.

'No, it is the law.'

Turnbull took a deep breath. 'Mr Collins, I believe James Dalbey, your client, is presently murdering people. Yesterday, he murdered an ex-coroner—'

'Brian Conway?'

'You knew him?'

'He was a good man, a professional. I had the pleasure of attending many of his inquests.'

'Then you will understand the importance of finding the chief suspect in the case, James Dalbey. I believe Mr Dalbey intends to kill again.'

Mr Collins appeared to consider this new information for a long time. 'I am permitted by law to reveal client information if it helps prevent the commission of a criminal offence. However, in this case, the information available to me does not clearly identify a proposed victim or isn't sufficiently detailed or compelling enough for me to form an opinion that a serious criminal offence will occur.'

'What? What are you saying?'

'I'm afraid the information is privileged, Chief Inspector.'

'Even if another person will die?'

'Even then.' Collins shifted his position in his chair and sighed. 'However, let me point you to an interesting snippet of case law.'

'I don't have time for a lecture on the law, Mr Collins.'

'Please bear with me, Chief Inspector, you may find the information useful. There is a famous case in Manchester, Rex v Manchester Crown Court. It was a little before your time, in 1999 to be precise. In this case, a client travelled to his solicitors' office after an alleged assault. The police asked the firm to confirm the time of his attendance to enable them to establish the facts. The firm declined on the grounds of privilege. The court found in favour of the police. The information was held not to be privileged because it was not a communication for the purpose of legal advice.' He stopped speaking and the smile appeared on his face again.

'I don't understand.'

Alan Jones nudged his boss. 'I think he's saying you can ask him anything that is not covered by legal privilege or confidential information, sir.'

'What is this bollocks? I'll get a warrant and he'll have to tell me.'

'I won't. And if any judge did grant such a warrant, which I doubt, we would fight it in every tribunal in the land. You would be spending the next two years of your life in court, Chief Inspector.'

Turnbull stood up. 'We'll see, Collins. You solicitors are all the bloody same. You protect the guilty but don't care about the victims. If someone else dies, you'll be the one with blood on your hands.'

Turnbull stormed out of the office. After a moment's hesitation, he was followed by Alan Jones. However, the detective sergeant stopped at the door for a second and turned back. 'Did Mr Dalbey visit this office at eleven a.m. yesterday, Mr Collins?'

'I haven't seen Mr Dalbey or Mr Monroe for the last eight months, Detective Sergeant. I have no idea where he is now.'

'Thank you, Mr Collins.' The policeman ran after his boss.

He didn't see the solicitor smile broadly as he sat behind his file-strewn desk. 'The police are always the same,' he muttered to himself, 'running around like headless chickens.'

It was true he hadn't seen James Monroe for eight months but he had spoken to him on the phone just last week. All they had to do was ask the right questions and they would discover far more.

On the other hand, they had given him too much information. It was time to make the call.

Chapter 68

In the briefing room at Stretford nick, Claire Trent and the head of the Police Tactical Unit, Sergeant Trevor Hall, were both hunched over a table, staring at a map.

Ridpath had stepped back a little to give them room, but could still see the details of the operation.

'Access is through a road from Longford Avenue. There's a coffee shop in the park. We'll use it as our base, advancing on foot from there to the houses. We'll also come in from The Quadrant along the side of the pitch and putt course as well as from Ryebank Road, past the Athletic Club. Any questions?' asked Hall, looking at his team.

His men shook their heads.

Claire Trent spoke up. 'It's already dark, what about lighting?'

'The path to the house is well lit, but obviously the park itself is not. If, for some reason, he escapes our cordon, I have two officers equipped with night vision goggles to help with any subsequent search. The weather's rough, wind and rain throughout the operation, which will help us as nobody will be out and about walking their bloody dogs. But it makes it more difficult to spot him if he makes a dash for it and tries to break through the cordon.'

'He won't escape though, will he?' asked Claire Trent.

'No, ma'am, he will not.'

'Any reports of activity?' asked one of the PTU officers. A man with tattoos curling up his arms and vanishing beneath a short-sleeved shirt over tight biceps.

'Nothing at the moment, Ian. We have eyes on the house. No movement reported.'

'I want him taken alive if possible, but understand this man has already tried to blow up a pathologist and a CSI as well as killing a coroner. Be careful, very careful.'

'Our bomb disposal officer will be in the first group to enter the house. Bob, are you ok with the plan?'

'Fine, Trev, but we need to watch out. This bastard has C4 and has used it before. The place may be booby trapped. Do not touch anything until I have given the all clear, understand?'

The assembled officers all nodded.

'What about the park itself? There's a kids' zoo nearby,' asked Ridpath, pointing to the map.

'The entrances are being sealed off and, as we speak, people are being asked to leave the park quietly without fuss. Luckily, it's raining so there aren't many people there.'

'Thank God for Manchester weather.'

'Right, one last thing. No blues and twos, this is a silent operation. Our objective is to capture this bugger. Ok? The time is now 17:30. The operation will commence at exactly 18:00 hours. Let's be careful out there. Anything to say, DCS Trent?'

'This bastard is a killer. You are authorised to fire but only if your life is in danger. I want this man in custody.'

The officers, all wearing their protective gear – matt-black Kevlar helmets, NIJ level IIIA bulletproof vests, black ski masks to cover the HOSDB approved jumpsuits and Nomex under-garments – nodded agreement and moved away to perform last-minute checks on their Heckler and Koch rifles.

Five minutes later they were pulling out of Stretford Police Station in their armed response vehicles, a palpable, almost physical air of tension in the group.

Nobody was talking, nobody looking at each other. All concentrating on their role in the upcoming job, focussed on what they were about to do.

Five minutes later they were edging through the police tape strung across the bottom of Longford Avenue where it entered the park, silently pulling up outside an old hut which now housed the cafe. The area and the nearby kids' petting zoo were deserted except for police officers.

As they stepped out of the vehicles, the wind and rain hit them. They hurried for the shelter of the nearby cafe.

'Anything from your observers, Sergeant Hall?' asked Claire Trent.

'Nothing, ma'am,' the officer said formally. 'All quiet, no sign of movement inside the house.'

The officers adjusted their equipment, checking each other carefully, making sure each piece of kit was operational.

'It's 17:55, ma'am, do we have your permission to begin?'

Claire checked her watch. 'You do, Sergeant Hall.'

The sergeant spoke into his Airwave. 'Team B, where are you?'

'Moving into position now, Sarge. ETA, one minute. Over.'

'Right. On arrival hold position until further orders. Over.'

'Copy that. Over.'

'Team C?'

'Passing the playground by the side of the pitch and putt course, Sarge. Over. Will reach our position by the wall next to the car park in one minute. Over.'

'Hold position on arrival. Over.'

'Will do. Over.'

Sergeant Hall turned to Claire. 'Teams B and C in position, ma'am. Permission to proceed?'

Ridpath noticed she was crossing her fingers.

'Permission granted, Sergeant Hall.'

'Right, Ian, you'll lead column A on the right, keep close to the wall. I'll lead column D. On arrival at the house, Barry will use the enforcer to gain entry. You will cover us.'

'Copy that, boss.'

Trevor Hall checked his watch. 'It's 17:58:30. By my reckoning, it will take us one minute to get to the house. Twenty seconds to assess the situation and then entry. All clear?'

His team nodded.

'Right let's move, Ron.'

Ninety seconds later, the teams went into action with military precision. They formed two columns of four officers each. In the left-hand column, led by Sergeant Hall, the second officer held the heavy red enforcer that would allow them to gain entry.

Sergeant Hall had studied the plans of the house. Pretty standard layout. Living room on the ground floor with kitchen at the back, three bedrooms upstairs, no basement.

They advanced down a narrow lane, keeping to either side, the rain gusting straight onto their visors. On the right, a lawn bowls club was empty and quiet.

Sergeant Hall whispered into his Airwave. 'Approaching the house now. Do you have eyes on us?'

'We can see you. Over,' replied Team C.

'Still no view for us. Over,' came the answer from the leader of Team B.

They must have positioned themselves too far back. Never mind too late – they needed to carry on.

He held up his hand, dropped to a kneeling position and stopped, his Heckler and Koch G36 levelled at the house.

It was quiet; no lights and no sign of movement. He quickly scanned the area. It was a lovely place to live, even in the middle of a gale in February, surrounded by parkland, trees and the dark of the night.

He banished the thought from his mind and concentrated on the job, waving the team forward. 'Going in,' he whispered into his Airwave.

Chapter 69

The judge was sitting on a chair in the middle of the room, his hands dangling down at his sides, the wrists fastened to each leg by a pair of handcuffs.

The man was quiet at the moment. A soporific, Risperidone in this case, given to him three hours ago in a cup of water, continuing to work. It made him docile yet still responsive.

Just as any judge should be.

The house was barely furnished. He had found it almost four months ago and immediately realised it was ideal. It was sufficiently isolated to give the sort of privacy he required without being too far away from everything. Located on the outskirts of Manchester, in the middle of one of the few patches of countryside left, the only strangers he saw were the occasional dog walker giving their animals exercise.

Bloody fools.

Being in the middle of winter helped. Not many people brave the outdoors of Manchester on a February evening when the wind is blowing, the rain sleeting down and the cold probing their bones like a stiletto.

What did amuse him though was it wasn't far from the crematorium. Each day, lines of black limousines and hearses would pass the house on their journey to the land of the dead.

The judge was about to join them, even though he didn't know it yet.

He listened for a moment.

Outside, Manchester lived up to its reputation; the wind whistled through the trees and the rain was beating against the window.

Inside, the man's breathing whistled in his chest. Did he have asthma or bronchitis? No matter. He wouldn't be troubled by his chest for much longer.

He checked the time.

5.58 p.m.

Two more minutes and he would leave to get some food for both of them. He'd feed the old man at nine o'clock, slipping in the last dose of Risperidone with his food.

He wanted the man to be as aware as possible tomorrow morning. After all, the judge was going to return to court once more.

But this time, he was going to be the one on trial.

Chapter 70

Ridpath was biting his fingernails. The thumb was already bitten down to the quick so he started on his index finger. It was a disgusting habit but one he couldn't quit. His mother had tried, how she had tried; painting his nails with some ugly tasting solution, shaming him with words, making him look at the chewed ends of his nails. But still, in times of stress, he returned to the habit.

Tonight was a time of stress.

He hated standing there, doing nothing except listen to the squawks and occasional communications on the Airwave as the macho men crept forward.

He looked across at Claire Trent. She was staring at the radio on the desk as if looking at it would make time go quicker. He glanced down to her hands. She still had both fingers crossed. He wouldn't have guessed she was a superstitious woman, but there she was with one of the most basic signs of hope.

On the Airwave, he heard the whispered message of 'Going in,' from Sergeant Hall. You could cut the tension in the cafe with a blunt pen knife.

Claire Trent was gripping the table now. Another officer, from Stretford, was tapping his fingers on his wrist, making an annoying sound.

Ridpath ran his fingers through his hair and sighed heavily, receiving a dirty look from his boss. Why couldn't they go in too? Waiting here was sheer torture.

There was a long period of silence, what seemed like hours and hours but actually couldn't have been more than thirty seconds.

This was suddenly broken by the sound of metal crashing into wood. They were using the enforcer to gain entry. Followed by shouts of 'Police, police.'

The sound of the door crashing open and more shouts of 'Police. Police.'

Heavy boots on a wooden floor. More shouts. Another door being slammed into a wall.

'Living room, clear,' a voice shouted.

'Kitchen clear,' from another voice.

Sounds of heavy boots pounding upstairs. 'Bathroom, clear.'

'Bedroom, clear.'

A long silence.

Another door crashing open followed by a high-pitched male voice. 'Jesus, what the fuck is that?'

Chapter 71

He checked the plan one last time. The six Ps had been drilled into him over and over again.

Proper planning prevents piss poor performance.

It was the mantra. Everything was timed to the minute.

Sure, things occasionally didn't quite go like clockwork. Glossop was a classic example.

They should have taken the lives of the complete CSI Team but they had missed them because the idiots had been slow to arrive and get to work. Ridpath intervening had not helped.

No matter.

He would get revenge on the detective later. He was saving Ridpath for last. That was the plan. He was going to be the one they savoured, tasting the pleasant bitterness of his death.

But he mustn't jump ahead of himself.

Stay in the now, he always reminded himself. The past and the future are where mistakes are made. The present is where the truth lies.

Outside, he heard a noise in the garden, a screech like the gate being opened. They deliberately didn't oil the hinges. A simple precaution but an effective warning.

He moved silently towards the window, slowly pulling aside the curtain.

At first, he could see nothing, but the twinkle of light in a pair of eyes gave the intruder away.

A fox stood in the gateway, his nose sniffing the air, whiskers twitching, checking whether it was safe to enter or not.

He pulled the curtain further open. The fox took fright, fleeing silently into the windswept night.

He checked his watch again.

Five minutes behind schedule. No matter, he would make the time up.

He checked the door to the cellar one last time.

It was bolted twice and locked. The judge would not escape.

He put on his coat and prepared to brave the rigours of the February night.

Tomorrow was going to be a brilliant day. He could feel it in his bones.

And so would the judge.

Chapter 72

Ridpath and Claire Trent ran out of the cafe, turning left to follow the same route taken by the Police Tactical Unit a few minutes before. But they didn't bother with concealment, instead they ran as fast as they could through the pouring rain, past the lawn bowling club on the right and the glasshouses on the left.

A group of PTU officers assembled in a group outside the house, checking their rifles and the rest of their equipment.

'Where's Sergeant Hall?'

'Upstairs, second bedroom on the left, ma'am,' one of them replied. He stepped in front of her with his arm out, 'But you can't go in yet. The bomb disposal officer still hasn't declared the place safe.'

Claire Trent pulled on her blue plastic gloves and moved the arm aside. 'Are you going to stop me, Constable?' She brushed past him followed by Ridpath.

They walked past the shattered red door, still hanging off one hinge and ran up the stairs.

Trevor Hall was waiting for them at the top. 'The house is clear. Ron is just giving the place a final check but there is no sign of explosives or firearms.'

'We heard you found something.'

He nodded. 'It's in here.'

They walked into a small bedroom on the right. There was no bed inside nor any furniture. Instead the whole room was painted the deepest, darkest black Ridpath had ever seen. The windows appeared to be boarded up so no daylight could enter.

Against one wall, a picture of an old woman was superimposed over the body of the Madonna painted in the style of an old Renaissance painting. A single candle in a red glass container cast a shimmering light upwards. Two other long, unlit, votive candles were on either side of the light.

Around the head of the woman, a halo glowed brightly.

'It's his mother,' whispered Ridpath.

'What?'

'It's Dalbey's mother. I recognise her face. She died not long after Dalbey was imprisoned. I remember he complained when I met him. He was angry the Ministry of Justice wouldn't allow him to go to his mother's funeral.'

The detective superintendent glanced at the scene again, her lips pursing. 'It's all a bit weird, almost incestuous.'

Ridpath stared at it for a long time, remembering his own childhood and the weekly masses forced on him and his sister by his mother until he rebelled when he was thirteen. 'You're going to hell, like your sister. You're a heathen,' she had shouted, crossing herself, 'may God in his infinite wisdom have mercy on your heathen soul.'

Finally he spoke. 'You weren't brought up a Catholic, guvnor?'

'No religion at all in my family. My father disapproved of it. He was a bit of a leftie. Went with the territory of being a university lecturer in sociology.'

Ridpath glanced across at her. That was the first time Claire Trent had ever told him about herself or her background. 'He's equating his mother with the Madonna, the Virgin Mary. This is a shrine to her.'

'The Virgin Mary?'

'No, his mother.'

'It's weird, almost Oedipal. Did we ever discover who was Dalbey's father?'

'I don't know if we ever asked.'

Sergeant Hall coughed behind them. 'The building is clear, n. Can I stand my men down?'

'Please do, and thank them for me. They did well.'

'Thank you, ma'am, I'll pass it on.'

'Can you also get a CSI team here, Sergeant, as soon as possible? I want this house done over like a kipper. No stone unturned. Understand?'

'Yes, ma'am.'

She turned back to Ridpath. 'At least we know Dalbey was here, and recently by the state of the house.'

'Yes, boss, but where is he now? And, more importantly, who is going to be his next victim?'

'That's what worries me, too. There's nothing left for me to do here, I'm going back to HQ.'

'I'd like to stay a bit longer, question the neighbours. Find out all I can about James Dalbey and what he was doing here.'

'Good, I want a debrief at the office at nine p.m. this evening, Ridpath. Don't be late.'

Chapter 73

He could feel them closing in on him.

The detectives would be out now, searching for the car. Checking CCTV. Interviewing possible witnesses. Knocking on doors from house-to-house. Going through his bank accounts. Looking up his mobile phone records. Talking to his friends (they wouldn't find any).

Doing everything and anything to find James Dalbey.

Eventually, they would succeed. He had made it as obvious as he could without painting a big sign over his head saying. 'It's me. I'm James Dalbey. Come and get me.'

And when they did discover his new incarnation, it was going to be too late.

Because James Dalbey was going to be dead.

Or as near as was humanly possible.

Chapter 74

Luckily, there were only six other houses in that area of Longford Park. After visiting them all with one of the local sergeants, Ridpath headed back to MIT.

On his arrival, Claire Trent stepped out of her room, barking out an order to all the detectives. 'Incident room in ten minutes. Is the board up to date, Chrissy?'

'Yes, guvnor.'

'Where's DCI Turnbull?'

'Getting something to eat, guvnor.'

'Make sure he's here.'

Ten minutes later thirty detectives were all sitting in the incident room waiting for the meeting to start. There was a sense of expectation as Claire Trent stood up.

'Right, as you may or may not know, we discovered where Dalbey aka James Monroe was staying until recently. We organised a PTU to go in but discovered the bird had already flown the nest. Ridpath, can you tell the team what you found in the house-to-house?'

'Not a lot. Dalbey kept himself to himself. Not surprisingly, the neighbours knew nothing about his past. Most said he was a quiet man, mouse-like almost, they hardly ever saw him. One neighbour reported him putting out his bin for the council a week ago but that was the last sighting.'

Harry Makepeace put up his hand. 'When did Dalbey move into the area?'

Ridpath checked his notes. 'About eighteen months ago according to the neighbours.'

'Just after he left prison?'

'That would be about right.'

'Did he have a car or van?' asked Emily Parkinson.

Before Ridpath could answer, DCI Turnbull came in wiping his mouth. 'Sorry, ma'am.'

'He drove a white Custom Ford Transit. But the neighbours didn't know the registration number.'

'It was AW 15 XEA,' Chrissy said, 'I checked with DVLR in Swansea. This was the only vehicle registered to James Monroe. And before you ask, we're running a cross check through ANPR for sightings of the vehicle in the last seven days.'

'When will we have it, Chrissy?'

'Soon, it just takes time, boss.'

'Kick them up the arse, Chrissy. I want those sightings and any new ones asap.'

'Yes, guvnor. I'll put on my arse-kicking boots.'

This drew a laugh from the other detectives.

'How was your visit to the solicitor, Paul?'

Turnbull was settling himself at the front of the room. He looked up for a moment surprised by the question and stood up. 'Not greatly useful, Claire. The solicitor cited privileged information when we asked for the address.'

'I could have told you they would and saved you a trip.'

'But the solicitor did let slip after questioning he hadn't seen Dalbey for eight months.'

Alan Jones looked up from taking notes. Turnbull glanced across at him but didn't say any more.

'So it's a dead end. Never mind, we have lots of other leads to follow. Emily have you compiled the list of possible future victims?'

'It's on the board to your left, guvnor. I compiled two lists. Those involved in the original case against Dalbey in 2008. Most are police or judiciary.'

Claire Trent turned round looking for the board, finally ılking over to stare closely at it.

'The second is the people involved when the case was re-opened in 2018.'

The two lists were side by side. One name was prominent on both lists. DI Thomas Ridpath.

'It's time to issue the Osman notices. I'll dig up a template for you to follow. Start contacting these people,' Claire Trent ordered, 'warn them about Dalbey and ask them to report if they have seen anything unusual recently. It's imperative they be careful.'

'Should we be arranging personal protection for all of them?' asked Emily.

'There are twelve names on the list. We don't have the resources or the manpower to provide a twenty-four-hour nanny service. I believe we should use what resources we have to focus on catching Dalbey. But send the letters, and if necessary, go to see these people, Emily.'

'Yes, guvnor.'

'Chrissy, how are you going on the search for Dalbey/Monroe?'

'We've checked his bank account. He withdrew over 20,000 pounds two weeks ago and it was the last transaction.'

'Are you sure we have the right man?'

'The bank is an HSBC in Chorlton and the address tallies. Rob contacted the manager at his home and he came in to check the files. Kept going on about how he was doing us a special favour. Dalbey/Monroe used the same driving licence as proof of identity.'

'Great, good work, Chrissy, anything else?'

'Well, like I said, we're going through ANPR for the vehicle movements in the last week and we're checking all the major phone networks for a James Monroe with the Longford Park address. But without his number, it's a bit like looking for a City fan in the Etihad wearing a blue scarf.'

'Not many of those, Chrissy,' said Rob Allenby.

'At least we've got some fans, Rob. How are United doing these days?'

A hubbub of competing voices sprung up around the room.

'Enough,' shouted Claire Trent, staring out across the assembled detectives. 'Let me remind you we're looking for a man who has murdered two people, injured two more and is probably going to carry on killing until we stop him. Ok?'

The room fell silent.

Into the silence, a mobile phone rang loudly, playing 'Mic Drop' by BTS, the sound becoming progressively louder.

Ridpath felt the vibrations in his pocket and looked up guiltily as all the detectives stared at him.

'Sorry,' he mouthed, looking at the screen.

Sophia.

He stood up and answered the phone, walking out of the meeting.

'Now DI Ridpath has answered his phone, perhaps we can continue our briefing. Next steps; Paul, can you chase up ANPR? We need any sightings of the vehicle in the last twenty-four hours. It's our best hope of finding Dalbey quickly.'

Before DCS Trent could continue speaking, Ridpath rushed back into the meeting. 'That was Sophia, she's found out where Dalbey is.'

Chapter 75

'I'm going to put you on speakerphone, Sophia, can you tell everyone what you just told me?'

'Everyone?'

'DCS Trent and the MIT detectives. We're all in an incident room at the moment.'

'So exciting.'

'Just tell everyone, Sophia.'

Ridpath heard his assistant take a deep breath. 'Ridpath asked me to check up on the details of visitors to Harold Lardner. I was going through the list and there were the usual suspects; a few women who were obviously the sort who get turned on by serial killers. I read once—'

'Yes, Sophia, tell them what you told me,' interrupted Ridpath.

'One name stood out. Hannah Christenson. She visited with a man called James Monroe.'

'Monroe is Dalbey's new name,' said Turnbull loudly.

'I knew, Chrissy sent me the details. Anyway, I checked up on this woman and she turned out to be a nurse on the intensive care unit at Manchester Metropolitan Infirmary—'

'Lardner was based in the Hospital Trust when he worked as a pathologist,' explained Ridpath to all the detectives.

'Perhaps he knew her,' Sophia's voice came from the speakerphone. 'So, using the coroner's name, I contacted the Hospital Registry and guess who was recently admitted to Manchester Metropolitan Infirmary's intensive care unit?'

The assembled detectives stared at each other.

'A James Monroe. The name and address are the same as the one Chrissy sent me.'

'What?' said Claire Trent.

'I said James Monroe was admitted to the intensive care unit about a week ago. He's in a medically induced coma.'

'A what? A medically induced coma? What's that?' shouted Turnbull.

'Why is he in a coma?' added Ridpath.

'I don't know is the answer to both questions. They wouldn't tell me what the diagnosis was, but I do know he is there.'

A silence descended onto the incident room.

'Sorry, did somebody say something?' Sophia's tinny voice came from the speakerphone.

'Great work, Sophia, thank you.' Ridpath switched the phone off.

DCI Turnbull's forehead creased with frown lines. 'What does it mean?'

'It means, if Monroe is Dalbey, he couldn't have killed Don Brown or Brian Conway,' said Claire Trent softly.

Chapter 76

Claire Trent, Paul Turnbull and Ridpath took the lift up to the ICU unit on the first floor of Building One in Manchester Metropolitan Infirmary. Of course, the DCI hadn't wanted Ridpath there.

'Is it necessary, boss?'

'For once, Paul, don't let your antipathy to Ridpath get in the way of doing your job.'

Turnbull looked abashed.

'Do you know what Dalbey looks like?' Claire Trent asked him directly.

'I've seen the pictures and watched the tape.'

'We all have, but Ridpath is the only one who has actually met him.'

So now here they were approaching the Nurse's Station. A ward sister looked up from her computer. Her name badge said Victoria Ojukwe. 'Can I help you?'

'I'm Detective Chief Superintendent Claire Trent.' She flashed her warrant card. 'I'd like to see one of your patients, a James Monroe.'

'This is an intensive care unit, all the patients here are receiving treatment for major illnesses or trauma and many of them need to be kept in isolation.'

'It is imperative I see James Monroe, now.' Claire Trent's voice rose an octave.

'Do you need any help, Victoria?'

A man dressed in a surgical coat stood at the entrance to the unit.

'These police want to see Mr Monroe.'

The man laughed. 'You want to question him? I'm afraid you're not likely to get many answers.'

'Why?' asked Ridpath.

'He is in a medically induced coma and unresponsive.'

'Could we take a look at him? We are looking for a man called James Dalbey but we believe he changed his name to James Monroe about a year ago,' Ridpath asked.

The doctor glanced across at the Victoria Ojukwe. 'That explains it.'

'Explains what?'

'The absence of medical records. The man told us he had been born abroad and never registered with the NHS.'

'We want to see him now.' Turnbull tried to enter the unit. The doctor moved in front of him.

'Entry into this unit is strictly forbidden. Only for medical personnel.'

'Do you want us to get a warrant?'

'If you must, go ahead. But this is my unit and I decide who goes and who remains on the outside. If you persist in your behaviour, Mr—'

'Detective Chief Inspector Turnbull.'

'—Mr Turnbull, I will call security.'

'But don't you get it, we're the police.'

'I don't care if you are the chief constable, Mr Turnbull, nobody tramps germs and God knows what other bacteria into my unit.'

'Let me tell you why we're here, doctor.' Ridpath interceded between both of them.

'It's Mr Sullivan, detective.'

'We're investigating the murder in the last week of two people and the wounding of two more, one of who was the pathologist for Derbyshire. We believe this man, James Dalbey, lso known as James Monroe, may have been involved.'

'Highly unlikely, detective.'

'Why?'

'He's been in a coma for the last five days. He is currently on a ventilator.'

'What's wrong with him?' asked Claire Trent.

'I'm afraid I've already told you far too much. The information is confidential. Now, if you'll excuse me, I have sick patients I must look after. Please call security Victoria.'

The nurse picked up the phone on her desk.

He turned to go back into the ICU.

'Mr Sullivan…'

The consultant stopped for a second and turned back to face Ridpath.

'As we said, we're investigating a murder and we need to ascertain your patient's identity, that is all. All we need is for of one of us, accompanied by you or one of your staff, to take a look at him. We won't need to ask any questions.'

The consultant considered the idea. 'Only one of you?'

Ridpath nodded.

'You would have to get suited up. The man is in isolation.'

'No worries, I'm used to hospitals.'

Chapter 77

It took Ridpath fifteen minutes to suit up, wearing the full PPE gear he needed before he could set foot in an isolation unit.

Outside, he could see Claire Trent was on the phone while Turnbull was staring into mid-air, absentmindedly cracking his knuckles.

The ward sister, Victoria Ojukwe, escorted him into the unit, giving him the guided tour as they entered. 'We have eighteen beds in this ICU with fourteen beds currently occupied. It's a state-of-the-art unit with more than 250 people staffing the facility 24/7.'

As he entered the place, Ridpath's heart skipped a beat. All the memories of his time in hospital returned to him in one tsunami of emotions. The smell of disinfectant, the constant beeping of machines, the squeak of shoes on tiled floors, the obsessive cleanliness of the place, producing the palpable fear he faced all the time he had spent on the Christie's cancer ward.

He visibly shivered.

The nurse stopped halfway through her tour, 'Are you ok?'

'Fine. Just brings back memories.' He changed the subject. 'How long has James Monroe been in here?'

'He was admitted on February 4, five days ago.'

So Dalbey couldn't have been involved in the murders of Brian Conway and Don Brown. How had he got it so wrong? He quickly asked the next question to cover his confusion. 'And what's he in for?'

She smiled at him. At least, he thought she smiled at him, because all he could see were her eyes above her mask. 'You know I can't tell you.'

'Surely telling me the illness can't be so terrible.'

'But you heard Mr Sullivan.'

'Doctors, they love their secrets, don't they? But when I was in hospital a couple of years ago, it was the ward sister who knew everything going on. She ran the place rather than the consultant, but they always get all the credit.'

'Tell me about it. Last week, I caught a junior doctor prescribing the wrong dosage to one of the patients. I had to quietly tell him to change it.'

'See, it was the same in Christie's with my ward sister, Mary Evangelista.'

'You were in Christie's?'

Ridpath nodded.

'Cancer?'

'Myeloma. But I'm in remission now, have been for the last eighteen months. Still have to go for my check-ups though.' Ridpath made a mental note to ask Polly when his next check was scheduled.

'You're lucky, myeloma is tough. I used to work at Christie's. Mary is lovely.'

'Isn't she? I don't know how I could have handled the chemo without her.'

Victoria leant in closer to Ridpath. 'Don't tell anybody I told you but he's a self-admitted private patient.'

'A what?'

'Somebody who's requested a medically induced coma and the neurosurgeon agreed with him.'

'So let me get this right, Dalbey asked to be put in a coma?'

The nurse nodded. 'When you have a grade three astrocytoma it can be for the best.'

He stared at her.

'A brain tumour. They are working out when they can operate. But the tumour is aggressive and its edges undefined.' She opened the door to a small ward with only three beds, two of which were occupied. 'Mr Monroe is near the window.'

Ridpath walked slowly across. A man wearing an oxygen mask was lying in bed, his head resting on a single pillow. At his side, the oxygen tube was connected to a ventilator. The machine rhythmically beeped and the lights on the screen flashed blue, red and green.

Ridpath stared down at the figure on the bed. He looked older and his hair was thinner but it was James Dalbey for sure.

Victoria Ojukwe joined him. 'Mr Monroe was intubated four days ago.'

'Intubated?'

'A tube was placed in his throat to help him breathe. As long as he's in the coma, he is dependent on the ventilator to keep him alive. He also receives a constant dosage of Propofol to ensure he remains in the coma.'

'Can he hear us? Is he aware we're here?' Ridpath whispered as the machine continued wheezing and beeping.

'I think so. Some of the nurses make sure they talk to the patients every day. Personally I can't see the point when they are in a coma, but some are convinced it helps.'

Ridpath looked down at Dalbey. For a moment, he thought he saw the man's eyelids flicker.

'Did he just move?'

The nurse laughed. 'Lots of people get spooked in ICU. The patients aren't dead, they're in a coma. Brain activity is still there; they still dream, but it's at a much lower level.'

The pager on her uniform started buzzing. 'I'll be back in a second.'

She rushed off out of the small ward. Ridpath was left alone with Dalbey, the only sounds the constant beeping of the machine and the pump of the ventilator feeding oxygen the tube in the man's throat.

'I know it's you, Dalbey,' Ridpath said out loud. 'I know you're involved somehow. But if you didn't kill Brian Conway, who did?'

There was a brief flicker of Dalbey's eyelids.

Could the man hear him? Ridpath was about to speak again when the nurse re-joined him quietly.

'Is this the man you were looking for?' She moved past Ridpath to check on Dalbey lying in his bed.

'It is.'

'I think it's time you left. You can take off your PPE in the same room.'

Ridpath walked out of the ward, taking one last look at James Dalbey lying in his bed, hooked up to a machine keeping him alive.

If Dalbey wasn't the man in the wolf mask, who was?

Chapter 78

Voices close to his head.

From the bottom of his well, he strained to hear what they said, imagining himself drifting upwards to get as close as he could.

One voice he recognised. The African nurse who had admitted him all that time ago. What was her name? Victoria, that was it, like the Victoria Falls, she joked.

He liked her. She didn't prod or poke him like the others. And when she changed his dressing or his catheter, her movements were always quick and precise.

He heard the squeak of shoe on polished floor. She was moving away, her perfume fading into nothingness.

But somebody was still there, watching him.

He heard the words clearly.

'I know it's you, Dalbey. I know you're involved somehow. But if you didn't kill Brian Conway, who did?'

It was Ridpath, he was sure of it. He tried to answer the detective but the words sat in his mouth unable to be voiced. He tried again, but still his lips wouldn't move, his tongue like a dead whale inside his mouth.

He could feel Ridpath's eyes on him, but he didn't care.

The plan had worked.

They were here.

Ridpath was here.

He felt a wave of elation flood through his body. Ridpath was going to be next. He didn't know it yet, but he was the last on the list.

Now he was sure they would achieve their goal.

The deception had worked.

More voices and a shadow over his head.

He knew what was going to happen next as the nurse adjusted the dial on his drip and he drifted back down to the bottom of his well again.

Chapter 79

'You are certain it was him in the bed, Ridpath?'

'It was him, boss, James Dalbey is not a man you forget.'

They were standing outside Manchester Metropolitan Infirmary, surrounding an ashtray overflowing with cigarette butts. Around them, doctors, nurses and hospital workers scurried, enjoying a break from the smell of disinfectant or hurrying home after a long, hard shift. The rain had stopped now, but the wind remained, blowing in a storm from the Arctic.

Claire Trent ran her fingers through her hair. For once, the ice-cool composure and perfect grooming were missing. The DCS was puffing furiously at a cigarette, her eyes staring at the ground as she worked out the implications of their latest discovery. 'And the nurse said he was admitted on the fourth?'

'She was clear on the date.'

'It means it couldn't have been Dalbey on the video of the murder of Brian Conway. We've been barking up the wrong tree all this time, boss.' Turnbull glanced across at Ridpath. 'All the work we did was a total waste.'

'But it felt right. All the evidence pointed to Dalbey. We were so sure.' Ridpath looked across to Claire Trent for support.

She ignored him, taking another swift drag on the end of her cigarette.

Turnbull seized his chance. 'We weren't sure, Ridpath, you were. If I remember, it was you who believed everything linked directly to Dalbey.'

'That's not fair, sir. The evidence—'

'What evidence?' Turnbull interrupted. 'The only thing linking the murders of Don Brown and Brian Conway was your intuition.' The word 'intuition' was sneered. Turnbull began counting off his fingers. 'There's no witness putting him at the scene of any of the murders, nor at the death of John Gorman's dogs, nor at Southern Cemetery. Second, there is no ANPR evidence of his van being in the vicinity of any of the crime scenes. Third, we have no fingerprints or DNA evidence, nothing forensic that links him to any of the crimes. And fourth, he was in a bloody coma when the murders of Don Brown and Brian Conway were committed. Now, I don't know about you, but being in a coma is about the best possible alibi there is.'

Ridpath thought furiously. 'But it had to be him. All the signs fitted. They all pointed to Dalbey. He was the only thing linking all four crimes. And what about the telephone message?'

'Somebody has been jerking your chain, Ridpath. They recorded the TV interview and used it as the voicemail message.'

Claire Trent looked at him. 'Perhaps, you made the cardinal error of forcing the evidence to fit your hypothesis instead of the other way round.'

There was no accusation in her voice just a gentle sadness.

'Exactly, boss. It's a rookie mistake. Jumping to a conclusion. The telephone message was a recording of the interview.'

She stopped Paul Turnbull from speaking by simply raising her hand. She threw the cigarette to the ground, crushing it with her elegant high heel.

'Paul, tomorrow I want you to go back over everything we have discovered. Right back to when John Gorman first asked us to look into the death of his dogs.'

'That crime may not even be linked to the murders, boss.'

'Of course it's linked,' Ridpath blurted out.

Again, Claire Trent held up her hand. 'Paul, go back through all the evidence we have. Question all the suppositions we made, dig deep into the evidence. There must have been something we missed.'

A smile appeared at the corner of Turnbull's mouth as he said, 'Will do, boss.'

Claire Trent stepped forward and waved to her driver who was sat in her car with the engine running down the street.

'What do you want me to do?'

'I think you've done enough, don't you, Ridpath? And tomorrow, I would spend some time at the coroner's office if I were you. There is still work for you to do there, right?'

Chapter 80

He took one last look at the judge snoring on the day bed.

At nine o'clock, he'd fed the man and watered him, taking him to the toilet and watching through the open door.

Not a pretty sight.

Of course, the old man had objected. 'Do you have to stand there? Can't I at least close the door?'

But he couldn't take any risks. Not now, they were so close.

Afterwards, he had given the man the water laced with Risperidone. Within minutes, he was fast asleep and would remain sedated for at least the next eight hours.

The judge might be a bit slow and dopey in the morning though, an after effect of the drug. They wanted him at least semi-alert and active. It was necessary for what they had planned.

So he had an epipen with adrenaline in it just in case.

Every contingency, every possibility had been taken care of in the plan.

While the judge slept, he brought the case down from upstairs and began to prepare the set up.

The camera was better this time, a Canon, XF400, they wanted the pictures to be clearer, to see every nook and cranny of the judge's emotions.

He set up the tripod and camera facing a plain white wall with just a single metal chair sitting in front. He wanted the bareness of this image for tomorrow. A judge with all the trappings of the legal system removed, leaving just one stark, indelible image of its real nature; an old man with his prejudices and foibles.

He checked the image on the Mac, zooming in slightly.

Perfect. He would finalise everything with the judge in his place tomorrow morning before the transmission, but, for now, he was finished.

Time to rest and prepare himself for tomorrow.

It was going to be a big day.

Chapter 81

Ridpath sat in his armchair facing a darkened television, a large glass of Lagavulin in his hand.

After the discussion with Claire Trent, he had driven home. Polly was waiting for him.

'You look as dark as last week's washing, what's up?' she asked, putting her arms around his neck.

'The case, it's all gone wrong.'

She didn't ask for any of the details. She knew he wouldn't tell her – not when the investigation was ongoing. 'Not your fault, you're a team, remember?'

'We're not a team when things go wrong.'

She pulled him closer to her. 'Look, you did your best. Tomorrow is another day. You can go back in to work and sort it all out.'

He forced a smile. 'Love you, Mrs Ridpath.'

'Mrs Lam-Ridpath, remember? I always fancied having a double-barrelled name and we Chinese don't hold with this taking of our husband's names rubbish. Unless, of course, your surname is Fuk, then you jump at any opportunity.'

He laughed. 'How was your day?'

'Same old, same old. The wicked witch of the West, also known as the Mrs Hardisty, has decided in her infinite wisdom, we are going to be giving up two days of our holiday for training in – you'll never guess?'

'What?'

'Yoga for teachers.'

'Sounds good, I'm sure the instructor will be cute.'

'But can you imagine me telling my ten-year-olds how to do the downward dog? That's really going to help them in their exams? Or what about the happy baby?'

'You could try to invent some new poses. The "here comes the teacher, let's hide" pose could be a winner. Or better still, the "confuse the Ofsted inspectors" pose.'

'Is that the one with my head up my arse?'

'Nah, it's the one with your head up the inspector's arse.'

'Touché, Ridpath. Good to see you haven't lost your sense of humour even when you've had a shitty day.' She took her arms from around his neck. 'Anyway, I'm going to do the "Lying flat out pretending I'm a lizard" pose in my bath. Don't stay up too late.'

'How's the girl?'

'Fine. I caught her holding hands with a boy today in the playground.'

'A bit young isn't she?'

'She's eleven, going on twenty-seven, Ridpath. They grow up far too early these days.'

'You're telling me. I'll pop up to see her.'

'She's asleep I think. Either that or texting her new boyfriend.'

'I'll take a look.'

As silently as he could, Ridpath climbed the stairs to Eve's room, quietly opening her bedroom door. His daughter was fast asleep gently snoring, her body curled up into a foetal position, head resting on a Frozen pillow, gripping her rabbit. Above her bed, a poster from the latest BTS album was illuminated by the soft glow of a night light.

She had grown up so quickly, too quickly. He missed the time when she was three years old and was discovering the world. Now she straddled the banks of childhood and woman-hood, with a foot on either shore. Too old to be a girl and too young to be a woman.

He closed the door and went back downstairs to find his whisky.

Twenty minutes later and he was sat in his armchair, the whisky still untouched in his glass.

How could he have been so wrong?

Everything pointed to Dalbey being the person behind the killings. He would have staked his life on it. But how could the man be the perp if he was in a bloody coma?

None of it made any sense.

And even worse, Claire Trent seemed to have disowned him. Not helped of course by Turnbull's active dislike. Perhaps he had played it wrong. He should been more accommodating, played the game, been the subservient little underling.

'Sod that,' he said out loud, taking a long swallow of the whisky, feeling it gently burn the back of his throat, like being kissed by a fire-breathing version of Marilyn Monroe.

The name rang a bell. Monroe? Why had Dalbey chosen that as his new name? What did it mean to him?

He let his mind wander over the events of the last few days. The image of John Gorman's dogs jumping from the back of the van. The small cairn of stones that once was Charlie's gravestone. The explosion in Glossop. The body of the former coroner swinging silently from the rafters.

It must have been Dalbey, mustn't it? Who else could it have been?

Chapter 82

The following morning, Ridpath's bones ached and his head hurt.

For the first time in a long time, he wasn't the first to get up. For some obscure reason that dubious honour fell to Eve.

Polly had woken late as well and was now rushing around the house like a demented ferret.

'Has anyone seen my teaching notes?'

'On the table, mum.'

'And my iPad?'

A long exasperated sigh followed by the crunch of a spoonful of cornflakes. 'Next to the notes, Mum.'

'My glasses, where are my glasses?'

'On your head, Mum.'

By the time Ridpath surfaced and walked into the kitchen, Eve was dressed and ready to leave, looking impatiently at her mum who was flapping around searching everywhere.

'Has anybody seen my butterfly brooch?'

Ridpath pointed to a scarf hanging in the hall.

'What's it doing there? I never wear it with that scarf.' Polly ran upstairs to get a coat from the wardrobe.

'We missed you this morning, Dad.'

'Mum hasn't had her coffee yet?'

'Nah, brain's still in fuzzy logic mode.'

'Have you eaten?'

'Cornflakes. With milk rather than water.'

'Do you want anything else?'

'Nah, I'm good. You not rushing off this morning?'

Ridpath shook his head. 'No meetings until ten.'

'I thought you were working a case?'

'I was,' he said before correcting himself, 'I still am, just not this morning.'

'Not like you.'

'Not like me,' he agreed.

The noise of heavy footsteps across the ceiling, followed by a loud clump as something was dropped.

'Anything special for you today?' he asked changing the subject.

'Nah, the usual. Me and Andrea are meeting up after school to do a project on the Suffragettes.'

'Emily Pankhurst and all that?'

His daughter nodded. 'Did you know she was born in Manchester?'

He nodded. 'Of course, where else?'

'We'll probably go into town to take some pictures of the new statue in St Peter's Square.'

'Take care.'

'Nah, we'll take the tram, it's quicker.'

'Smart arse,' he said, messing up her hair.

Polly finally clumped down stairs. 'Are you ready, Eve?'

A long roll of Eve's teenage eyes. She rose from the table and leant in to whisper, 'You need to make her coffee in the morning, Dad. She's useless without her fix of caffeine.'

A shout from the hall. 'I heard that. Hurry up, we're going to be late.'

A quick kiss on the cheek. 'Cheer up, Dad, you look like death warmed up.'

And she was off, out of the front door and into the waiting car. Polly ran back still putting on her jacket. Another kiss on the cheek. 'Bye, Ridpath, see you later. I'll cook a Marks and Sparks takeaway tonight, ok?'

'Sounds good,' Ridpath said to the retreating back.

The door slammed and he was left alone in the hallway, suddenly feeling lost for a second. He walked back into the kitchen and made himself a coffee. He didn't feel like eating anything, not this morning.

He had stayed up far too late last night and drunk far too much whisky, the sour taste was still in his mouth. He had gone over the case again and again in his mind, searching for something he had missed or a point where he had gone wrong. But everywhere he looked the logic and the detective work were correct.

And yet, Dalbey was in a coma in the hospital?

He sat there drinking his coffee, going over the events of the past few days again and again.

It wasn't until later, in the middle of his shower, that an idea came to him from something Harold Lardner had said. Once it did, it was so obvious, he couldn't understand why he hadn't thought of it earlier.

Chapter 83

Exactly ten a.m.

He focussed the camera on the man's face, making sure the image was sharp so he could see every nook and cranny, every wrinkle and fissure.

Without the ridiculous horse hair wig, judicial robes, and all the perfectly designed theatre of a court of law, the man looked weak and fragile. He hoped the judge would find his voice. A trial was the best sort of theatre after all.

He pressed the record button on the camera and the feed went live. He looked down at his laptop and adjusted the framing slightly, zooming out a fraction to show the judge in a medium shot.

There was something poetic in the slump of his shoulders and the way he hung his head.

In the corner of the image a small eye indicated the number of live viewers, just twenty-five at the moment, but he was sure it would increase as the teaser progressed. There were enough ghouls out there to watch a free show and he made sure they would know about the event by posting the link onto 4chan pages with the promise something special was going to be broadcast.

He decided to begin, clearing his throat nervously before he began. 'Today, we have with us Sir Robert Brooking.'

At the sound of his name, the judge raised his head slightly. The adrenalin he had been given an hour ago fighting with the remains of the soporific in his system and winning. 'What? Where am I? Who are you?'

Another cough. 'Sir Robert used to preside over criminal trials as a judge at the Crown Courts. He has sent many a guilty criminal to reside at Her Majesty's pleasure in Strangeways, or Belmarsh, or Wakefield. He even sent some people to jail who were innocent, didn't you, Sir Robert?'

'I don't know – don't know what you are talking about.' The judge shook his head, trying to clear it of the fog of the man's words.

'It is the innocents we are concerned with now, Sir Robert…'

He glanced down at the viewership counter, over 500 now and rising steadily.

'That is why we have decided to reverse the tables for once and put you on trial. The court will sit in thirty minutes at 10.30 a.m. You will be tried and sentenced for your crimes before a jury from all over the world.' He moved the camera to look directly into his own masked face. 'Join us at that time and hear the evidence for the prosecution and, of course, for the defence. You will then decide this man's fate. The wolf has spoken.'

He slowly zoomed into the judge's confused face, lingering on the watering eyes and the furrowed lines across the forehead. He hoped the man would come out of his stupor and mount a defence, even if the verdict had already been decided in advance.

Isn't that what happened normally?

He checked his viewing figures.

There were 1,238 ghouls. In half an hour, once the video had been seeded by the sneezers on 4chan, the number would be far higher.

It was time to give them the show they were looking for.

Chapter 84

At MIT, Detective Chief Inspector Paul Turnbull called an early briefing.

Emily Parkinson joined, along with the other detectives working on the case. The boards at the front of the incident room hadn't changed, James Dalbey's picture still at the centre. No new information had been added.

'Right, quieten down people, time to get started.' Turnbull clapped his hands to bring the briefing to order.

Parkinson noticed Claire Trent wasn't sitting in her usual place at the front. Her chair was still there but empty. She checked her watch. Ridpath was late too. Did he know about this meeting?

'Shouldn't we wait for Ridpath?' she asked.

'We'll get started, I'm in charge of the investigation not him,' Turnbull said firmly. 'Right, I've called this briefing to fill you in about the developments in the case which occurred last night. As you know, we eventually discovered the whereabouts of our target; James Dalbey aka James Monroe. He is in a coma in the intensive care unit of Manchester Metropolitan Infirmary and has been there for the last five days.'

Harry Makepeace put his hand up. 'What's that, boss? If he's been there, he can't have been the man in the mask on the video.'

'Well spotted, that man.'

'Have we confirmed how long he's been in the hospital?' asked another detective.

'The length of the stay has been confirmed.'

Emily Parkinson put her hand up. 'So if he didn't commit the murder of Brian Conway, was he involved in the other crimes?'

'A great question, DS Parkinson. I'm starting to wonder myself.'

'You think we've been chasing the wrong man all along?'

'It looks that way, yes.'

A murmur went around the assembled detectives. 'So all the work has been wasted?'

'No work is ever wasted, Rob. But it does mean we have to start again.'

A louder murmur this time.

Paul Turnbull held up his hands. 'Listen, this happens in an investigation. Sometimes, we get led astray by assumptions people make.'

'Are the four crimes even linked, boss? We've always assumed the same perp killed John Gorman's dogs, vandalised Charlie's grave and killed Don Brown and Brian Conway. And that the perp was James Dalbey,' said Harry Makepeace.

'But they must be linked, Harry,' Emily answered him. 'Are you trying to tell me four people involved in a case twelve years ago are all attacked or murdered and somehow the crimes aren't linked?'

'Could be a coincidence. We don't know they are related, do we?'

'Come on, coincidences like that don't just happen.'

Paul Turnbull held up his hands again. 'People,' he shouted, 'we are going to examine every assumption we have made, including whether these crimes are linked our not. We are going back to basics. Evidence and only evidence is going to guide our investigation. Not hunches or assumptions or guess-work. Cold hard facts are what we are looking for.' He stabbed his index finger in his palm as he spoke these words. 'And to answer your question, DS Parkinson, we will start by treating these crimes as four separate cases until the evidence tells us otherwise. Clear?'

'But, they must be—'

'Clear?' Turnbull raised his voice.

'Yes, sir,' Emily mumbled staring down at her notes.

'Right, we're going to deal with these as two cases of murder, one of vandalism and one of violence against animals. As with any case, the investigations of the murders will take precedence. Harry, I want you to take charge of the investigation into the death of Donald Brown. Re-interview all the witnesses, check their statements, talk to the woman again who saw the man sitting in the car and see if she can give us a better ID. If we can get a photofit, we'll put it out into newspapers and hopefully, somebody will come forward.'

'Will do, boss.'

'Alan, I want you to take over the Brian Conway case. Here the ANPR work is key. We need to find the vehicle the killer or killers used to get to the house in Saddleworth.'

Chrissy put her hand up. 'You want me to continue with the ANPR comparisons, we're nearly finished.'

'Stop it, until we've proven the cases are linked.'

'But, sir, if we stop, we'll lose our best chance of finding the link between the four cases,' interrupted Emily.

'As I said, DS Parkinson, I am not convinced the cases are linked. We've been led on a wild goose chase based on hunches and assumptions. Given our limited resources, we will concentrate our efforts on the murders. The chief constable wants us to solve these cases and solve them quickly.'

'What about the Osmans? They're ready to go out.'

'Hold onto them for now. No point in spooking people needlessly.' He turned back to Alan. 'I also want you to go through Brian Conway's cases. Find out if he made any enemies. Also check out his personal life; a single man, never married, you know what I mean.'

Emily Parkinson's mouth dropped; she was about to say something when he turned to her.

'Emily, I want you to liaise with the hospital, find out more concerning Dalbey.'

271

She nodded without saying anything, writing a note in her book.

'What about the John Gorman case and the desecration of Charlie's grave, boss, what are we going to do?' asked Harry Makepeace.

'Put them on the back burner for the moment. No point in spreading our resources too thin.'

There was a knock at the door and Hannah Rowland, one of the young civilian staff working on the digital team, entered. All eyes turned to look at her.

'Sorry for interrupting the briefing, DCI Turnbull, but we found something on the dark web and we think you need to know.'

'What is it?' barked Turnbull.

'I don't know if it's important but a High Court judge is going to be put on trial.'

Chapter 85

'Morning, Ridpath, we weren't expecting to see you today.' Sophia was already sitting behind her desk.

'Still working here, Sophia, I thought I'd show my face. You're in early again.'

'Mum's still being a pain. Wants me to meet this chemical engineer. The man keeps his pens in the top pocket of his shirt and his mobile phone in a pouch on his belt.'

Ridpath did a quick mental check where his pens were, realising he didn't have any. 'The fashion police will have to arrest him.'

'You're telling me. That's a ten stretch if ever I heard one.'

Ridpath pointed to the coroner's office. 'Is Mrs Challinor in?'

'Is she ever not here? I sometimes think she has a bed under her desk. When you've finished, there are some deaths I have to go through with you, plus Don Brown's family are asking when we will release the body for burial.'

'Ok, let me see her first, then we'll chat. I may also have something for you to do.'

'Sounds interesting. Does it involve foreign travel?'

'If you count Liverpool as foreign, then yes it does.'

He knocked on Mrs Challinor's door. A loud 'Come in' came from inside.

The coroner was in her usual position, behind her desk going through a file. 'Morning, Ridpath, didn't expect to see you today.'

'I thought I'd do some work here.'

'*Persona non grata* at MIT are we?'

'How did you know?'

'Claire Trent rang me last night. Said it might be best if you spent a few days working here. What happened?'

'She didn't say?'

The coroner shook her head. 'And I didn't ask.'

As Mrs Challinor spoke her email pinged loudly.

'It's another link,' she whispered, reaching for her mouse.

Chapter 86

He kept the camera focussed on the judge. The man was more like his old self, but had still not fully recovered the aggression, arrogance and sarcasm he had used so effectively in his courts to demean the defence.

It was amazing the effect only one day of being deprived of his liberty had on the man. Now he would know what it felt like to be dragged out from the stench of the cells below court to the bright, eviscerating light of the judicial system.

He glanced down at his ghouls, otherwise known as viewers. There were 7,800 and the number was rising rapidly. The teaser had worked. Time to send out the link to the specially invited guests; all those who had been involved in James Dalbey's case. Time to scare the living shit out of them. And the dead shit too.

Checking the focus one last time, he pressed send. After the last show with Brian Conway, he was sure they would need no encouragement to click the link.

He put the wolf mask over his head. It was hot inside but he could put up with the discomfort for the next thirty minutes. The mask did add the element of theatricality the production needed.

The light went green. His specially invited audience had clicked the link. It was time for the show to begin.

Raising the gavel in his hand, he brought it down heavily on the table in front of him, cleared his throat twice, and began. 'I call the court to order. Today, we have with us Sir Robert Brooking.'

At the sound of his name, the judge lifted his arms and rattled the handcuffs against the chair. 'Release me, now, damn you. I order you to release me.'

A nervous clearing of the throat. 'All in good time, judge. But first, we are going to put you on trial. Sir Robert was a recorder in the High Court. For those unacquainted with the bizarre rituals of the British legal system, that is a senior judge in charge of serious criminal trials at the Crown Courts. He has sent many a guilty criminal to prison. He even sent some people to jail who were innocent, didn't you, Sir Robert?'

'I told you to release me now.' The judge rattled his handcuffs.

He could see the anger in the man's eyes. Marvellous. 'It is those who were innocent we are concerned with now, Sir Robert.'

He glanced down at the viewership counter, over 12,500 now and still rising.

'That is why we have decided to reverse the tables for once and put you on trial. The charge is that you did knowingly and with malice aforethought convict one, James Dalbey of Manchester, for a crime you knew he did not commit.'

'A lie, a brazen lie.'

'How do you plead? Guilty or not guilty?'

'It's a lie and I do not recognise this court. It's a sham, a pantomime of justice.'

Another cough. 'No, Sir Robert, the prosecution will show the real pantomime was in your handling of the case in 2008 and it led to the incarceration of an innocent man for ten years for a crime he did not commit. I will ask you once again. How do you plead? Guilty or not guilty?'

The judge sat there in silence, not saying a word.

'In the absence of a plea, and in the desire to seek a fair trial, the court has decided to accept a plea of not guilty. You will be able to present your case for the defence, Sir Robert. The verdict will be decided by a jury of your peers, now numbering...' he glanced down at the viewing figures. 'Twenty-two thousand four hundred and fifty-six men and women. The trial will commence now.'

Ridpath was staring at the screen open-mouthed. 'That's the judge from Dalbey's original trial. Sir Robert Brooking.'

Mrs Challinor didn't react, her eyes deep in thought.

Ridpath took out his mobile and called Claire Trent. She picked up after two rings. 'Boss, Mrs Challinor has been sent another link. The judge from Dalbey's original trial is now being tried himself.'

'I know, Ridpath, we're watching it here at MIT. The digital team found the pictures on the dark web. It was advertised this morning.'

'We didn't know he was missing?'

'When his wife arrived home, she reported it to the local nick but they decided to wait until after the weekend before flagging it in the system. Just in case he'd done a bunk with his mistress. Idiots.'

'Boss, I had an idea this morning. What if Dalbey had an accomplice, an assistant? The same way Harold Lardner used to operate—'

'We have no evidence.'

'But we do, boss. The CCTV from the abduction of John Gorman's dogs. There was somebody else in the car. And I remembered something Lardner said as we were leaving. It was "Remember it's about pain, he takes no pleasure in doing what he does. It's all about pain. His pain and theirs." You see, he used the plural boss. At the time, I thought he meant the other victims. Now, I wonder if he meant his accomplice or accomplices.'

Ridpath felt Mrs Challinor's hand touch his arm. 'I recognise the voice of the man in the wolf mask. It's come back to me who it is...'

Chapter 87

He checked the number of viewers – still rising. A little cough to clear his throat again. 'Sir Robert Brooking, you had an interesting career, didn't you?'

'Did I? I am so glad you approve.'

The sarcasm was back. Marvellous.

'Marlborough. Pembroke College, Cambridge, member of Kent Court Chambers from 1970. A barrister specialising in maritime law, weren't you?'

The judge tilted his chin slightly and stared into the camera, and raised his eyes to look at the man behind the camera. He tried to lift his arms to shield his gaze from the lights but the handcuffs restrained him. 'Let me go.'

'I'm afraid that is not possible until the verdict has been reached. You are in a court, milord. But this time you are not the judge but the person facing trial. Shall I continue?'

The judge frowned.

He read from the bio he had printed out, coughing before he began. 'Sir Robert Brooking. Took silk in 1983 and quickly found favour with the Thatcher Government as an advocate for tougher sentencing for law and order offences. You were particularly busy during the miners' strike, sentencing one man to six months for the theft of a loaf of bread and two bars of chocolate.'

He glanced down at the viewing figures. There were 28,000 now and rising quickly. The ghouls were gathering from around the world.

'What's all this about? What's going on?' The judge tried to lift his arms again, the handcuffs rattling against the metal chair. 'Let me go! Let me go now!' he shouted.

'You were generally chosen when the government of the day required a compliant judge who would always deliver the necessary verdict. Whether the verdict had anything to do with justice was dubious. But you did your duty; to be seen to be upholding the rule of law, whether the law was justified or not.'

'I'm not going to listen to this poppycock for a second longer. Release me now.'

He continued ignoring the man's shouts. 'Knighted in the Birthday Honours of 2008 for "services to justice", you remained on the bench for the best part of twenty-nine years before finally retiring as a recorder in 2012. During your time, many innocent men were sentenced for crimes they did not commit. You were particularly fond of confessions obtained under duress. What was it you said? "A confession is still a confession regardless of the circumstances under which it was obtained. No man confesses to a crime he did not commit." You did say those words did you not?'

The judge stopped shouting and raised his head. 'I did and I would say them again.'

'I thought you would. Even if it led to the conviction of an innocent man?'

'No justice system is perfect, mistakes get made, but the vast majority of criminals get the sentences they deserve. In my opinion, we are often too lenient.'

He glanced down at the viewing figures; 42,396 and rising higher all the time. 'It's time for you to confess, Sir Robert, but rest assured, this is a crime you did commit. You are not innocent.'

The judge's face was going redder and redder. 'This is not a court of law. You know nothing of justice.'

'And I would say with the utmost lack of respect, neither do you, your honour.' The man in the wolf mask paused for a moment. 'Do you remember one case? That of James Dalbey?'

'I tried many cases.'

'But do you remember the Dalbey case?'

The judge shook his head.

'Let me remind you. A man accused of murdering a young woman, Alice Seagram. He confessed to the crime when questioned by two police officers, Detective Chief Superintendent John Gorman and Detective Chief Inspector Charles Whitworth.'

'It was a clear-cut case.'

'But didn't James Dalbey retract his confession, saying he knew nothing about the murder? And didn't you, in your summing up, stress the relevance of the confession to Dalbey's guilt?'

'What of it? There was other evidence. Fibres. DNA. The time of death. I believed the man had committed the offences with which he was charged.'

'All evidence discovered or planted by the real murderer, Harold Lardner, who, ten years later, was arrested for committing the crimes. Dalbey was innocent all along, wasn't he?'

The judge shrugged his shoulders. 'Mistakes happen. No criminal justice system is perfect.'

'But you ignored evidence showing the confession had been coerced. No lawyer was present. No recording was made. Only the two officers heard what Dalbey had supposedly said.'

'It was before the days of the mandatory recording of statements.'

'But wasn't there a possibility Mr Dalbey had been forced to confess his crime?'

'No, the confession itself was an act of guilt which, when combined with the fact he was found in a lock-up garage where the murder had taken place, convinced me he had committed the crime. Subsequent courts found my belief to be untrue. But you have to look into the context of the time—'

'So you confess to making a mistake? Incarcerating a man for ten years for a crime he didn't commit?'

'Is that what you want to hear? Every day mistakes are made in our justice system, some are rectified, most are not. I was a judge for twenty-nine years, of course I made mistakes.'

'Thank you for your confession of guilt, your honour. You will now be sentenced by this court.'

He looked down at the viewing figures, over 65,000 now and rising exponentially. The ghouls of 4chan were out in force. Most would be recording the proceedings to forward to all the usual suspects later; Facebook, Twitter, Reddit, YouTube and the rest. The recordings would be seen by millions before they were taken down. But, as with everything on the net, they would never be totally eradicated. That was the beauty of the web. The judge's admission and subsequent sentence would be online forever.

'What? What did you say?'

'I will address the jury.' The man in the wolf mask moved in front of the camera. 'It is now the turn of you, the worldwide jury to decide this man's fate. The procedure is easy; press like for innocent and retweet for guilty. Unlike most trials a simple majority will decide the verdict. Remember, like for innocent and retweet for guilty. You have one minute to record your verdict, commencing – now.'

As these words were spoken, the judge began to howl, 'I'm innocent, I was only doing my job, a servant of the law…'

Chapter 88

As the trial continued on the screen, Ridpath moved his phone closer to Mrs Challinor. 'I'm putting the coroner on speakerphone, boss.'

'Hi Claire, I recognise the man's voice, the man who is wearing the wolf mask. It's Tony Seagram.'

'Are you sure Mrs Challinor?'

'It's the tone and the delivery, he's got a slight Welsh accent plus he has a peculiar nervous tic before he speaks. A slight cough, likes he's clearing his throat. I couldn't remember where I had heard it before, but it came back to me. He made a speech at the interment of his sister, Alice, he kept doing the same thing. Clearing his throat before he spoke. I should have recognised it earlier when Brian Conway—'

'What is it Chrissy?' Claire Trent interrupted the coroner's explanation. An indistinct conversation mumbled down the line, then the detective superintendent spoke again excitedly. 'Chrissy has checked his LinkedIn profile. He went to Aberystwyth University and also did a Master's in Theatre Studies there. She's looking at his Facebook page.' A slight pause. 'No entries for the last nine months.'

'We need to track him down. Phone records, bank accounts, car hire, anything and everything,' ordered Claire Trent.

'Don't forget to check the TV studios where he used to work.'

'Don't teach me my job, Ridpath,' she barked. 'Well, get on with it you lot, I want Tony Seagram found.' Claire Trent commanded, 'Ridpath, keep watching the video with Mrs Challinor. See if she remembers anything else that could help.'

Mrs Challinor grabbed his wrist again. On the screen, the man in the wolf mask had moved in front of the camera and was now standing directly in front of the judge.

'What's going to happen?' Mrs Challinor whispered.

Chapter 89

A little cough. 'Sir Robert Brooking, judge of the Queen's Bench, the jury has spoken. By a vote of 62,478 for versus 3,576 against, you have been found guilty of injustice.'

The man in the wolf mask moved out from in front of the camera to reveal the judge hunched over and looking down.

'Your actions were a shocking dereliction of your duty to those who were accused of crimes. Have you anything to say in your defence?'

The judge mumbled a few words.

'Speak up please so the world can hear.'

The judge raised his head and spoke clearly. 'This is not a court I recognise. It is a kangaroo court. I refuse to dignify it with any statement.'

'Thank you. Interestingly, we refuse to dignify you as well. There is a famous statue of the blind woman holding the scales of justice in her hand on top of the Old Bailey in London. It is supposed to indicate that justice is blind and all receive the same respect from the court regardless of their wealth, status or position. In your case, this was manifestly untrue. Your justice was not blind. But it soon will be.'

'Don't talk nonsense, man. Who are you to sentence me?'

The man in the wolf mask bent down and picked up something at his feet. He showed a thin metal tube to the camera and set it alight.

'Is that a welding torch?' asked Ridpath.

Within seconds the metal glowed white hot, a small, bright flame protruding from the end.

'You are hereby sentenced to have your sight removed. Justice was not blind in your courts and now you will be blind in life. If you die from your injuries, so be it. Justice will have been served. The sentence is to be carried out immediately.'

'He's going to kill him,' shouted Mrs Challinor.

The man in the wolf mask advanced on the judge, the welding torch glowing in his hand.

The judge shouted, 'No, no, what are you doing? I order you to stop immediately. You must sto—'

He plunged the heating iron into the man's right eye, hearing the sizzle as it cut through the iris and into the aqueous humour. The judge wrenched his head back, screaming at the top of his voice.

Suddenly, the screams died in the judge's throat and he went limp as the intense pain forced his body to the safe haven of unconsciousness.

A quick glance back to the camera and the man in the wolf mask brought the flame closer and closer to the left eye.

Chapter 90

After the judge had been blinded, the link faded to black.

Mrs Challinor and Ridpath were left stunned and silent. It was Ridpath who spoke first. 'I have to get back to MIT, they'll be needing me.'

'Go, Ridpath.'

'Are you ok, Mrs Challinor?'

She nodded without looking at him, busily searching for a file on her desk.

'Are you sure?'

'Just go, Ridpath,' she finally looked up and smiled, 'I'll be fine.'

He made the gesture of thumb against ear and little finger pointing towards his mouth. 'Call me if you need anything.'

'I will.'

He turned to go.

'One last question before you leave.'

Ridpath slowly turned back.

'Was the judge on the Osman list compiled at MIT?'

'How did you know about that?'

'It's rather obvious, isn't it? Tony Seagram seems to be targeting all those in the legal system who were involved in the investigation of his sister's death or the subsequent arrest of James Dalbey.'

As ever, Mrs Challinor understood exactly what was happening. 'He was on the list but I don't think any Osman warnings have been sent out yet.'

She paused for a moment. 'Am I on the list?'

He nodded. 'I am too.'

'Not surprising in your case.'

'Shall I send a copper round to keep a watch over you and this office?'

She busied herself sorting out the files. 'I'm sure the police have more important things to do at this point in time and I am perfectly capable of looking after myself. Weren't you leaving for MIT, Ridpath?' she asked abruptly.

'Call if you need anything.'

'I will. Make sure you take care of yourself. I have a feeling Tony Seagram hasn't finished yet.'

'That's my worry too, Coroner.'

Chapter 91

Back at MIT, the place was a hive of activity, all centred on one goal; find Tony Seagram.

Bank accounts were requested, telephone records checked, even his gas and electric bills were pored over.

Nothing was found.

His social media accounts on Facebook and Twitter were dormant. The last entry in both a cryptic message about 'not being able to face the future any more.'

To Ridpath, it looked more like a suicide message than one of a man embarking on a murder spree.

Finally, Claire Trent called him into her office. Paul Turnbull was already there.

'You saw the link to the murder this morning?'

'I watched it with the coroner.'

'Your thoughts?'

He glanced at Paul Turnbull. She saw the look and said, 'Speak freely, Ridpath.'

'I'm now convinced Dalbey was involved in the planning of these murders, if not their actual execution.'

'An unfortunate choice of words.'

'Sorry, boss. I meant even though he's lying in a coma, I'm certain James Dalbey is behind all this. When I met Tony Seagram two years ago, he was smart but not organised enough to plan these murders.' Ridpath scratched his head. 'What I don't understand was the lack of any clue. Each time up until now, we've been pointed in the direction of the next killing. But there was nothing this time.'

'There was, Ridpath. I received the pathologist's report into the death of Brian Conway this morning. A piece of paper was found in his mouth. Printed on it were the words, "Is Justice Blind?"'

'Why didn't we know earlier?'

Claire Trent glanced across at her DCI. 'A breakdown in communication apparently.'

'None of it matters until we capture Seagram, does it?' growled Turnbull.

'No, that has to be the priority.'

'I'm so glad you agree with me, Ridpath.'

'Stop it you two.' Claire Trent slammed her fist down on the table. 'This stops here and now. Understand?'

'Yes, boss.'

'Yes, Claire.'

After glaring at both of them, she fixed her gaze on Ridpath. 'I need you to go to visit Mrs Seagram before the tabloids get to her.'

'To do what, boss?'

'Interview her and see if she knows anything about her son. Take Emily, put a team together and search the house for any clues to his whereabouts.'

'She won't be happy, boss.'

'Her happiness is the least of my concerns at the moment. Well, what are you waiting for?'

Ridpath stood up to leave.

Claire Trent glanced across at Turnbull who kept his head down. 'When you've finished and reported back your findings, you can go home, Ridpath. It's obvious at the moment, you need a break.'

'But, boss, there's—'

'That's an order.'

'But—'

Her voice rose. 'Don't try my patience. You have my orders, carry them out.'

'Yes, ma'am.'

Chapter 92

With Emily Parkinson by his side he knocked on the door to Mrs Seagram's house and it was opened immediately. 'I was expecting you lot.'

Ridpath raised his eyebrow.

'I watch the news too. Tony's name is all over it.'

There had been a leak from somebody in the team. Emily had a call from the office. Claire Trent was furious. Paul Turnbull was swearing to publicly castrate whoever leaked the story, even if it were a woman.

But now the newspapers and TV were all over it. It was only a matter of time before they started to gather like a pack of hyenas outside Mrs Seagram's door.

'You'd better come in.' She pointed to the team of constables behind Ridpath. 'Can you ask them to wipe their feet? I don't want to spend the rest of my life cleaning their shit off my carpets.'

She walked back into her sitting room.

Ridpath turned to the team. 'Search everywhere for anything and everything to do with Tony Seagram. But do it respectfully, lads. This is a clean search.'

'Aye, skipper,' the lead sergeant, a Geordie, replied. 'We'll be as clean as Mrs Mop.'

'Leave the sitting room till last.'

Half the team trooped upstairs and the rest headed for the kitchen and outbuildings.

Ridpath and Emily Parkinson followed the woman into her living room. She was already seated in her chair, staring out of the window.

He decided not to waste time. 'Do you know where Tony is, Mrs Seagram?'

She shook her head, tears forming in her eyes. 'No, and I wouldn't tell you if I did.'

'You said before, he vanished about six months ago.'

'Lost his job and went rapidly downhill. Was drinking too much, taking drugs. He couldn't handle the guilt you see.'

'Guilt?'

There was a loud thump on the ceiling followed by the heavy tread of coppers' boots. Mrs Seagram stared upwards before continuing. 'The loss of Alice, then reburying her. James being locked up for so long when he was innocent. You know Tony gave evidence at his trial. He was always convinced it was his evidence that swayed the jury. It was why he worked so hard to free James later when he was convinced the man had nothing to do with the death of his sister.' She paused for a moment, sitting upright in her chair to recover her composure. 'After the death of his father, Tony went to pieces.' She turned to face Ridpath, her eyes blazing. 'My son was successful, intelligent, hard-working and you lot destroyed him. I detest every single one of you.' A long pause. 'I hope he kills you all, leaves your families as empty as mine.'

The woman's teeth were bared like an attack dog ready to strike. A tap on the door broke the tension.

The Geordie sergeant entered cradling a Smith & Wesson nestling in a cloth. 'We found this canny piece upstairs in a drawer, Ridpath.'

'What are you doing with a firearm, Mrs Seagram?' asked Emily Parkinson.

'It makes me feel safe. I often keep it by my bed at night.'

'Where did you get it?'

'I told you Harry was an armourer in the REME. He loved guns. We often used to spend weekends shooting with the gun clubs up in the Derbyshire Hills with Tony. Alice didn't like them though so she never went with us. It is licensed you know. They all are.'

'They?'

'There's two more in a safe out in the garage.'

'Is Tony armed, Mrs Seagram?'

'I don't know. Why don't you ask him?'

The interview ended soon after. Ridpath, Emily Parkinson and the team spent the next hour searching the house from top to bottom but discovered nothing new.

As he was leaving, Mrs Seagram stood by the door. 'You won't find him you know, not unless he wants to be found. Tony was always good at blending in. It's why he did so well at his job. One last thing, Inspector Ridpath.'

'What's that?'

'This is all your fault. None of this would have happened without you.'

She slammed the door in his face.

He was left staring at the frosted glass panel, hearing the first shouts of the newly arrived reporters at his back.

'What did Mrs Seagram have to say?'

'Is she supporting her son?'

'Who's going to be his next victim?'

He hated every single one of them.

Chapter 93

The body of the judge was found that evening in a wooded area close to the Manchester Ship Canal in a suburb called Partington.

It had been placed in an upright position with the back leaning against an ash tree. A man walking his dog had come across it almost by accident when the dog had suddenly veered off his usual path and went charging down through the woods bordering the Red Brook.

Claire Trent and Paul Turnbull, accompanied by a hungry pack of reporters, were there twenty minutes after the discovery. Dr John Schofield, the duty pathologist, arrived slightly later with a CSI team. Immediately the body was covered by a white tent while the doctor suited up.

After less than five minutes inside the tent, the doctor came out and walked slowly over to where the detectives were standing.

'I've pronounced him dead at 7.35 p.m.'

'Anything you can tell us?'

'Look, it's early days but my bet is he died from shock. The heart of an old man wouldn't have been able to withstand the pain of having his eyes cauterised.'

Paul Turnbull rubbed his shiny bald head, freshly shaven this morning, another small red nick above the ear. 'Time of death?' he asked.

'I can't give you a time until I've performed the post mortem. Any time between the event and now with a time close to the event being more than likely.' He gestured towards the white tent. 'I thought I'd come out and let you know. I need to go back in and finish the paperwork as well as make my preliminary examination before we let the CSIs loose and move the body to the morgue.'

'Thank you, doctor.'

The doctor turned to go before stopping and turning back. 'I've also completed the post mortem on Don Brown, the report should be in your office. Cause of death was a myocardial infarction as I predicted. A heart attack in the common parlance, brought on by exposure to extreme cold. The toxicology has also come back. There was a large dose of Propofol in his system. It's a drug used—'

'—to induce a coma.' Turnbull finished his sentence for him.

'How did you know?' said the doctor.

'We've come across it elsewhere,' replied Claire Trent. 'If you could complete your post mortem on the judge and send us the results as soon as possible doctor, we would be grateful.'

'I'll do it this evening. You will have my preliminary thoughts tomorrow morning.'

He walked away back to the single white tent, now illuminated by the portable lights and generators of the CSI team.

'What do we do now, Claire?'

'I'll need you to organise this area, Paul. We need to interview the dog walker and canvas the local estate, maybe somebody spotted something. I'm going back to the office. See if we have discovered any new information on Tony Seagram. The team must have found something by now.'

'They would have called if they did, Claire.'

She nodded. 'You're right, but I'm going back anyway.'

Claire Trent stared back at the mob of reporters and television news crews being kept back by a thin blue line of coppers from the local nick.

'Now I need to fight my way through the mob, Paul, to do my job. It's going to be a long night.'

Chapter 94

In the middle of the press of reporters and television crews, one man stood staring at the white tent.

Earlier that day he had transported the judge to this particular location and placed the body in the wood.

James had predicted the man would die as soon as the sentence was executed, but he lasted more than three hours, groaning and moaning, until Tony Seagram could stand it no longer.

He was about to stab him through the heart when the noises stopped abruptly. He checked the man's pulse.

Nothing.

'Finally, about bloody time.' He'd levered him up into a wheelchair, covered him with a paisley blanket and wheeled him out to a van parked outside the house.

That afternoon, the clouds had cleared and it was a bright, if cold, day. A good day to dump the body of a judge.

He used the chair lift to place the judge in the back of the van, checking the notes on the plan to see if he had accomplished everything on his list.

After he had placed the judge's body leaning against the tree in the specially chosen place, he would return to the house to make preparations for tomorrow.

It was the final act of the plan.

The final act of his little drama.

After tomorrow, he would be free.

And they would be dead.

Chapter 95

When the interview and search of Mrs Seagram's house was finished, Ridpath briefed Emily Parkinson what to say in the report and decided to obey the instruction to go home.

Both Polly and Eve were surprised to see him.

'You're back. After we saw the news, we thought you'd be late this evening.'

'I thought you wouldn't come back at all,' chipped in Eve.

'They sent me home. Said I wasn't needed, that I should rest.'

'Claire Trent?'

Ridpath nodded.

'She's right. After a good night's sleep, you'll be back to the old Ridpath, fit and raring to go.'

'Didn't you hear the part about not being needed?'

His wife took a deep breath before looking him in the eye. 'Listen, Ridpath, you are needed. Your family needs you. Myself and Eve need you. For one night, the Greater Manchester Police can manage on their own. You can save the world tomorrow. Tonight, you can enjoy a relaxing evening with us. We can eat a special microwaved lasagne, drink a bottle of cheap Spanish plonk and devour some Haagen-Dazs chunky monkey for dessert.'

Ridpath smiled. 'It's gourmet night chez Ridpath?'

'I've got a three Michelin starred microwave.'

'Mum, I hate to tell you this, but those stars are actually ice crystals. That setting is for defrosting food.'

'I wondered why the lasagne was always cold in the centre.'

'Sit down, Mrs Ridpath. Myself and my sous chef, Eve, will prepare your evening meal. Would you like a glass of Chateau Plonk while you wait?'

'That would be appreciated. Wine helps clear the lungs of chalk dust.'

'Coming right up. Sous chef Eve, come with me.'

So Ridpath prepared the meal adding a salad he made from a wedge of red cabbage, some sesame seeds and a dollop of mayonnaise only slightly past its sell-by date.

For the first time in a while they sat down as a family and talked, Ridpath forgetting, for a moment, Tony Seagram, James Dalbey, and all the rest.

It was only when Eve and Polly had gone to bed and he was sitting alone in the darkened living room that the demons returned.

With a vengeance.

Had he missed a clue?

Had he not worked hard enough?

Had he not followed through properly, missing vital evidence?

A deep sense of failure washed over him. Had he lost the knack for police work in his two years with the coroner? Was Turnbull right, was he now too much of a maverick to ever work as part of a team again? Was he just a pile of worthless shit?

A vast wave of despair flowed over and through him.

He hadn't felt like this since the middle of his chemo when he felt so sick and tired he just didn't want to carry on. Only Polly and Eve kept him going, their smiles through the glass window as the poison leeched into his body, making it all worthwhile.

But what had it all been for?

For him to fail when he had been tested? For him to let the Seagrams, Mrs Challinor, and all his colleagues down?

He looked across at the golden bottle of Lagavulin sitting half drunk on the shelf. He could take the pain away with its bitter honey. He could chase the demons away with its bur at the back of his throat.

He stood up and stopped.

Getting drunk wasn't going to solve anything. The only thing to do was to return to work tomorrow.

Work harder.

Work smarter.

The answer was out there, he just had to find it.

His mobile phone buzzed. A message from Emily Parkinson:

> Body of judge found. DS Trent happy about discovery of guns. Ballistics being checked, Still at work. Emily.

He messaged back.

> What was the clue with the body this time?

She replied.

> No clue found yet. Perhaps the judge was the last?
> Will you be in tomorrow?

He thought for a moment. Would he go in to MIT? Perhaps it would be better to spend time with the coroner. After all, officially he had less than a week left to work with her.

He shook his head.

Turnbull wasn't going to get rid of him so easily. Not when there was work to be done. He messaged Emily back.

> Of course, will be there at 9 a.m. You can brief me at that time.

She replied a minute later.

> Good. See you.

Perhaps Claire Trent was right. He just needed a good night's sleep. Tomorrow was another day.

But at least he had Polly and Eve to come home to, filling his days away from MIT and the Coroner's Office with joy and happiness. When every day was filled with death and dying, they reminded him that life, in all its beautiful strangeness, carried on.

He switched off the lights and climbed the stairs to his bed, thanking his lucky stars for the two most important women in his life.

Tomorrow would be another day.

Tomorrow would be a better day.

Chapter 96

In his bed in Manchester Metropolitan Infirmary, James Dalbey surfaced briefly from the bottom of his deep, dark well as the nurse changed his catheter.

He couldn't feel anything but he was aware she was attending to him.

For a moment, he thought about waking up and sitting up in bed to request a bacon sandwich with extra butter melting into the thick doorstop of bread.

But the moment passed and the taste of the bacon butty vanished from his mouth.

How he enjoyed playing them and playing with them.

They had deprived him of ten years of his life. Even worse, they had kept him from the only person he had ever loved or who had ever loved him. His mother.

The old James Dalbey had trusted people.

The old James Dalbey had loved his mother.

The old James Dalbey had tried to be a good man.

They were going to pay for the death of the old James Dalbey.

Each and every one of them, one by one.

The diagnosis of a brain tumour a month ago had knocked him back. But immediately he had seen the possibilities. What better alibi than being in a coma? Tony had always wanted to execute the plan on his own anyway, he enjoyed the infliction of pain and hurt. After they killed the dogs and commenced the implementation, he bowed out. No more prison for him.

And he was going to get away with it.

He had a plan.

A shadow loomed over him, playing with something above his head.

As the Propofol kicked in again, and he began sinking down to the bottom of his well, a fleeting thought crossed his comatose mind.

Were they all dead yet?

Chapter 97

The next morning Ridpath made breakfast for his daughter and his wife before driving into MIT. He felt rested and strangely relaxed. Getting a good night's sleep had been the right move. For the first time in ages, he felt sharp and alert.

The radio was full of the story of the murder. The killing had been broadcast around the world through the internet. Even as the social media companies blocked the footage in one place, it popped up in another. The only other story dominating the airwaves seemed to be the arrival of a new disease in China. Already the authorities there had locked down one of their major cities in an attempt to control its spread. He couldn't imagine the same thing ever happening in England.

As he stepped into MIT at exactly nine a.m., the office was buzzing, there were even more detectives than before, many of whom he didn't recognise. They were all rushing around, sometimes bumping into each other in their haste to do their jobs. Chrissy was over behind her desk, buried beneath a wall of files. For a second she raised her head and saw Ridpath. Her mouth tightened and her eyes rolled upwards as if to say, 'What the fuck is happening?'

He found Emily Parkinson in a corner of the department, hiding behind a computer, typing furiously.

She stopped as he approached. 'What's going on?'

'It's a nightmare, Ridpath, there's just so many people but we don't seem to be getting anywhere.'

'That doesn't surprise me. The more bodies on a case, the harder it is to co-ordinate everybody. Who are all these people?'

'It's become national now, so they've drafted in teams of detectives from every division. There's even somebody from the Met over there. We've basically got every police force in the country looking for Tony Seagram. He vanished from sight about six months ago and hasn't resurfaced anywhere since. And that lot there—' Emily pointed towards a group of six people huddled in a corner, '—are the communications team.'

'Communications team?'

'Since the trial of the judge was posted on the web, the media are all over this like flies on shit. That lot are just answering their enquiries. I've heard we're going to get four more "press liaison officers" and another ten dedicated phone lines.' She formed quote marks with her fingers.

Ridpath whistled. 'This shit has hit the fan. And the judge?'

'As I messaged you, his body was found in a forested area close to the Manchester Ship Canal, a place called Partington.'

'No clues on the body?'

'Forensics found nothing. Dr Schofield is performing the post mortem, we should get the results in soon.'

As Emily spoke, Turnbull appeared in the entrance to his office. 'Listen up people, Dr Schofield has emailed over his preliminary report. The judge died from a heart attack brought about by shock. We're still waiting on toxicology but I'm not hopeful it will give us anything.'

He spotted Ridpath and Emily and beckoned with his finger. 'You two in the incident room now. Claire Trent wants to see you.'

DS Parkinson stood up and pulled down her jumper. 'I wonder what bollocking the dragon lady is going to give me now.'

'How's Claire Trent bearing up?'

'I think you're going to find out.'

Chapter 98

In the house out in the wilds of Altrincham, Tony Seagram was making the last-minute preparations and checking the list on the plan.

He'd been following the news on Sky TV all morning. He didn't bother watching the BBC any more, it was far too slow in its reporting and had turned into little more than a government mouthpiece.

A face on the screen was reporting the worldwide reaction to the death of the judge. Shock, horror and anger seemed to be the words most used, followed by a long explanation of the Beast of Manchester case with stock images of James and Harold Lardner.

For a second, a photo of Alice appeared on his television. His beautiful sister was alive again, if only for the few seconds of a television report.

The journalist finally spoke about the failing of the judicial system in the case. Good. The message was getting through.

After today, they would have even more to talk about.

A spokesman for the police came on. He used the usual platitudes; ongoing investigation, working hard, teams of detectives, sympathy for the family. Every time, they stood up and said the same thing only in a different order.

He switched the man off in mid-sentence, returning to the plan.

He went through the list once more, checking he had packed everything he needed.

It was done.

He was ready.

He put on the camouflage jacket over his white t-shirt and took one last look at the room. The camera was still there against one wall pointing at the single chair where the judge had sat.

He checked his watch. Nine a.m.

It was time to leave.

He didn't bother locking the door behind him, he wasn't coming back.

Chapter 99

Death.

It was God's last big joke on all of us. We all knew we were going to die, but nobody knew when.

From the bottom of his well, James Dalbey focussed on death.

It was something he'd thought about a lot before he entered his coma.

The death of Alice.

The death of his mother.

The death of the dogs. And Don Brown. And Brian Conway. And the judge.

So many deaths, but in the greater scheme of things, so few.

He wished he could have killed more. Not in the physical sense of pulling a trigger, kicking a chair from beneath a hanged man, or blinding a judge. Tony was far better at the physical aspects of killing. His friend enjoyed it far more.

Even helping with the killing of the dogs had made him nauseous.

No. He wished he had planned to kill more.

A station full of coppers.

A court with a row of judges.

He chuckled to himself. What was the collective noun for solicitors? A lie of lawyers. A corruption of counsellors. A dishonesty of public defenders?

Whatever.

He was suddenly aware of the beeping of machines and the whispers of doctors. He knew they were planning his surgery soon. They would cut open his brain to take out the tumour growing within.

He chuckled again. The metaphor of a malignant cancer growing in his mind appealed to him.

Little did they know, how malignant it was.

He wished he could've killed more.

Chapter 100

Ridpath and Emily Parkinson followed their DCI into the incident room. Claire Trent was sitting behind a desk. Her face was a pasty shade of white and it looked like she hadn't slept in a hundred years.

The whiteboards were still the same as before except now a close-up picture of a smiling Tony Seagram was placed in the centre.

'Right, I want you both to go to Ashworth and interview Harold Lardner again. It's time to test your theory that he knows something.'

'I'm sure he does. How's the rest of the investigation?'

She sighed and tugged the skin between her eyes. 'Look, Ridpath, I'll be honest, I've got nothing – except the mayor, the chief constable and half the world's press up my arse.'

'There were no clues at the place where the judge's body was found?'

'None that we found. The post mortem hasn't revealed anything new either.'

'But Seagram has been leaving clues at the scene of every murder.'

'Not this time.' She stood up and walked over to a table with a map stretched out on top of it. A map of the area was marked with a large 'X' where the body was found as well as a grid of the search area in the woods and the homes already interviewed in the house-to-house.

She prodded it forcefully with her index finger. 'The judge was found here at 6.32 yesterday evening by a dog walker...'

Ridpath looked down at the table and stared at the map, not believing what he saw. 'The wood, boss.'

'Yeah, he was propped up against a tree, an ash apparently.'

'I know, but the name of the wood.'

Through her tired eyes Claire Trent gazed down at something she had looked at one hundred times over the last twelve hours, seeing it new for the first time.

'It's called Coroner's Wood.'

Chapter 101

Claire Trent was staring at him. 'You think the name of the wood is important?'

He nodded his head. 'Tony Seagram always leaves a clue to his next victim with the last one. This time there was nothing except the place where the body was found.'

As the realisation of what he had just said dawned on Claire Trent's face, Ridpath's mobile phone beeped with a new message.

> Please come to Court #1 in the Stockfield Coroner's Court at 10 a.m. It is important that you are there on time. Margaret Challinor.

Strange, why was the coroner messaging him? He looked at the message again. Even stranger, it seemed to be a group invitation. Mrs Challinor never contacted people in this way.

'What is it?'

'I've just received a message from Mrs Challinor, she wants me to go to Stockfield.'

Turnbull clicked his tongue loudly. 'You have work to do here, Ridpath. MIT is in the middle of the most important investigation it has ever undertaken and you want to waltz over to the Coroner's Office the minute she calls you? I think you need to get your priorities in order.'

Ignoring his DCI, he pressed the speed dial button to call Mrs Challinor.

No answer.

He tried again.

Still no answer.

Maybe she was already in court, preparing for a case. He rang Sophia, knowing she would already be sitting at her desk, if for no other reason than her mother was still trying to marry her off.

No answer again.

'Nobody is answering their phone, I need to go over there, boss.'

'You think she's in trouble?' asked Claire Trent.

'I don't know, but the name of the wood where the judge was found worries me.'

'Go and check it out.'

He moved to leave the office.

'I don't believe it, you're letting him wander off to see the coroner, just when we need everyone here.'

'We have enough warm bodies, Paul.' She turned back to Ridpath. 'It doesn't smell right to me either. Go and check it out.'

'I'm coming with you,' shouted Emily Parkinson.

Claire Trent nodded. The DS ran to join him.

The last thing Ridpath heard as he ran out of the door was Claire Trent on the phone. 'I need a Tactical Unit at the Coroner's Court in Stockfield, NOW.'

Chapter 102

In the car racing to Stockfield past the Etihad Stadium, the blues and twos screaming above their heads, Emily Parkinson leant into him and shouted, 'I hope you're right, Ridpath.'

'I hope I'm wrong.'

The time on the car's dashboard said 9.35. In this traffic, he would have to hurry to get to the coroner before ten a.m.

He swung the car off the A6010 to avoid the grid lock of the junction at Belle Vue, taking a short cut to Hyde Road and pulling across the flow of the traffic to race down Mount Road.

'You broke at least fifteen traffic laws back there.'

'You going to book me?'

'Not this time.'

'Can you call Sophia again? See if she's answering.'

Using Ridpath's phone, Parkinson pressed redial. The phone rang and rang until a voice machine cut in.

'No answer.'

'Shit.'

Despite taking a short cut, Ridpath still had a wall of red lights to pass before he could get to Stockfield, each one decided it would turn red just as he approached. As cars pulled to the side, he inched through the traffic flow.

At one red light, one stupid driver decided he had right of way and narrowly missed the oncoming police car.

'Bloody idiot,' shouted Ridpath through the windscreen.

Emily Parkinson called Sophia again.

Still no answer.

Ridpath switched off the sirens a mile away from the Coroner's Court. It was exactly ten a.m. He screeched to a halt, parking on a double yellow line, and jumped out of the car, racing up the steps.

The reception area was empty. Normally, by this time of the day, Jenny would have taken up position to repel any visitors.

Ridpath walked past the desk and down the corridor to his office. 'Mrs Challinor,' he shouted, 'Sophia…'

There was an eerie silence about the place as if it had been abandoned suddenly like the *Marie Celeste*. 'Mrs Challinor,' he shouted again.

Silence.

His office was empty but Sophia's blue knapsack was slung across the back of her chair and her computer was on.

'Where is everybody?' asked Emily.

He walked through to the Coroner's Office without answering. For the first time he could ever remember, Mrs Challinor wasn't sitting behind her desk.

His phone rang.

'Mrs Challinor, we've been looking for you, where are you?'

'Hi, Tom. I'm in court no. 1 with the others, can you come here now, I have something important to show you.'

'But…'

'Come here, Tom, now if you can, it's important.'

'I'm in the office. I'll be there in three minutes.'

'Great, I'll see you soon.'

The phone went silent.

Tom? Mrs Challinor never called him Tom.

Chapter 103

Alarm bells were going off in Ridpath's head.

He'd never heard such tension, such pleading in Mrs Challinor's voice. Normally she simply told him to come to her office in a professional, almost abrupt way.

And why had she called him Tom twice? He hated it when people used his first name. The only person who did was his mother and she called him Thomas, never Tom.

He looked at Emily Parkinson, who was already heading down the corridor to walk across to court no. 1.

'Hang on,' he shouted after her.

'Mrs Challinor, doesn't she want us to meet her?'

'But something's not right. Don't ask me what but it doesn't feel right.'

He stood there for a moment, his eyes darting left to right. Was Mrs Challinor in trouble? Or was he completely over-reacting and it was just a normal meeting? A police tactical unit was heading to the Court right now. Was it a false alarm?

If it was, Turnbull would have him for breakfast. And for lunch.

Had he just said goodbye to his career?

But why had she called him Tom? And what about the place the judge was found, Coroner's Wood. Was that just a coincidence?

As Claire Trent had said, it just didn't smell right.

He remembered something Mrs Challinor had told him. He ran down the corridor, past Jenny's desk.

'Where are you going? What's happening?' Emily Parkinson shouted at him.

Where was it? It should be somewhere around here. He wrenched open one door. Nothing but brushes, mops and wooden shelves stacked with council approved cleaning liquids.

He ran to the next door and pulled it open.

'What are you looking for?' asked DS Parkinson joining him.

He was staring in front of a small cupboard. On each shelf was mounted CCTV equipment, with two small monitors at the top. On one of the monitors, a man was standing in front of a group of people seated in the jury box.

The man was wearing a wolf mask.

'What are we going to do, Ridpath?' asked Emily staring at the monitor.

Chapter 104

Two minutes later Ridpath was walking up the steps to the main entrance to court no. 1 on his own. He took his time, making sure people could hear him.

At the top of the stairs, the large double doors were closed. He halted for a moment in front of them.

He hoped this was going to work. He had briefed Parkinson on what she had to do.

Now it was his turn.

One thing they needed above everything was time.

He took a deep breath and pushed the doors open.

'Come in, Ridpath.'

The man wearing a wolf mask was standing in front of the witness stand, brandishing a gun in one hand and a mobile phone in the other.

Opposite him, in the jury box, Mrs Challinor sat with Jenny Oldfield, Sophia, an older man Ridpath didn't recognise and John Gorman.

A little cough. 'You've finally arrived. I'd almost given up waiting for you. But of course, we couldn't start until our star witness arrived, could we?'

Ridpath glanced behind him as the door shut noisily.

'And don't think about running. If you do, I will quite happily shoot Mrs Challinor first, followed by former Chief Superintendent Gorman. The others I'll save for dessert.'

He pointed the gun directly at Mrs Challinor. She didn't flinch, staring straight back at him.

Another nervous cough. 'Cat got your tongue, or was it a wolf? Now come in and put these on. I'm sure you know how they work.'

He reached down and threw a pair of handcuffs to Ridpath.

'You can join the others in the jury box, fastening one end of the handcuffs to the rail as they have done.'

Ridpath noticed for the first time Mrs Challinor and the others all had their arms resting on the jury rail.

As he walked towards the jury box Mrs Challinor said, 'I'm sorry, Ridpath, he forced me to call you.'

'How touching. An apology at a time like this.'

A large backpack was resting next to the jury box. As he got closer, Ridpath recognised the unmistakable smell of putty.

'I see you've noticed the elephant in the room, otherwise known as a rather large bomb. Enough to wreck this place and everyone in it quite comfortably. Or I should say uncomfortably.' He gestured for Ridpath to put on the handcuffs.

'You're not going to get away with this Tony.'

'Ah, I see you finally worked out who I am, Ridpath. I guess you won't mind if I take this off. It's awfully hot inside.'

He removed the mask letting it fall to the floor.

'That's better. We thought the theatrics of the mask worked well for the internet audience, didn't you? Before I came out this morning, I noticed new memes popping up everywhere. While fame was never our intention, it can't but help the cause.'

Ridpath risked a glance up to the door leading from the courtroom to the coroner's ante-room but hadn't seen any movement. The coroner's desk was raised above the rest of the court so he couldn't see all of the door, just the top.

Where were they? Where was Claire Trent?

He focussed back on Tony Seagram. 'What was the cause? To kill innocent people?'

A cough and the man began to talk. It was as if he'd been waiting to tell them the story for his whole life. 'That was the point, Ridpath, have you not been listening? None of these people were innocent. None of the people here are innocent. They were all complicit in the cover-up of my sister's death and the jailing of an innocent man, James Dalbey.'

Ridpath noticed a slight movement from the door behind the coroner's desk. Was it opening?

'You keep saying "we" and "our". Was Dalbey involved in this?'

'Wouldn't you like to know? Perhaps I am using the royal we? As in we only have to press the send signal on this phone and the C4 in the backpack will blow you all to bits.' He held up the phone for all to see.

Ridpath glance up again. He couldn't see if anybody was there.

'Why don't you let us go, Tony? You've made your point now. The judicial system failed your sister and James Dalbey.' Mrs Challinor was speaking. Had she seen the door open?

'Ever the voice of reason, Coroner. But I don't think I'll let you go. See in this court I have the people who caused my sister and James the most pain. We all know about John Gorman and his steadfast approach to upholding the rule of law. Pity that didn't extend to my sister.'

Ridpath looked across at his ex-boss. The man was as white as a sheet, struggling for breath.

'Next to him, we have the Crown Prosecution Service's solicitor, David Grenham. I'm so glad you received my email invitation to be here.'

'You said the coroner wanted to speak to me.'

'She does, but not yet. It was shameful of you to withhold evidence from the defence Mr Grenham. Evidence that would have cleared James.'

'I...I...'

In the background, Ridpath could hear the sound of sirens coming closer. Tony Seagram had noticed them too. 'Looks like the cavalry are on their way. Did you call them, Ridpath or was it Emily Parkinson?' He looked at his watch. 'Shame they will arrive too late.'

Ridpath noticed a movement behind the coroner's desk. Who was there?

'And then there's the coroner, Mrs Challinor. So keen to do the right thing, she managed to trick Harold Lardner into confessing in this very court. But justice doesn't end here, Coroner, what about the victims? What about their families? My father died just after we re-buried Alice. His heart was broken, but you, and all the rest of you, had already moved onto your next case. The justice system grinds on, grinding its victims into dust behind it.'

Another movement behind the coroner's desk.

'You can come out now, whoever you are?'

No answer.

'If you don't come out now, I will shoot Ridpath dead in five seconds.'

The barrel of the gun was levelled at Ridpath's heart.

'One.'

'Two.'

'Three.'

'Four.'

Tony Seagram cocked the trigger of the revolver, a loud metallic click echoed around the courtroom.

Ridpath could see the hard metal ring hanging down from the revolver's grip. Was this a military gun?

'Fi...'

Emily Parkinson jumped up from behind the coroner's desk. 'Don't shoot, don't shoot.'

'Detective Sergeant Parkinson, I wondered where you were. You're going to have to stop following Ridpath round like a love-sick puppy. But if you would care to join him in the jury box, we will bring these proceedings to a conclusion.'

Slowly, Emily Parkinson descended the stairs.

'Put these on.' Seagram threw her another pair of handcuffs.

'Sorry, Ridpath, I thought I should help.'

Outside the window, the sirens were louder now, cars screeching to a halt, the sound of slamming doors.

'Give yourself up. You're not going to get away, Tony.'

'Right on time, the cavalry have arrived, Ridpath. Exactly as James said they would in the plan.' He held up the mobile phone. 'It's now time for the final act.'

Chapter 105

'Trev, get your sharpshooters in position on the surrounding buildings. I want eyes on the interior of the building. Who's inside?'

'Yes, ma'am.'

'Harry, check if the other buildings in the complex are clear. Move everybody out. And find the CCTV that Emily told us about. Where is she anyway?'

'I'll find her, boss.' He ran off towards the administration buildings.

'Paul, make sure we have a cordon tight around here. I want those people—' she pointed to a group of reporters and television camera trucks who had followed their cars from HQ, '—pushed back at least one hundred metres.'

'It means closing the main road through the town.'

'Do it, but get onto Traffic, divert cars away from this area.'

'Operation Centre will be here,' she pointed back to the cafe behind her, 'until further notice.'

He ran to marshal the coppers near their cars.

Her phone rang. She looked at the name and mouthed a silent swear word. 'Yes, sir,' she said answering it. 'Yes sir, doing it at the moment. No, no there's no need for the assistant chief constable to take charge, everything is under control.'

A long pause as she walked slowly away, nodding her head at the voice on the other end of her phone. 'Arsehole,' she said to the receiver after ending the call.

She looked at the detectives and uniforms surrounding her. 'Well, lads, it's all down to us. We'd better not fuck this up, or else we'll all be working in Cheetham Hill for the rest of our careers. Alan, they're sending a hostage negotiator to us, he'll arrive in twenty minutes, make sure he has everything he needs.'

'Yes, boss.'

Sergeant Trevor Hall, the head of the Armed Tactical Unit, strode calmly back to the position. 'We're in place overlooking the court now. My men are trying to see what's happening inside.'

'I can help,' said Harry Makepeace, running to join them. 'We've found the CCTV room for the court. We've got live pictures from inside.'

'Show me, Harry.' Claire Trent picked up an Airwave. 'Keep in touch, Trev, let me know exactly what your men can see.'

They ran off towards the administration building, running up a few steps and into reception. 'It's this way, boss.'

Harry Makepeace veered off to the left down a corridor. A couple of constables were standing outside what looked like a broom cupboard. They moved back respectfully as they saw Claire Trent.

Inside the broom cupboard was a rack of recording equipment with two small monitors sitting on top. The monitor on the left was marked 'Court Number One'. On it, in black and white, Claire Trent could see a wide-angled shot of the inside of the court.

'They must use it to check the proceedings. There is sound somewhere but we can't find how to activate it,' said Harry Makepeace staring at the dials on one of the black boxes.

'Don't touch it, I don't want to lose the feed.'

She looked on as a man was standing in front of the jury box, obviously haranguing the people sat inside. She could see Ridpath, Margaret Challinor, John Gorman and Emily Parkinson in the box, plus three other people she didn't recognise. One of them she guessed was Sophia Rahman, Ridpath's assistant at the Coroner's Court. Gorman seemed to be sitting in a slumped position. Had Seagram shot him? She pointed towards the screen. 'What's that?'

Harry leant in to take a closer look. 'I dunno. Looks like a rucksack or a backpack.' He leant in even closer. 'It must be Tony Seagram standing at the front. He's got something in his hand.'

On screen, they could see Seagram had stopped speaking and was now holding up a mobile phone.

'Shit,' said Harry, 'does the backpack have more C4?'

As Claire Trent was about to reply, her Airwave squawked. 'Hall to Commander. Over.'

'Commander here. What is it, Trev?'

'We have eyes on the perp, ma'am. Over.'

'We can also see him on a monitor.'

'He seems to be holding up a mobile device in his left hand and a pistol in his right. Over.'

'We agree—'

'Just a minute, ma'am. Over.' There was a muffled conversation, before the Airwave squawked again. 'Position number three has a shot, ma'am. Over. Repeat. Position number three has a shot. Over.'

Claire Trent thought quickly. Tony Seagram was moving again, walking up and down in front of the jury box, before once again stopping and raising his left arm.

'Permission to take the shot, ma'am. Over. Requesting permission to take the shot.'

Chapter 106

Tony Seagram pointed the pistol directly at them. 'This was foreseen in the plan. Looks like none of us is going to escape after all.'

On his right, John Gorman went a deathly white and clutched his chest. He let out a loud gasp and slumped to his right across Jenny Oldfield.

Ridpath jumped up to help him, but found his left hand still attached by the handcuffs to the rail of the jury box. 'He's having a heart attack, he needs help.'

Tony Seagram stared across at John Gorman, and, for the first time, looked worried, before quickly regaining his composure. 'Sit down,' he gestured with the gun.

Ridpath stayed where he was.

This time the pistol was levelled directly at Sophia. 'Sit down, now, or she will be the first to die.'

Ridpath glanced across at John Gorman. The man's lips were turning blue.

The pistol in Tony Seagram's hand fired once, the loud bang echoing around the courtroom. A bullet buried itself in the plaster of the wall behind Sophia's head, showering fragments down on to all the prisoners sitting in the jury box.

Jenny and the solicitor screamed.

Mrs Challinor shouted, 'No!'

Instinctively, Ridpath ducked.

Only Sophia remained where she was, staring at Tony Seagram.

'Sit down. The next shot will go into Sophia's face, destroying those pretty features.'

Ridpath raised his hand and sat down. 'Why don't you let the women go and get help for John Gorman? They've done nothing wrong.'

'Neither have they done anything right. As for Gorman, I wanted to kill him at the same time as we killed his dogs, but James said to wait. We had to build up to his death, destroy his life first.' He stared at the ex-detective superintendent lying slumped over, his head resting in Jenny's arms. 'Looks like the man's heart has finally given up on him. It gave up on James and Alice twelve years ago.'

'Let them go,' pleaded Ridpath.

'I'll release you all, soon, don't worry.'

He held up the mobile phone with his left hand, the finger hovering over the send button.

'Wait,' shouted Ridpath, 'what did I do wrong? You've spoken about everybody else, but what about me? I was the one who helped to convict Harold Lardner, released James Dalbey and finally found where Alice had been kept hidden all those years.'

Tony Seagram smiled. 'Yes, you did all that, Ridpath. But you were the worst of all. Because for you, justice was all about punishing the guilty, but what about the victims? What about my dad? Or my mum? What about James? What about the other women who were killed? Did you charge him for their murders? What about their relatives?'

'We didn't have enough evidence.'

'But were they not victims too? You see, your justice is all about discovering guilt not finding retribution or atonement. It's not justice at all.'

Ridpath noticed for the first time, Tony Seagram had lost the nervous cough at the beginning of all his sentences.

'Enough talk, it's time to end all this.'

He raised the mobile phone, his finger poised to press the send button, moving closer to the backpack and the jury box.

'I'm going to count to five. After that, I'm afraid, it will all be over. One...'

'Stop, don't do it, Tony.'

'Two.'

'Killing us won't change anything.'

'No, it won't, but it will make me feel better. Three.'

'Why should you kill us, just because you don't want to live any more?'

Tony Seagram laughed. 'Because I can. It's my justice. Four.'

The finger hovered over the send button.

Chapter 107

'We've lost the shot, ma'am. The target has moved. Repeat we have lost the shot. Over.' Sergeant Hall's voice crackled through the Airwave.

Claire Trent stared at the black and white monitor, not daring to breathe. Tony Seagram had now moved closer to the jury box, holding the mobile phone above his head and talking all the time.

'Can't we get any sound?' she said irritably.

Harry Makepeace leant forward and pressed two buttons at random.

The picture went blank.

'Get the picture back, Harry, what the hell did you do?'

'I don't know, boss,' replied Makepeace, pushing every button in the row.

Sergeant Hall's voice came over the Airwave again. 'Position two has a shot. I confirm position two has a shot. Over.'

Claire Trent took a deep breath. The screen was still blank. Harry Makepeace and the other constables were staring at her.

'Sergeant Hall, you are authorised under Section 3 of the 1967 Criminal Law Act to take the shot. I repeat critical shot authorised. Over.'

There was no response from the Airwave.

Chapter 108

'Four,' repeated Tony Seagram with a beatific smile on his face, teasing his audience in the jury box, his finger resting lightly on the send button.

Ridpath leant forward trying to grab Tony Seagram but the handcuffs hooked around the jury box rail held him back, making a rattling sound. 'Don't do it,' he pleaded.

Seagram jumped back staying just out of reach. 'I'd like to say it's been fun knowing all of you, but that wouldn't be true. I've hated every second of my life on earth. And I've hated you lot even more.'

Jenny screamed.

Mrs Challinor shouted.

Sophia just stared at Tony Seagram as he laughed.

'Five,' he said quietly.

The shot, when it came, made hardly any sound.

A soft thud as the metal of the bullet struck flesh.

A look of surprise, almost disappointment, crossed Tony Seagram's face and he collapsed on his knees to the ground, blood spurting from a hole in the right side of his neck. He dropped the gun, clamping his hand over the wound. The blood seeping through his fingers.

He fell to one side, with the mobile phone still in his hand. For a second he lay there unmoving. Then his head slowly rose and he looked directly at the phone, the blood still pouring from the wound in his neck.

Ridpath saw the finger twitch on the send button. He jumped over the jury rail and reaching out as far as the handcuffs let him, kicked the mobile from Seagram's hand, sending it scudding across the oak floor.

Seconds later, the door to the court crashed open and armed officers poured in, shouting, 'Police. Police. Stay where you are.'

Ridpath raised his arms and looked down at the body of Tony Seagram.

The man's finger still twitched as he tried to press the send button of the mobile phone no longer in his hand.

Four Days Later...

Chapter 109

Ridpath was sat on the couch. On his left, Eve was propped in by four pillows and covered in her favourite blanket. Next to him, Polly was leaning on his shoulder.

On the TV, *Zombies 2* was playing again. It was another movie night. Ridpath had asked for a different film but Eve had insisted on this one. Addison's white hair was so rad, apparently.

On screen, the girl who thought she was a werewolf but wasn't, was falling in love with a zombie who wished he wasn't but was. They all seemed to be dancing and singing about it at a 'Prawn', which was a sort of strange, monster prom.

Eve was entranced. 'Mum, can I dye my hair white?'

'No,' answered Polly from her position on Ridpath's shoulder.

'But you told me you're going to dye yours red.'

'That's different.'

'You're going to dye it red?' said Ridpath, looking down on his wife's head. When they'd first met it was a bright Irish green.

'Yeah, half-term's coming and I feel like a change.'

'Ok,' answered Ridpath, before returning to stare at the screen. He'd lost the plot of what was happening, not that he had been following it closely anyway. Memories of the events at the court kept intruding.

Polly lifted her head off his shoulder and stared at him. 'What's up? You have a face like yesterday's washing.'

'I keep wondering if I could have done more. Worked out Tony Seagram was behind it earlier. I should have known.'

333

'How could you know?' She paused for a moment as if remembering something. 'How is John Gorman?'

'Still in hospital. The stroke paralysed his left side. Even if he lives, he's going to be unable to walk any more.'

'Sad. I always liked him and Charlie.'

'You never admitted that before.'

'Yeah? Well, I did, more than I like Claire Trent.'

'She's a bit of a hero now. Lauded by the press for taking decisive action.'

'The killing of Tony Seagram?'

A loud hush came from Eve's direction, followed by, 'This is the important bit. The zombies and the werewolves discover they have something in common.'

'That they are the world's worst actors?' suggested Ridpath.

'Daaaddd...'

'What about James Dalbey?' asked Polly.

'Last time I checked, he was still in a coma in MMI. When he comes round, they are going to perform surgery on the tumour immediately. It's 50/50 whether he will survive. Even if he doesn't, Paul Turnbull has made it his life's mission to find enough evidence to charge Dalbey with conspiracy to commit murder.'

'I wouldn't like Turnbull chasing after me.'

'He's also looking at other possible conspirators; the consultant who put Dalbey in the coma, Harold Lardner and even the doctor at Ashworth. Nobody knows at the moment how many people were actually involved.'

'Daaaddd, you're missing the best bit. This is where Addison discovers she's not a werewolf.'

Ridpath took a deep breath. 'Can you pause it for a second, Eve.'

'Do I have to?'

'Only a second.'

The film stopped in mid-werewolf dance move.

'I've made a decision.' He paused taking a deep breath. 'I'm not moving back to MIT yet. I'm staying with the coroner and liaising with MIT.'

Polly sat up and gave him a big hug. 'That's great news. But why? I thought you wanted to go back? You love being a copper.'

'I still do and I'm not ruling it out in the future, but I've thought about it and I don't know if I'm ready yet. Mrs Challinor still hasn't found a replacement, and frankly, I can do far more good working with her than being another cog in the MIT machine.'

'Would Paul Turnbull have anything to do with this decision?'

'I'd be lying if I said he wasn't part of it, but I've handled bad bosses before and he would be no different. But it's a much more positive decision than that. I can simply do more working with Mrs Challinor. I have much more freedom. And besides, it means I can spend more time with you two.'

Polly hugged him again. 'That's great news, Ridpath. I'm so happy you've decided what you're going to do. Have you told anybody yet?'

'No. I thought you should know first.'

'I'm sure Mrs Challinor will be glad, but how will Claire Trent take it?'

Ridpath shrugged his shoulders. 'Dunno, I'll cross that bridge when I come to it. But she's got her head so far in the clouds, I'm sure I'm the least of her concerns at the moment.'

Polly was silent for a few seconds. 'I have news too,' she finally said. 'The ex-deputy head of the school rang me yesterday. She has a place at her new primary school teaching Year 4 and asked if I would be interested. Only slightly more money, but what's great is the primary is in Altrincham so I can drive Eve to her new school in the morning and pick her up at night to take her home.'

Eve perked up at this news. 'So I won't have to take the tram?'

'Some days you will if I have to work late, but most days I can bring you home.'

Eve did a little dance on the chair. 'Yay.'

'It means I'll have to wake up even earlier to cook breakfast for you both. No more rushing out at the last minute.'

'True, Ridpath, but you like doing it anyway. Gives meaning to an otherwise rather meaningless morning, doesn't it?' She smiled, licking her lips. 'Talking about food, I couldn't half murder some dim sum now.'

'You want me to cook them?' said Ridpath.

'I thought you'd never ask.'

'What about the movie, Dad? You're going to miss the best bit.'

'I'll get over the disappointment.'

He stood up and walked out into the kitchen. Polly's mother had bought some frozen *har gau* and *siu mai* from Wing Wah supermarket that week. All Ridpath had to do was steam them.

He put a large pan of water on to boil, and searched for the bamboo steaming baskets in the cupboard. He emptied the frozen pork balls and the prawn parcels into separate baskets and placed them over the water in the steamer.

He was about to get the chili sauce from the fridge when the door bell rang twice.

'I'll get it,' he heard Polly shout from the living room.

I wonder who that could be? They weren't expecting any visitors that evening. He leant over the steaming dim sum to look out of the window.

Mrs Seagram was standing at the door.

What does she want?

He heard Polly's footsteps in the hall and the latch turning on the door.

And then it hit him.

'Polly, don't open...' he shouted, running out from the kitchen.

Before he could finish the sentence, he heard two shots ring out, one after the other.

He rushed out into the hallway. Polly was lying on the floor, a small strawberry-red stain spreading slowly across her white blouse.

She tried to lift her head to look at her chest.

Ridpath knelt down next to her. 'Stay still, Poll, stay still.'

As he looked up, he saw the barrel of a Webley revolver staring at his head, a thin trail of smoke wisping up from the barrel.

Mrs Seagram's face was contorted in fury. 'You know how it feels now, Ridpath,' she snarled.

He watched as she cocked the hammer again and raised the gun to point directly at his head. Her arm continued moving upwards and she placed the barrel in her mouth and pulled the trigger.

Behind him, Eve appeared in the doorway, staring down at her mother.

'Eve, ring 999, quickly,' shouted Ridpath.

Eve just stood there.

'Ring 999, now!'

The door closed and Eve ran to find her mobile phone.

Ridpath grabbed a coat and bundled it up, pressing it down on Polly's chest to try to staunch the flow of blood.

As he did, she lifted her head and whispered something, the red blood bubbling between her lips.

'It'll be ok, Polly, lie still, the ambulance is coming, lie still…'

Eve appeared at the doorway again. 'The ambulance and police are on their way Dad.' A long pause. 'Is Mum going to be ok?'

'Eve get a blanket. We need to keep your mum warm.'

Eve ran upstairs, past her mother's body lying on the floor in the hallway.

Polly raised her head and whispered something again.

'Stay still, Poll, the ambulance is coming.'

Ridpath lowered his face to hers.

She lifted her head again and whispered. 'Kiss me.'

He pressed his lips against hers, feeling how cold they were.

In the distance, he could hear the sirens calling to each other.

CANELOCRIME

Do you love crime fiction and are always on the lookout for brilliant authors?

Canelo Crime is home to some of the most exciting novels around. Thousands of readers are already enjoying our compulsive stories. Are you ready to find your new favourite writer?

Find out more and sign up to our newsletter at canelocrime.com